Once

the hotel

it idle.

"Would you like to come up?" said Livingston.

"I would like to but I'm not going to."

He gave her a crooked smile. "Why not?"

"It wouldn't be right," she whispered in the dark confines of the car.

"What wouldn't be right about it?" For the second time that night Livingston took his hand and placed it on her knee. "I don't think you're in a relationship or you wouldn't be driving me around at all."

She gave a delicate snort. "I'm not in a relationship. Hell, I'm not even causally dating." Grace added hesitantly, "I'm afraid."

"Afraid of what? I don't bite." His eyes in the darkness made him look like a panther and he was obviously ready to pounce.

"I don't know you and I've never been the type to have a one-night stand."

"What makes you think that's all it would be?"

"How often do people actually meet in a club and have things work out?" She searched his eyes with hers.

"I don't know," he answered. "How often does lightning strike?"

She gave a start of surprise at hearing these words. *My thoughts exactly.*

He slid one finger along the edge of her panties and then his index finger inside her. She instinctively turned towards him to give him full access and gently began to probe her moistness. She squirmed and writhed as his finger played with her and she almost came. Then she stilled his hand and said, "I don't want to be disappointed."

Livingston pulled his hand away and licked the finger that had just left her aching body. "There's more of that when you want it."

WHEN LIGHTNING STRIKES!

MICHELE CAMERON

Genesis Press, Inc.

INDIGO LOVE STORIES

An imprint of Genesis Press, Inc.
Publishing Company

Genesis Press, Inc.
P.O. Box 101
Columbus, MS 39703

All characters in this book have no existence outside the imagination of the author and have no relation whatsoever to anyone bearing the same name or names. They are not even distantly inspired by any individual known or unknown to the author and all incidents are pure invention.

ISBN: 13 DIGIT : 978-1-58571-369-1
ISBN: 10 DIGIT : 1-58571-369-4
Manufactured in the United States of America

First Edition

Visit us at www.genesis-press.com
or call at 1-888-Indigo-1-4-0

DEDICATION

I dedicate this novel to my maternal grandmother, Reverend Eloise Gilliard Montgomery Greene of Lake City, South Carolina.

"Eastern Star"
May you rest in peace . . .

8/4/2009
Michele
Cameron

ACKNOWLEDGMENTS

I would like to give special thanks to Deborah Schumaker, executive editor at Genesis Press, Inc., aka Deborah Johnson, author of the novel, *The Air Between Us.* She's an outstanding multi-tasker . . .

CHAPTER 1

At the sound of her telephone ringing, Grace cast weary eyes to the clock on the nightstand. Glancing at her caller I.D. she breathed a deep sigh of resignation, grabbed the receiver and barked, "I'm on my way!"

"Girl, you are always *so* cranky. You better get rid of that attitude if you plan on finding Mr. Right tonight. Men like women who are not only beautiful to look at but also know how to act."

Babs's chiding words only made Grace feel more irritable, and her next words showed it.

"Maybe I ought to stay home then. It's not as if I think I'll find Mr. Right during happy hour, anyway."

"Don't be such a snob, Grace. He could be out there."

"I haven't seen him yet!"

"You probably did see him," Babs snickered. "He was just with some other chick." Then, changing the subject, she asked, "What are you wearing?"

Grace replied with obvious disinterest in her voice, "I haven't decided."

"I have a new emerald green mini-dress that I bought at Sak's. It rocks!" Babs practically cooed.

"I'm very happy for you," Grace replied dryly. Before Babs could make a comeback, Grace's phone beeped.

"That's Solange calling. I'll meet you at Sutra's in about an hour," she said as she disconnected.

"Hey, sweetie!" The cheerful voice of her best friend immediately lightened her mood.

"Hey back."

"I'm on my way out the door. Are you dressed yet?"

"Not really. I just got off the phone with your annoying-ass cousin, Babs."

Solange chuckled before saying, "I love her to death, but she *is* annoying as hell."

"She's ridin' me because I don't feel like going to the same club for the third Friday in a row. I just don't see the point."

"The point is tonight *may* be the night." Solange paused before saying, "I don't know, Grace, but I have a feeling that we should go out because something momentous is going to happen for one of us."

"Give me a break. I hardly think that I'll meet my future husband in a club," Grace repeated.

"Why not? You're out there and I know what a great catch you are."

"If I'm such a great catch, why am I almost thirty years old and single?"

"Because you're so picky," Solange retorted.

Grace drew in a deep sigh of tiredness. "I don't think what I want in a man is unreasonable. Decent job, no more than two kids by the same woman, keeps up with politics, tries to maintain good credit, though with the economy the way it is that's becoming a hard thing to do, and oh, go to church other than Mother's Day and

Easter. Besides, who are you to talk? You want the same thing."

It was true. One of the reasons she and Solange got along so well was because they had parallel visions of what they wanted in life and how to get it. Step one, graduate from college with honors. Step two, get a job in their profession making enough money to not worry if Social Security ran out before they were able to draw on it. Step three, live the single life and get all of their partying out of their systems. Step four, meet and fall deeply in love with the man of their dreams and move to the suburbs in Atlanta to an area where their children and pets could have the freedom to play. The fly in the ointment was that they hadn't figured it would take them so long to accomplish the latter.

Grace had found once she got in the dating game after college that even if you were beautiful and intelligent, the competition for good black men was stiff. Suddenly the picture of her dream house with a big yard, a fence, and a boy and girl romping with a cocker spaniel flashed in front of her eyes. She stood in the driveway and when her husband got home from work, their children ran to greet him and were each met with a kiss. Next he leaned forward and planted a firm kiss on her upturned mouth, then scooped each child up and carried them inside with Grace and their dog following him to eat the dinner she had lovingly prepared.

Her reverie was abruptly interrupted when she heard Solange ask, "What are you wearing?"

"Good grief, who cares?" Then she softened her tone and said, "I thought that I'd wear my black pantsuit with a silk scarf."

"Don't wear that," Solange ordered, ignoring Grace's previous caustic tone. "You'll look as if you're going to a business meeting. Besides, once we get inside the club you'll start dancing."

"Dancing? I haven't done that the last few times that I went out."

"Men ask you, you just always turn them down."

"Yeah, right," Grace retorted dryly. "Those men are so freakin' lazy that they sit there and stare at you, waiting for you to make the first move. But when a slow song comes on they forget the cat and mouse game and beat it over to you and try to drag you on the dance floor so that they can cop a feel. That's why I say no."

Solange laughed again and admitted, "There is some truth to that." Then, switching the subject back to something that they could do something about, she said, "Wear that black silk dress that you bought at Bloomingdale's. It makes you look like someone who just walked off the runway."

"Oh, all right," she acquiesced. "I'll meet you in at the club in about an hour or so!"

"Okay. I'm still at the office, but I knew that I'd be running late today so I brought my clothes," Solange said before she hung up.

Fifty-five minutes later, Grace walked past clusters of people standing outside the club. She took no notice of the small groups of men who paused in their conversations when she strutted by. True to her word, she had donned her black silk dress, but she had jazzed it up with a pair of fishnet stockings and high-heeled, black, eel-skin stilettos. Silver jewelry accented her outfit and because her hair was naturally curly she wore it in the afro look that had recently become so popular.

Grace stood almost eye to eye with a six-foot-tall man who stood at the door, took her twenty dollars, and nodded at the bouncer to let her pass. Once inside the club, she spied Solange and Babs sitting at a table waving their hands to get her attention.

Drawing in a deep sigh of boredom, she plastered a happy smile on her face as she went to join them, not wanting her mood to spoil their outing.

After her second pomegranate martini, Grace surveyed the nightclub and dance floor crowded with couples obviously attempting to have a good time no matter what. It looked as if it was going to be another Friday evening with her girlfriends and no decent man in sight.

Babs expelled a long breath. "Damn, even I have to admit the pickin's are real slim tonight. Everyone's already paired up."

"They're paired up, but do you notice with whom?" Solange raised her eyebrow in query.

"No, what do you mean?" Grace asked.

Solange surreptitiously nodded her head at a couple all over each other at the bar. "Last week that girl in the hot pink dress was all over that guy in the plaid shirt sitting on the other side of the bar. Now she's with the guy in the green suit. And the guy in the green suit was with that girl in the red dress, who is with the guy in the plaid shirt. And they all know each other because in the past, I've seen them sitting at a table together."

Babs stared at the couples with narrowed eyes as she tried to figure out if what Solange was saying was accurate. Then she responded in awe, "You're so observant, Solange."

"Good grief!" Grace declared. "They're recycling couples." Suddenly she stood and stated with disgust, more than with necessity, "I'm going to the ladies' room! Order me another drink." Weaving her way in and out of people, she stopped to let a somewhat inebriated guy pass her. Right when his path came abreast of hers, he stopped, turned bleary eyes to her and said, "Hey, bitch. I'd love for you to lick my lollipop."

Appalled, Grace recoiled. As she drew herself up to make a scathing remark, another guy came up to them and said, "Ignore my friend. He's getting married tomorrow and he's had too much to drink." The man grabbed his friend by the arm and pushed him out of Grace's path. "He's not usually like that." Then he offered with a shamefaced smile, "Sometimes bachelor parties bring out the worst in people."

Grace stared at the apologetic look on the man's face and somehow, from deep within, she held her temper and decided not to make a scene. Giving the embarrassed-looking friend a curt nod, she aggressively pushed her way past them and headed towards the ladies' room, head bent. Suddenly she collided with something rock hard. Had it not been for the hands of steel that grabbed her, she would have surely toppled to the floor.

Grace flung back her head and locked her eyes with the most beautiful light-brown ones she had ever seen. Time seemed to stand still as she gazed at him. *Good God! He's like a black James Bond.*

Her safety net made no effort to let go of her as he too stared, mesmerized by the alluring picture she made. The bemused expression on her face looked similar to the one people had early in the morning after a passionate night of lovemaking.

The electricity was such that Grace now knew first-hand what it must feel like to be struck by lightning.

Suddenly a high whistle from an interested bystander broke their trance and she was steadied to an upright position and released. Feeling overwhelmed by the intensity of the encounter, Grace hurriedly muttered an apology. "Excuse me, I didn't mean to bump into you." Before he could respond, she made a beeline to the ladies' room.

From nervousness, she now really did have to use the ladies' room. Once she relieved herself, she stood at the sink. As she washed her hands, she stared at her reflection in the mirror. Beads of sweat had formed on her forehead and her flushed face hadn't had this much vitality since she was in college and still had high hopes that when she met a new man, he might be the soul mate she was searching for. She grabbed a paper towel and dabbed at her forehead, careful not to smear her makeup. Then she took the palms of her hands and pushed up her breasts. After she adjusted her dress, Grace took a deep breath before heading back to Solange and Babs.

Once settled back at the table, Grace picked up her waiting drink and downed it in one long draught. She stared steadfastly at her empty glass, curbing her desire to spot the location of her brief captor.

"Damn, where have you been?" Babs demanded. "We started to send out a search party for you, but I didn't want to leave the room. There has been an interesting development since you left the table. Take a look over at the bar. There is one fine chocolate Hershey Bar in here that I've never seen before."

She knew who Babs must be talking about, and her heart dropped. *If Babs wants mystery man, I'm out of luck. She's so aggressive that she beats out all the other competition. I wish she hadn't come out with us tonight. Maybe then I could've had a chance.* Grasping at straws, she thought, *Maybe it's not him she means.* Grace deliberately tried to sound nonchalant as she asked, "Whoever do you mean?"

"Look over there at the bar, silly," Babs ordered.

"Grace, there's something vaguely familiar about him," Solange said, "but I can't figure out what it is."

"Well, maybe you'll find out," Babs muttered excitedly, "he's looking this way. And here he comes."

Grace lifted her head and looked in the direction of the bar, then stammered incredulously, "It's my brother Jethro."

"Your brother!" Babs's eyes were open wide with anticipation. "You never even mentioned that you have a brother."

"He's not my blood brother, but we were raised as brother and sister."

"That's why he looked familiar to me. I've seen pictures of him in your apartment. He's really changed," Solange murmured. "His pictures made him look scrawny."

Grace sized Jethro up as he made his way to their table. It was true. In the years since she had last seen him he'd really matured, and she loved the confident way he strode towards her. Family emotion made her eyes water and a lump form in her throat. "He used to be so skinny. My baby brother has really grown up."

Solange and Babs looked at each other and responded in unison, "Baby brother, I'll be damned!"

Babs laughed, pointing at Solange. "You owe me a Coke!"

Ignoring them, Grace stood and opened her arms.

Jethro enveloped her with his and, for the second time in one evening, she felt safe. For a moment, neither spoke. Then Jethro squeezed her slightly before he pushed her away.

Tears of emotion filled her eyes and trickled down her cheeks.

With one thumb, Jethro gently wiped them away.

Then turning to Solange and Babs, Grace proudly introduced him. "This is my brother, Jethro. Jethro, this is," she said, pointing at each, "Solange and Babs."

Jethro reached over and warmly shook their hands, "Call me Jet."

"Jet? You've gone and renamed yourself, huh?" Grace chuckled.

"It was my line name and I just sort of kept it."

His voice is even deeper than I remember. It's as if he's a different person, yet he still has that gentle demeanor.

"Would you like to take a seat?" Babs coquettishly batted her eyes at Jethro. With a knowing smile in her direction he easily lowered his long frame into an empty chair.

Nervously, Grace's mind began to work overtime. *I'll catch him on the sly and warn him that she's husband hunting. She's not the kind of woman his mother would have wanted him hooked up with. Babs as my sister-in-law?* Grace visibly shuddered at the thought.

"What's the matter?" Jet's attention was immediately diverted from Babs back to Grace. "You're not cold, are you?"

"Not at all."

"Well, I wouldn't be surprised if you were cold, running around half–dressed and all," he said jokingly.

"I bet if I wasn't your sister, instead of chastising me, you would probably be cheering at my skimpy dress."

"I probably would." He laughed agreeably.

"What in the world are you doing here? I thought that you were in Chicago?"

"I was, but because of the recession my job at the Sears Tower folded, so I'm heading back this way. I'm sick of the hustle and bustle. I kind of miss the South."

"Atlanta isn't exactly country," she demurred.

"I'll be okay if I stay in Marietta. It's close enough to the city, yet it still has a suburban feeling."

Jethro looked around and signaled a waitress hovering nearby. When she came over he said, "Another of what everyone here already has and four bottles of Corona."

"You want four bottles of beer?" Grace gave him a stern look. "That's too many to be drinking one after another."

He chuckled and said, "You still call yourself looking out for me? I'm a grown man and know how to handle myself. Besides, two of them are for my frat brother Livingston. I don't know where he went to, but he'll show up sooner or later."

Just at that minute, all the attention of the ladies at the table was captured by Mister Tall, Dark and Handsome himself.

As he strolled towards them and his eyes pinned Grace's, butterflies did a tap dance in her stomach. *He's with Jethro*?

"Oh, my God!" Babs exclaimed. "There are two of them."

Grace and Solange's eyes met across the table. *I've always wanted to introduce Solange to my brother because they'd be perfect together. But I can kiss that good-bye because neither one of us would sleep behind Babs. She has too many notches on her bedpost.* Her thoughts were drawn to a more pressing problem. Babs was now batting her eyes at Livingston, who stood at their table. *Well damn it. She can't have him. I saw him first.*

Jethro was in the process of making introductions. "Livingston Lockhart, this is Babs and Solange. And this is my sister, Grace."

"Grace and I have already had the pleasure of meeting." Livingston's eyes twinkled and Grace felt herself blush from head to toe.

"Really? When was that?" Jet asked curiously.

Now there were three sets of quizzical eyes on Grace, and they all noticed her discomfiture as she shifted nervously in her chair.

Reaching behind him Livingston, with one swift movement, grabbed an empty chair from the next table and positioned it close to Grace, then placed his hand consolingly on her knee. "I almost knocked her down outside the bathrooms."

At his touch, Grace felt an instantaneous heat in her vagina and relished it.

The music playing had been a mixture of rhythm and blues and salsa, but suddenly the lights dimmed and soft music enveloped the room. Giving Livingston a tremulous smile she asked with slight trepidation, "Would you like to dance with me?" She was aware the minute the words were out of her mouth that there was a small start of surprise from Solange and a look of shock on Babs's face.

Swiftly Livingston stood up and said, "It would be my pleasure, young lady."

Placing her hand in his, she let herself be drawn to her feet. Out of the corner of her eye, she saw a man approach Solange, who gave him a negative shake of her head. The next thing that registered before she melted into Livingston's embrace and closed her eyes was Babs and Jet joining them on the dance floor.

As they sinuously moved to one song after another, Grace buried her head in his chest. The scent of his cologne wafted to her nostrils and made her dig in deeper. She felt the warm stirrings that had invaded her body when they bumped into each other earlier rise to full throttle.

"I'm going to be in town for a week on business. Will you spend time with me while I'm here?"

She only nodded her head in assent, then buried herself again in his chest. She felt as if a steel pole was lodged between them as he drew her closer. *Thank God he's attracted to me.*

Hours later, they were standing outside in a small group waiting for Solange to rejoin them. Grace shivered in the unusually cool breeze and, because she hadn't worn a bra, she felt her nipples poking through the thin fabric of her dress.

"Here, put this on," Jethro ordered and handed Grace his jacket.

"Thanks, Jethro," she muttered gratefully.

"Jet," he corrected her.

She looked at him in surprise. He had an unusually sharp edge to his voice, but she put it down to tiredness. After all, he had just flown in from Chicago earlier that day.

Babs looked in Solange's direction and spoke grumpily, "She had all night to hook up with ol' boy but waits until it's two o'clock in the morning to get his number."

Just before Solange made her way over to them, the man handed her a folded white sheet of paper and she placed it in her purse and snapped it closed.

"That's a first," Babs said.

"What?" Solange looked at her and said, "Oh no, it's not what you think. He's a headhunter. Hell, I'm always networking. That's the real reason I come out here week after week, unlike your reasons." She gave her cousin a knowing look.

"To each his own." Babs turned to Jet with a deceptively innocent look and purred, "Do you mind walking me to my car, Jet? The only parking space that I could find is a good distance away."

Jet hesitated for a moment and studied Grace and Livingston.

"Grace is going to give me a ride back to the hotel," Livingston explained. "I'll see you in the morning, probably around brunch."

"Fine," Jet said before he stalked off in the direction Babs had pointed to earlier. Babs followed.

Grace looked at Solange. "Are you good?"

"I'm good," she replied, "but call me when you get home."

The car ride to Livingston's hotel was filled with sexual tension. Every song playing on the radio was made for lovemaking. The air felt so thick that Grace wanted to pull to the side of the road, have her way with him, and get the sex out of the way.

"I'm on the left at the Radisson."

Once Grace pulled into the circular loop in front of the hotel, she shifted her Cherokee Jeep into park and let it idle.

"Would you like to come up?"

"I would like to, but I'm not going to."

He gave her a somewhat crooked smile. "Why not?"

"It wouldn't be right," she whispered in the dark confines of the car.

"What wouldn't be right about it?" For the second time that night Livingston placed his hand on her knee. "I don't think you're in a relationship or you wouldn't be driving me around at all."

She gave a delicate snort. "I'm not in a relationship. Hell, I'm not even casually dating." Grace added hesitantly, "I'm afraid."

"Afraid of what? I don't bite." His eyes in the darkness looked like a panther ready to pounce.

"I don't know you and I've never been the type to have a one-night stand."

"What makes you think that's all it would be?"

"How often do people actually meet in a club and have things work out?" She searched his eyes with hers.

"I don't know," he answered. "How often does lightning strike?"

She gave a start of surprise at hearing these words. *My thoughts exactly.*

Livingston continued, with a teasing inflection in his voice, "It only takes one time to kill you."

At these words, an eerie feeling went through her. His words made her decision. "I can't," she replied with a negative shake of her head. Then, so softly Livingston had to lean in to hear her, she said, "It's been so long. I don't want to disappoint you."

"I hardly think that would happen, Grace. Sex is like riding a bicycle. Once you get started your natural instincts take over." Livingston took his hand and stroked her thigh in the darkness. She stilled his hand.

Livingston pulled his hand out from underneath her dress. "There's more of that when you want it." He nodded his head in the direction of the hotel. "Meet me in the hotel lobby for brunch tomorrow, around twelve o'clock, if you would like to see me again." Then he opened the car door and left.

CHAPTER 2

Solange's yawn gave Grace an attack of conscience. "I'm sorry to wake you up, but you did tell me to call you when I got home."

"That was just a subtle warning for Mr. Lockhart. I wanted him to know that I'm keeping an eye on you and he better not pull any funny stuff. But the way you two were looking at each other, I honestly didn't think that I would hear from you until morning."

"You almost didn't. It took sheer willpower for me to deny that man tonight. I haven't wanted anyone like that in eons."

Sounding more wide awake now, Solange said, "Then why did you say no? You're two consenting adults and you know there's nothing wrong with a little bump and grind."

"I didn't want him to think I sleep with a man the first night I meet him. If I gave it up for him like that, he would probably think that I give it up easily for anyone."

"You're probably right," Solange agreed. "If you want something lasting, then you have to play the game."

"Now why is that?" Grace wailed. "Men can pick up woman after woman, and, as long as they practice safe sex, they're considered a stud. But I've been without a man for a year and if I had given in to my sexual yearnings, I would be considered a ho."

"That's just the way it is. It's not fair, but it is life," Solange responded in a resigned tone. "How long is he going to be here?"

"For a week."

"If you're really interested," she paused, "you're going to have to give him a real good memory to make him want to come back to see you."

"How long should I make him wait?"

"Well, it isn't feasible to play the 'I don't know you well enough to sleep with you' game because you could never know him that well in a week. Just go with your instincts."

For the second time in one evening, she had been told to follow her instincts. But instead of confiding that to Solange she said, "My first instinct was to pull over to the side of the road and do him. My next instinct was to stop by the drugstore, get a box of condoms, and use every last one of them before he leaves town, but then again . . ."

"Then again what? It sounds like a plan to me," Solange chuckled.

"I don't want Jethro to find out or lose respect for me."

"Do you think Livingston is a kiss-and-tell kind of guy?"

"It's been my experience that they all tell someone. And since that someone happens to be my brother, who was with him, who introduced us, I think that he just might."

Solange mused, "I don't know about that. I think it's kind of creepy to tell a guy he's banging his sister. There should be a law against that."

"I'll tell you what the law should do. It should prohibit a guy being as good looking as Livingston Lockhart. That's the real crime."

"And the fact that he's hanging out with another guy as fine as he is makes it even more of a crime. I can't believe how fine your brother is and how come you never told me that."

"For one thing, he looks different. For another thing, he acts different, and finally, I don't think that I've ever looked at him that way. To me, he's just my brother."

"Well, as far as I'm concerned, it's too late now, because Babs has her hooks in him."

"Don't be too sure about that. I mean, did you see the look on his face after Babs asked him to escort her to the car? He didn't seem that interested and, even though I haven't really kept up with him since his mother's death, I know that he has always had a mind of his own."

"That may be true, but very few men have been able to resist Babs's advances."

"That may also be true, but for some reason she doesn't seem to be able to hold their interest very long."

Later, as Grace stood at the bathroom mirror cleansing the makeup off her face, she thought, *I hope Jethro turns Babs down, and then I can pave the way for Solange. They'd be much better suited.*

At eleven forty-five, Grace stood at the lobby desk. "Will you please call Livingston Lockhart's room and tell him Grace Foxfire is here to meet him for lunch?"

"Yes, ma'am," the hotel clerk replied.

Once she hung up the phone the clerk said, "He said that he will be down momentarily."

"Thank you." Grace nervously smoothed her sweating palms down the sides of her dress. "I feel like I'm going through early menopause," she muttered.

Crossing over to the other side of the lobby, she stared at the gift shop figurines on display. Suddenly, she felt breath on her neck and, swinging around, she bumped into Livingston, who was standing behind her. Once again in a 24-hour time period, she needed the help of Livingston Lockhart to keep her steady on her feet.

Chagrined, she stared into his eyes and said, "You certainly have a way of saving me from bodily harm."

"I'm just saving you for myself." His eyes danced merrily at his not-so-oblique innuendo.

"I think I can get on board with that."

The sound of a man clearing his throat made them aware that once again they were being observed. Looking over in the direction of the sound, Grace was caught off guard to see Jethro and Babs. Babs had her hand curled possessively on his arm and Jet's expression was inscrutable as he watched her and Livingston.

"Hey, girl." Babs waved airily at Grace, obviously happy with the way things had worked out.

Disappointingly, Grace noticed that Babs had on the same dress she had worn the previous night. A disapproving pout settled on her lips.

Today, Jethro really looked the part of a jetsetter. He had obviously showered and changed and he now wore a pair of yellow and blue striped shorts and white sneakers.

"Hey, man." Livingston's teeth glinted in a smile as he too took in Babs's appearance. "We're going into the hotel restaurant and have brunch. Would you like to join us?"

"That would be great!" Babs replied enthusiastically. "I'm starving." She strutted with head held high towards the restaurant.

Once they were seated and had ordered, Jet said to Grace, "I was going to call you today. I have to go to Lake City because I have some business that I need to settle and wondered if you'd like to ride along."

"I don't know about that," Grace replied, averting her eyes.

"You have to face the past sometime, Grace," Jet said softly.

They looked at each other, and it seemed as if they were the only people seated at the table.

Babs looked at Jet and demanded, "Tell me again how the two of you are brother and sister."

"It's not a happy story." Jet took a drink of his mimosa before continuing. "Our fathers were in the military together. When Grace was almost five and my mother was pregnant with me, our dads were doing routine aircraft testing on the base. Somehow the flight plan got messed up and their plane collided with another in mid-air. There were no survivors."

Babs leaned forward and gave Jet a soulful look. "I'm sorry I brought that up. Imagine the two of you growing up without fathers. That must have been very hard."

"It's hard to miss something that you never had. Grace had a rougher time than I did because she had vague memories of hers. And at least, for a time, we had our mothers. Some people have nothing."

"Are you named for your dad?" Babs asked quizzically.

With a smile of resignation he answered, "No, I really am named after Jethro from *The Beverly Hillbillies.* It's been the bane of my existence my entire life."

Grace piped in, trying to lighten the atmosphere brought on by Babs's question. "Esther, Jet's mother, was put on complete bed rest the last four months of her pregnancy. The military only offered basic cable, and they used to play reruns of that show over and over again." Grace's eyes misted over as she thought of her play mother. "I can still remember her laugh. She had an unforgettable tinkling laugh that made you want to join in when you heard her." Grace reached over to grasp Jet's hand.

He returned her squeeze. "From the earliest time I can remember, when people would ask my mother why she named me after that country boy, she would just smile and say, 'Because out of all the characters on the show he made me laugh the most, and even though I was flat on my back for months, I was happy because I was bringing the most important person that I had left into this world.' "

"So are you going to Lake City to see your mother? I would so love to meet her."

Jet's tone saddened. "Our mothers are also gone. Grace lost her mother when she was thirteen, and I lost mine five years ago to breast cancer. It's just the two of us now."

At hearing these words, another thick silence descended on the group and Livingston broke the tension. "Grace is going to show me around this week."

Mindful of Jet's watchful stare she offered, "His timing is perfect because I'm off work next week because of spring break."

Livingston's eyes shone with anticipation. "Sometimes timing is everything."

She quipped, "Sometimes timing can be your best friend."

Now Jet and Babs watched them.

Livingston continued, "I'd like to take in a show while I'm here."

"I think that can be arranged." Grace replied. "Have you ever seen *Wicked*?"

"No, I haven't seen *Wicked,* but I certainly feel wicked," he teased, moving his eyebrows up and down in a Groucho Marx impression.

Grace chuckled at his imitation.

"Maybe we can make it a foursome." Livingston offered the invitation, looking at Jet.

"I would love that!" Babs gushed.

Jet promptly responded, "I'm afraid I can't. I have a lot of business to take care of this week."

Jet noted the dejected look that came over Babs's face, but he couldn't help it. He didn't have time for meaningless dalliances. He had scores to settle, and he had no intention of letting anyone or anything distract him from his mission.

CHAPTER 3

Grace and Livingston strolled hand in hand through the High Museum of Art. Room after room displayed breathtaking Renoir, Van Gogh and Monet canvases. Tugging on Livingston's hand, she walked over to a Monet placed perpendicular to another painting. "Look at these two pictures by Monet." She exclaimed at the hues of soft green, sky blue, and rose. "The landscape is so dreamy, it makes you want to reach out and touch it."

"You better not," Livingston cautioned and nodded his head over to the other side of the room where a sentry watched the patrons as they viewed the art. "Actually, this one," he said, pointing, "is a Monet and this other one is a Manet. They're two different artists, but they are from the same impressionistic school."

"How did you know that?" Grace looked at Livingston in surprise.

"Well, for one thing, it states it on the card below it." He smiled teasingly. "Do you wear glasses?"

"Only when I'm not trying to look my best. It wasn't until last year that I finally needed them for reading."

"I guess years of reading all those students' papers has finally taken its toll."

"Yep, that's what did it. Every time I put my glasses on, I remember that commercial that used to play all the time when I was growing up that used the line, 'Women who wear glasses seldom get passes.' "

"Do you have them on you?" Livingston asked.

"Yes," she murmured.

"Let me see you with them on."

Grace hesitated, and then fished around the bottom in her pocketbook until she found and withdrew her eyeglass case.

Taking the case from her, Livingston opened it, took out her glasses and placed them on her face.

With the boost from her glasses, Grace inspected every inch of Livingston's face. His nose was a little crooked, but, in her eyes, he was absolutely perfect. Her heart fluttered when she saw him begin to lean towards her. Automatically closing her eyes, she felt the firmness of Livingston's lips as they touched hers. At first they were soft, but as they became more insistent, her hands moved up to encircle his neck and she clung to him. After what seemed to be an endless time, she felt him withdrawing and she locked his lips with hers, willing him not to let her go. Finally she released him, but their eyes remained locked.

Finally he spoke, and his voice was even more throaty than usual. "So you see, the commercial was wrong. Not only do women who wear glasses get passes, they return them with a passion that is very much appreciated."

Later that evening, Grace was resting on her sofa watching her favorite talk show, *The View,* when her doorbell rang. Hitting the pause button on her DVR she walked down the short hallway. When she saw through the peephole that it was Jet, she opened the door and beckoned him in with a smile.

Reaching out to hug him, she was a little taken aback when his return hug was a little lukewarm.

"Hey, Jethro, I mean Jet," she corrected herself when he gave her a sharp look. "What are you doing here?"

"I need to talk to you, so I took a chance that you would be alone."

She replied, a little surprised by his tone, "Why wouldn't I be alone?"

Jet gave her a look of intense interest. "Maybe because you've been quite busy with Livingston."

Grace didn't realize it, but a dreamy look stole across her face at the mention of Livingston's face. She responded, "He said that he had some work to do tonight. Something about drawing up plans for the arena his company is building. He needed to fax them the measurements before the close of business today," she said, closing the door behind him. "Come in and take a seat."

Once inside, Jet looked around appraisingly and his expression softened. "I like the way you decorate. There's something a little familiar about it."

She smiled at him and said, "You're probably seeing the influence of your mother. She certainly took me to enough furniture stores, flea markets, and red tag sales. Would you like something to drink? I'm having wine."

"That'll work," Jet said as he sank into Grace's plush leather sectional sofa.

"I kind of wondered when you were going to make it over here," she yelled from the kitchen as she opened the refrigerator door. "I've hardly seen you since you came to town."

"I asked you to ride to Lake City with me, but you declined." Jet tried to keep the admonishing tone from his voice, but it seeped through anyway.

Grace came to stand in front of him, handed him his glass and sat next to him on the couch. "It's too hard for me to go there. It's too soon," she replied with downcast eyes.

"It's been years, Grace."

"It seems like yesterday," she responded, picking up her wine glass and draining it. "There's nothing left for me there."

"Our mothers' graves are there."

"What's the good of that? It's not as if they can talk back to you or anything. A grave is nothing but a rock with a person's name on it."

There was a long silence in the room, and the tension was tangible. "When are you going to forgive her, Grace?"

A stony silence was his answer.

"It's about time you let it go." Jet picked up Grace's hand and held it.

Her hand was tiny in comparison to his, and she felt a lump in her throat. Her breathing was constricted.

"She couldn't help it," he murmured softly.

Now the eyes Grace laid on him were a mixture of tears and anger. Her voice was high-pitched and strained. "She couldn't help it? She couldn't help drinking all day *every* day? She couldn't tell that she needed to stop? When the doctor said, 'Abigail, you need to stop drinking,' and he told her that she had a chance to save her liver if she quit, her reply was, 'I'm going to die of something anyhow.' "

"She tried, Grace. While I was in pharmacy school I learned a lot about what to look for when it comes to addictions in people. I think that your mother was a textbook manic depressive and was never properly diagnosed."

"Even if that is the case, hello, everyone knows that you shouldn't drink every day."

"True," he agreed, "but addictions have a way of creeping up on you. After your father died, she lost the will to live."

Her voice raspy, Grace said, "Women lose their husbands all the time and they go on. Your mother did. Not only did she live for you, but later she took me in and treated me like I was her own daughter."

"That's true, Grace. But remember the time your godmother called her and told her that she'd heard through the grapevine that some jealous girls were going to jump you when you got off the school bus? When we pulled up to the bus stop, your mother was standing there with a baseball bat, ready to protect you."

"Yeah, I know. But you forgot to include that at three o'clock in the afternoon she was still in her nightgown and had on a seersucker housecoat over it and pink rollers in her hair."

"But she was there, Grace. That should tell you something."

"Yes, it did. It told me to make sure I never needed her to come to the bus stop to look out for me again. The kids teased me for weeks at school about the sight she'd made."

"You have to forgive her, Grace. Only then can you begin the healing process."

"That's easy for you to say," Grace spoke with extreme sadness in her voice. "Your mother wasn't the embarrassment mine was."

"My mother, much as I loved her, wasn't perfect either. She over-mothered me. I couldn't play football because she was afraid that I would break a bone. She wouldn't let me be on the basketball team because I had asthma."

"At least she was there for you. My father couldn't help dying, but my mother didn't care enough about me to fight to have a life with me."

Jet intently searched her face. "Have you had any more nightmares?"

"Not since the night before your mother died." Suddenly Grace emitted a sound of pain.

Jet pulled her close and held her as gulping sobs almost strangled her. As she cried, he patted her back softly and laid his head on top of hers. Finally her deluge subsided into small sniffles.

Pushing him away, Grace wiped her cheeks with the back of her hand.

Without speaking, Jet walked into the bathroom and pulled a handful of tissues from the box. Handing them to Grace, he watched her wipe her face, then blow her nose. The loud sound in the room eased some of the tension, and when Grace saw a small grin on Jet's face she gave a half-smile. "Sinuses," she explained.

"You still suffer from that?" he asked, a little surprised. "I'll write you a prescription for that and one pill a day will relieve your pain."

"Thanks, I'd appreciate that. The over-the-counter medication just doesn't seem to do it for me."

"You might need outpatient surgery to rectify the problem."

"Thanks but no thanks. Hospitals give me the heebie jeebies."

Another long silence filled the room.

"I have some news," Jet spoke quietly.

"Oh?" She gave him a tremulous smile.

He cleared his throat. "I too have had my demons to deal with. I found out that my mother went to the doctor when she first found a lump in her breast and was told it was nothing. Then she went back and was told again that it was nothing but hormones and early menopause so she shouldn't be concerned. By the time she went for a second opinion, her cancer had metastasized and it was too late.

"I was so angry when I found out that my mother didn't have to die when she did, I became very self-destructive. When I almost flunked out at Morehouse, my counselor called me in. Once he'd heard what happened, he called his cousin who's a lawyer. We sued the doctor and put him out of business. It took three years, but I finally got my retribution." Jet reached into his pocket, pulled out a check and handed it to Grace, whose jaw dropped in surprise as she stared at all the zeroes. "I got him," Jet said.

Grace was somewhat taken aback by the flinty look in his eyes.

"I got that coldhearted bastard that let my mother die. This settlement can't bring my mother back, but I've made sure that he can't do what he did to my mother to another woman." Now Jet gave Grace a look filled with meaning and said, "I've laid my ghosts to rest. Can you?"

As Grace stood in front of her bedroom mirror oiling her body, her thoughts were of Livingston. Tonight would be their fifth outing, and so far she'd enjoyed every minute spent in his company. She was pleased that since the first night that she had driven him back to his hotel he hadn't asked her up to his room or put any sexual pressure on her, even though for the last two dates she'd secretly hoped that he would.

Reaching into her dresser, she withdrew a pair of thong underwear, and after ripping the tag off she thought, *New drawers for a new man.* She knew that technically she couldn't call Livingston her man, but she now felt comfortable enough with him to bring their relationship to the next level. Her heart beat a little faster at the thought of making love with Livingston. Ever since they had slow danced the night she'd met him, she'd been sneaking looks at him and could tell by the bulge in his trousers that he had everything a man needed to please a woman, which made her sexual desire for him escalate even more.

Grace had been the perfect tour guide as she had shown him around Atlanta. Her biggest thrill came when they visited Martin Luther King Jr.'s birthplace. As they had walked through the house in companionable silence, the experience made her realize just how long it had been since she'd had a male companion that did the things she wanted to do without complaining the whole time.

Once fully dressed, she inspected herself in the mirror. She had decided to wear a dress to dinner because Livingston had a habit of running his hand up her thigh to caress her and she didn't want to dress in a way that stopped him from doing that. Her second thought was to not wear a bra, but she changed her mind because there was so much lace décolletage in the front of her ivory dress that her nipples would be visible to anybody. *My breasts are for Livingston only to see.* Then she completed her outfit with her four-inch heels. She loved the fact that even wearing them, Livingston towered over her. It made her feel protected as he pushed through crowds of people on their sightseeing tours.

Suddenly Grace sank down on the bed. *What am I doing? This man doesn't even live here. He's leaving tomorrow. The last thing in the world I want is to love a man who's a plane flight away. Right now there are no highs in my life, but there are no lows either. I'd rather have that than bring on any more pain in my life. But I'm so damned horny.* Grace's eyes focused on a piece of lint on her carpet. *What are your choices, Grace? Sleep with Livingston, who you feel is worthy, and have meaningful lovemaking, or have lukewarm sex with another man just because you couldn't hold out any longer waiting for Mr. Right.*

Her telephone ringing shook her out of her musings and, grateful for the distraction, she reached for the receiver. "Hello."

"Hey, stranger," Solange said teasingly, "you must have gone and gotten yourself a life. I haven't heard from you all week."

Grace responded just as playfully, "You could have called me, you know. Telephones work two ways."

"Yeah, I know, I know. I just didn't want to interrupt your quest to lock down that man Livingston."

"Is it possible to lock down a man that resides in another part of the country?" Grace retorted wryly.

"It depends," Solange replied musingly. "A lot hinges on how good the blow job is."

Grace's response was a burst of laughter, and Solange joined in. Once they were finished, Grace said, "You know, not all men are like that."

Solange snorted, "Hell, I never met one that didn't want it."

"Me, either, really. But trust me, I don't do him if he doesn't do me."

"I know," Solange agreed. "I get pissed off when a man jumps in bed, hurries up and lies on his back like King Tut and I hook him up. Then when it's my turn he thinks that all he has to do is the other thing and be done with it. I don't care how long he can go, it doesn't make up for that. And if he ever gets lucky again, he gets the conservative package."

"I hear you, girl. When I *was* having sex, I got into the habit of acting like I found the idea abhorrent and the man had to do me first. Then if he did, he had to show me what he wanted."

"*Was* having sex? Are you trying to tell me you and Livingston haven't done the nasty yet?" Solange sounded astounded. "Isn't he leaving tomorrow?"

"Yes, he is," Grace replied in a mournful tone. "I kind of thought that tonight would be the night, but I'm having second thoughts. I've never been a fan of the one-night stand."

"I don't think it qualifies as a one-night stand if the person doesn't live here. I think that instead it's considered a passionate encounter that one never forgets."

"I don't want my heart broken," Grace murmured softly.

"No one does, Grace," Solange replied.

CHAPTER 4

"I haven't had any of the food yet, but this restaurant is rich with atmosphere. I love your choice." Livingston nodded approvingly as he swung his head around to view the strategically placed African art. Authentic-looking artifacts placed in nooks and crannies gave the room a feeling of ethnicity that was lacking in many chain restaurants.

"I love Saga. The food is everything you could ask for. If you take a look at your menu, you'll see the food here is a mixture of African and southern fried cooking."

Livingston picked up his menu off the table and opened it. "I guess I should look at the menu, but I've been too busy viewing the alluring picture you make." He put his menu back down on the table. "I've decided."

"Already?" she laughed. "Don't you think that you might want to take a little while longer to decide?"

"Nope." He pinned her eyes with his. "I'm a make-up-my-mind-in-a-hurry kind of guy. It doesn't take me long to know what I want."

When Grace dropped her eyes from the intensity of his, Livingston reached across the table and clasped her hand. "I find it hard to believe that a woman like you doesn't have a man."

Those words stung Grace and she withdrew her hand from his. "You claim you don't have anyone special back in Chicago. Why are you available?"

"Because I wanted to be available." Livingston smiled at the look of censure she had on her face. "Don't get me wrong. I know that you have plenty of men to choose from. I guess I'm just surprised that you're not married or engaged or something."

"I don't want to settle. Even if I never get married, I won't settle," she finished with a set look on her face.

Livingston reached over and reclaimed her hand. "Me either."

Over dinner, the conversation reverted to the easy manner that they had become accustomed to in the last week. As they ate dishes of curried goat, lamb chops, dirty rice, and a mixture of southern-style vegetables, they picked what they wanted off each other's plates. Any person viewing them would have thought they had been lovers for some time.

Full to the brim, Grace topped her meal off with a second glass of the Riesling Livingston had ordered. As she watched him clean his plate of a second helping of food and then reach for the dessert menu, she smiled at him and said, "How you manage not to be fat is a wonder to me."

"Usually Jet and I work out at the gym for an hour or so every day." Livingston absently scratched his shaved head with one hand as he perused the menu. "I haven't seen much of him this week, though. I've had to go alone."

A look of displeasure crossed Grace's face. "He's probably with Babs."

"I don't think so. I haven't seen her at the hotel since we all had brunch together."

"Good," she murmured to herself, but Livingston heard her.

"I thought Babs was your girl?" he asked with a raised eyebrow.

"*Solange* is my girl. Babs is her cousin."

"If you don't really care for her, why hang out with her?"

"I like Babs, but she's just sort of messy. Whenever she's around, so is drama and I just don't know if Jet can handle her," she ended with a worried tone in her voice.

A look of astonishment flooded Livingston's face and he guffawed. "Jet not handle her? You've got to be kidding. Jet's a real ladies' man. Every time I see him, he's with a different chick."

"Jet?" she repeated dumbly. "Every time you see him, he's with a different chick?"

"Honey."

The natural endearment slipped out and even if Livingston didn't notice it, she did, and her heart did a somersault.

"You keep thinking of him as Jethro, that shy country boy. Once he became a dog, along with the name change, he changed."

"Not for the better, so it seems," Grace replied in a disgruntled voice.

Livingston attempted to smooth Grace's ruffled feathers. "He's just being a typical bachelor. There's no reason to call Doctor Phil or anything. If I hadn't fallen for you, I'd be hangin' right along with him."

The waiter came over to the table, and, handing the menu to him, Livingston said, "I'll have the hot fudge brownie with vanilla ice cream and two spoons."

Beset by emotion from what Livingston had said and not knowing what else to say, Grace said the first thing that came to her mind. "I swear, you act as if every meal is your last."

Livingston opened his eyes wide in exaggeration. "It just might be. You never know which day *is* your last. I mean, I could be gone tomorrow."

"Don't say that," she retorted harshly, "not even kidding around. Don't you ever say that!"

"I'm not going anywhere, Grace. Believe me."

"I'm sorry," she began to apologize for the sharpness of her tone, but he held his hand out to silence her apology.

"You don't need to say anything, Grace. I know the story. I'm Jet's big brother, remember? We have no secrets from each other."

They walked hand in hand to the car. In the dusk, she stared at Livingston's profile and wondered, *Is there anything wrong with him? So far he hasn't jumped out of his crazy bag and for some reason I don't think that he will.*

Livingston felt Grace's eyes on him and turned to look at her. She was unaware that her eyes mirrored the desire that he had for her. Feeling the sexual tension that ran between them, he lifted her hand to his mouth, kissed it, then let it fall back down to his side.

Once seated in the Acura SUV he'd rented for the duration of the time he was in Atlanta, Livingston smoothly pulled out into traffic. No words were spoken between them as they listened to the local jazz station.

Grace sank into the leather interior of the car, and her mind reverted to the conversation she'd had with Solange. *I need to give him a reason to come back. I have never felt so in tune with another man and I don't know if I ever will again. I want to take a chance on him.*

Once they had arrived back at the hotel, the valet eagerly walked up to the car. With a smile and a folded bill Livingston handed him the valet key. "Thank you. I'll call down to the desk when I want my car brought back around."

"Will do, sir," he replied as he tipped his hat.

Drawing in a deep breath, Grace looked at Livingston, the valet, and then back at Livingston. Then she spoke directly to the valet and said, "We won't need it again tonight."

The man unsuccessfully tried to hide a smile as he noted the immediate look of glee cross Livingston's face.

They stared at each other in the quiet elevator as they rode up to the eleventh floor.

Livingston knew that Grace was nervous, but he was nervous also. He had never been as bowled over by a woman as he was by Grace, and because of that he hadn't pressured her for sex. If she had been the kind of woman that he felt wasn't worth the wait, he would have accepted at least one of the numerous advances from the women who were patrons of the hotel.

The outings with Grace that week had been the most fun he'd had in years. Several times he'd felt like taking the ball out of her court, throwing her on the bed and making love to her in such a way that the next time they did make love, the situation would be reversed. Two things had held him in check. One was his respect for her. He knew that initially she might enjoy being overpowered. In a way, it would have let her feel less guilty about sleeping with a man she'd known less than a week. But later on down the road, she might resent it and him, and that wasn't a risk he was willing to take.

Also, there was Jet. He was the brother Livingston had never had. Even though he was three years older than Jet, they had been through a lot together and their bond was strong. If push came to shove, each would give his life for the other. He knew he needed to play no games with his brother's sister.

Grace's declaration to the valet made it easy for him. He now felt no trepidation about the steps he'd take to secure her in his life.

Once inside Livingston's hotel suite, Grace bent over to take off one of her shoes but he stopped her. Guiding her over to the settee, he gently pushed her down. Dropping to one knee, he removed one shoe and began to massage her foot. First, he gently massaged under the bottom of her foot, pressing and rubbing her bones. After he rubbed her foot from heel to toe, he put it down and reached for the other, to which he gave the same painstaking attention. When he was finally done he took his head and buried it deeply in her lap. Livingston took a long sniff, breathing the aroma between her legs.

The only sound in the room was a faint whirr from the air conditioner vent. Grace lightly rubbed his bald head, then molded her hands around his skull as if she were an artist revering a masterpiece.

Not lifting his head, Livingston spoke. "I have something to tell you."

Livingston felt Grace's body tense up and hurriedly explained, "It's good news. At least I hope that you think so." Even though he had rushed to ease her anxiety, he now indulged himself with a pause as he searched her face because he knew that she'd jumped to the wrong conclusion, that he would be leaving in the morning and she might never see him again.

"The owner of the architecture firm that I work for called me yesterday. He wants me to stay in Atlanta and be in charge of the branch here, first to oversee the building of the arena, and then the other projects that are in the works."

Grace's heart thumped so loudly she felt that he must be able to hear it. She could barely speak because she was afraid to get her hopes up. Stuttering, she asked, "What was your answer?"

He gave her a long, probing look. "What do you want my answer to be?"

Tears formed in her eyes and she had to blink them away. "Please stay," she whispered. "I want you to stay."

"That makes two of us."

Livingston stood and pulled Grace up to lean on his tall frame. Bending slightly at the knees, he scooped her up in his arms.

Grace could only choke out, "Oh my!"

Livingston gave her a half smile and self-assuredly strode to the darkened bedroom. The only light came from between the drapes. Pulling the comforter and sheets back, Livingston gently laid her on the bed.

When their eyes connected in the dim light of the bedroom, she knew something wonderful was going to happen. She asked tremulously, "Do you have protection?"

"Always," he responded. He reached into his overnight bag at the foot of the bed and pulled out a box of condoms, which he placed on the nightstand.

Livingston quickly divested himself of his clothing and stood proudly before her. Silently he watched her as a hawk might watch his prey. Then quietly he asked, "Are you sure you're ready?"

Any doubts she might have had were quickly dispelled by the calm, soothing tone he used.

"I am now," she softly responded.

Livingston reached his hand down and began to tug at the front zipper of her dress. Once the zipper reached the hemline, he pushed the top over her arms and Grace leaned forward, eager to help him rid her of her encumbrance. When the dress was around her hips, she raised them slightly. Deftly sliding the dress off her, he threw it on the floor and with one hand he unhooked the front clasp of her bra. Then he placed his hands on the sides of her thong panties, pulled them down and threw them to land on his heap of clothes. Only then did he slide into the bed next to her.

Livingston slowly moved his body over hers, careful not to crush her with his weight.

Sliding her arms around his shoulders, Grace closed her eyes when his lips touched hers. They felt demanding, insistent, yet gentle before he moved his tongue slowly into her mouth. Livingston didn't dart his tongue around in circles, but took his time and leisurely explored every inch until she felt as if she knew his tongue as well as she knew her own. Then she felt his hands as they began to wander. He kneaded her breasts the same way he had earlier massaged her feet, one at a time, and her body arched forward, aching, loving, and longing for more of his touch.

The familiar wetness she felt whenever she was in his company burst like a dam and then overflowed. Surprised, she stiffened in reaction and embarrassment.

For a long moment, Livingston stared in her eyes, then moved his face downward to taste the liquid she had just spilled.

"Good Lord!" was the only way she could express the pleasure she was experiencing from Livingston's expert use of his tongue.

Grace moaned, and moaned, and moaned, and after an eternity, Livingston reached for the box of condoms and quickly sheathed his manhood.

Once she realized he was moving over her again, Grace opened her legs wide, giving him as much access as she possibly could.

Livingston entered her in one fluid movement, and because she was soaking from desire, she felt no discomfort, even though Livingston's manhood was the longest she had ever seen. Immediately he began to stroke. His movements were long, rhythmic ones that had a steady beat and Grace quickly matched his movements. Once again, she felt on the brink of imminent climax. Then Livingston withdrew his shaft.

"Why?" she stuttered.

"I want to prolong this as long as I can," he spoke soothingly. Then before she had a chance to get angry, he reentered her saturated body and began to grind into her with long, deep, strokes.

Grace had slid her arms around his shoulders as he rode her. She clung to him and matched him stroke for stroke until once again a river of satisfaction flooded her body and saturated the sheets.

Only then with a grunt of pleasure did Livingston let go and join her.

Later that night, she was awakened from her fitful sleep by the wandering hands of Livingston.

Grace, who was sleeping on her stomach, felt Livingston's hands cup her buttocks. He began to knead them, and, when she felt him planting kisses on her back, her desire quickly resurfaced. Wanting to feel him inside her, she began to turn over but he stopped her. Manipulating her body so that she was on her knees, he entered her.

Livingston remained completely still as he waited for her to adjust to him. When he could tell that she was comfortable he began to move. Their tempo was slow, then fast, then slow again, and when she began to come, he joined her.

The next morning, the sound of the shower roused her from her deep slumber. Stretching her arms above her head, she winced from the unfamiliar soreness. Her eyes rested on the wrappers of the three condoms they had used. The memories of the previous night quickly surfaced and she settled her head back on the bed and allowed herself the luxury of reliving that time.

Livingston emerged from the bathroom with a towel draped around his middle. “Good morning, sleepyhead.”

“Good morning to you also.” She felt unsure of what he expected, but she knew she felt too shy to get up buck naked and start putting on her clothes.

Livingston stood at the dresser mirror and began to put lotion on his torso. His eyes locked with hers in the mirror and he told her, “My plane leaves in about three hours so I need to get a move on if I'm going to make it.”

She started to get up, gathering the bedclothes around her.

“There's no need for you to hurry to get up. I'm thinking you might be a little sore from last night's activities.”

The twinkle in his eyes made Grace blush.

Livingston let his towel drop and, in the morning light, Grace inspected every inch of his body. As he stepped into his underwear, his firm buttocks looked like those of an Olympic athlete. She relished every minute of his reverse striptease.

Once he was dressed, Livingston walked over and sat on the side of the bed. He took his hand and placed it under her chin. "Last night was wonderful, Grace."

"For me too," she said shyly before dropping her gaze from his.

"I'll be back in less than a month. Wait for me," he ordered.

"I couldn't do anything else."

He pressed a kiss on her forehead, picked up his suitcases and walked out of the hotel room.

CHAPTER 5

"He ain't coming back!" Babs said as she came out from the bathroom of the apartment she shared with Solange.

"He is too," Grace stated with conviction. "Not only will he back, but we will be together."

"How long do you think that's going to last?" Babs snorted with derision. "I wouldn't pin your hopes on you and Livingston being together forever. There's a lot of competition in Atlanta and once he gets acclimated . . ." Her voice rose on the word "acclimated."

"Don't say that to her," Solange said, giving Babs a look filled with anger. "He's moving here for her. He wouldn't do that if he didn't think that they were going to have a lasting relationship."

Grace quickly responded, "I didn't say that he was moving here for me. Things just sort of panned out that way."

"But you did say that he could have turned it down if he wanted to, right?"

"That was my impression," Grace said.

"So there you have it." Solange smiled encouragingly. "People moving out, people moving in," she said.

"Who's moving out?" Grace glanced hopefully in Babs's direction as Babs turned on the television to her favorite show, *Maury*.

"Turn that mess down, Babs," Solange ordered.

"Oh, all right," she said as she hit the mute button on the remote control.

"You remember that headhunter that I was talking to at the club?"

"Sort of," Grace responded, her brow furrowed in concentration, as she tried to remember something other than having met Livingston that night.

"He tipped me off to a job and I interviewed yesterday for a job in New York."

"That was fast," Grace said with a stunned look.

"The word is that for months this firm has been looking for a computer analyst with a background in business to co-manage and eventually take over their stumbling White Plains branch. The salary is twice what I'm now making."

"But New York is so far away," Grace whined. "I'll never get to see you."

"You could come with me. Great teachers are always in demand." Solange gave her a knowing look. "But I know you won't."

Babs looked at Grace and said, "If Solange does move to New York, when your lease is up, do you want to move in here?"

Deciding to be political, Grace demurred, "I don't think so. I'm thinking about buying a condo or townhouse because I'm tired of paying rent. It's like throwing your money down a rat hole. I've been saving my summer school money up for the last few years, and I've built quite a little nest egg for myself."

"What the hell am I supposed to do?" Babs glared at the two of them.

"Since the apartment is in my name, if I get the job I'll continue paying my half of the rent until the lease is up in a couple of months. That should give you enough time to get your act together," Solange said.

Turning her attention back to the matter at hand, Grace asked, "When will you know if you got the job?"

"I'm waiting to hear," Solange said, obviously trying not to get her hopes up.

Babs abruptly cut in. "Have you talked to Jet?"

Treading carefully, Grace said, "Yeah, he stopped by my place the other day and we spent some time together."

"Huh, that liar text messaged me that he was too busy right now to hang out. Then he goes over to your place."

"I told you about giving it up so easily." Solange gave her cousin a stern look. "And you wonder why men don't call you back."

"I'm a free sprit, Solange. It's not my fault that I don't want cobwebs on my stuff like you have. Or you would have if I didn't hear that mechanical boy of yours buzzing in the bedroom with you two or three times a week."

Seeing the look of fury that crossed Solange's face, Grace tried to head off the argument that was sure to ensue. "I don't think that Jet considers spending time with me hanging out," she explained, trying to soothe Babs's ruffled feathers. "We had some family business to discuss."

"Y'all not even family," Babs answered, refusing to be appeased. "He's got a lot of nerve not wanting some more of this," she said as she pointed at the area between her legs. "I rocked his world. And trust me, that wasn't an easy thing to do. I didn't have much to work with, if you know what I mean." Babs took her thumb and placed it at the tip of her forefinger, indicating that was the size of Jet's penis.

Solange gave Babs a look of extreme reproach. "Sometimes I'm really ashamed to call you my cousin, Babs."

"That's really a nasty thing to say." Grace said, glaring at Babs. "Your nickname sure fits you, because you babble too damn much."

"Don't get mad at me because your *brother* ain't got it going on and is dumb. I guess he's just like his namesake."

Stung by her comments about Jet, Grace retorted, "Jethro wasn't so dumb that he didn't know that Miss Jane was chasing him." Then pausing for effect, she added, "And that he didn't want her."

To this, Babs just sucked her teeth and turned the television up so loudly no other conversation was possible.

"Walk me to the door," Grace mouthed to Solange.

They stood in the doorway and Solange whispered, "I'm sorry about that."

"Don't worry about it." Grace spoke with a tinge of sadness in her voice. "That's just sour grapes talking. It must be really sad to keep trying the same thing over and over again and never have it turn out the way you want it to."

Solange agreed by simply nodding her head.

An inexplicable sadness and intuition filled Grace's body. Trying to be happy for her friend, she looked at her and said, "You're going to get the job. I feel it in my bones."

Three weeks later, Grace and Solange sat at Starbuck's drinking their second cup of coffee. "I'm so proud of you for snagging that position, but I don't know what I'm going to do without you." Grace sniffed, trying to hold back tears.

Solange lightly touched Grace's hand. "We'll always be friends." There was a tense silence at the table. "You know that you can call me day or night if you need to talk to me about anything."

Grace kept her head bent and studied a coffee spot on the table.

Trying to lighten the atmosphere Solange asked, "When is the black Yul Brynner coming back?"

Immediately Grace lifted her head and her expression visibly brightened. "He called yesterday. He said that he'll be back a week from tomorrow."

"Where is he going to live?" Solange asked curiously.

"He's moving in with my brother. Jet's secured a pharmacist job and is renting a nearby condo until he can find something that he wants to buy." Grace shrugged her shoulders. "They've lived together before, so it's no big deal."

"Sounds like a plan. You guys will be one big happy family."

Grace said, with a look of happiness, "I'm counting the days until I see him again."

"I guess so," Solange said dryly. "I had a good feeling about him the night we met. I think that he's a keeper."

Grace gave her friend a look out of the corner of her eye. "You know, Solange, like hangs with like. Jet *is* available."

"Not since he slept with Babs, he isn't."

"So he made a mistake. Can you imagine how many men we've dealt with that have been with women like Babs? Unfortunately, with today's man shortage she's not an anomaly."

"You're right. But it's one thing to know and another thing to suspect. That's kind of right in your face. Besides, I'm getting ready to blow this Popsicle stand and if Jet's not willing to move to White Plains it would be a waste of my time and vagina for me to get to know him."

Grace leaned forward so the teenagers sitting at the next table couldn't hear her. "I know what you mean. I never got around a lot, but I wish I could get back my sex from every man I've ever given it to other than Livingston."

"You can't take back sex," Solange responded regretfully.

They both broke into laughter, and Solange dabbed at the moistness gathered at the corners of her eyes because of the laughter.

Grace stopped long enough to ask, "What has Babs decided to do?"

"She's going back to Decatur and moving in with her sister."

"I would hate to have to always live with someone. Can't she afford a one-bedroom apartment on her own?"

"She makes a decent living, but she blows it on nonsense. Every week she buys something new to go out in, and her truck payment is ridiculous. Also, it costs her over eighty dollars a week for gas and the economists see no end in sight. That's one of the reasons why I took this job. Hell, I don't want to move to New York. I don't have any people there or even know anyone. I'm just doing this so I can start building a decent retirement and Social Security package, if it's still there."

"Starting over can be a good thing," Grace said, reaching over to clasp her hand.

"It's going to have to be," Solange replied sadly before returning her squeeze.

Grace stood in front of the stove putting the finishing touches on breakfast. Carefully scraping scrambled eggs onto a plate, she walked over and placed it in front of Livingston.

He was reading the paper, and lowering it, he smiled at Grace, picked up a strip of bacon, and resumed reading.

She sat in his oversized shirt and boxers and, with her chin in her hand, quietly watched him.

Feeling her eyes on him, he folded the paper and put it on the empty chair on the other side of him. "What?" he asked mildly as he gave his breakfast his full attention.

"Oh, nothing." She crossed her legs to sit Indian style in her chair. "I was just thinking how sexy you look reading yesterday's stock market results."

"Is that right?" he replied with a grimace. "Maybe to you I look sexy, but what you're probably seeing is worry. I have too much in one place. If it crashed I would be destitute. After reading the stats on my accounts, I think that maybe I should split some of my money up."

"Is it that serious?"

"Not quite," he reassured her. "After the banking crisis, I funneled a lot of my money into different accounts, but I think I need to spread it around even more. It's just better to be safe than sorry." Then out of the blue he said, "I think that we're encroaching on Jet's single life, so I'm thinking about moving out."

"You think that you're in the way?" she asked, slightly affronted on her man's behalf.

"Maybe one is company but two is overkill," he responded, giving her a wry look as he finished his breakfast.

Now she was really indignant. "He's hardly ever here, so I don't see why that would be the case."

Just then the roar of a motorcycle pulling up outside announced Jet's arrival.

When he opened the door and strode inside the apartment with his helmet in his hand, he looked like a stunt driver in an action movie. Dressed in a black leather jacket, jeans, and black boots, he oozed manliness. Grace thought, *If he wasn't my brother and I didn't have Livingston . . . He looks fine as wine.*

Jet threw his helmet and it landed on the sofa in the adjoining room. Breathing in a deep sigh of tiredness, he eased himself into the chair on the opposite side of the table from where they sat.

"Rough night, man?" Livingston gave Jet a look.

"Pretty much. I broke up with Asia last night."

"Tough deal. I know you've been going with her for more than a minute."

Grace said in a demanding voice, "I sort of liked her. Why did you break up with her?"

"She's not the one, so I decided not to waste any more of her time. You'd think she'd be grateful." He sighed in annoyance.

Grace said caustically, "No woman wants to be dumped, Jet."

Livingston intervened. "If you broke up with her last night, why are you just getting here?"

"She was pretty upset, so I stayed the night and waited until this morning to leave." He gave Livingston a man's look. "I didn't get a wink of sleep all night long."

Now exasperated, Grace asked, "When are you going to settle down?"

"When I get the right woman," he returned just as acidly.

"How will you know if you have the right woman if you don't take the time to let the relationship develop?"

"I'll know from the very beginning." He scrutinized Grace's face and then Livingston's. "That's what happened for you guys, right?"

Livingston spoke to Jet as if they were the only two people in the room. "It did for us, but it doesn't always happen that way, dude."

Jet didn't respond.

"We just want you to be happy, Jet," Grace added softly.

"Leave it alone," he said sharply. "I met the right woman, but she's with another guy, so I gave up." A look of hurt crossed his face, but was quickly replaced by an impassive expression.

As the clock on the wall chimed ten o'clock, Grace reached for the coffee pot and refilled Livingston's mug. She caught Jet watching her movements with an enigmatic look.

Then, Jet eyed Grace's morning attire and said cynically, "Don't you ever go home?"

Taken aback, Grace stuttered defensively, "I'm sorry if I'm in the way."

Jet responded irritably, "Well, I can't walk around naked or anything with you around."

"You want to walk around naked in front of Livingston? What's up with that?" she teased, trying to lighten the atmosphere, which had shifted from an easy camaraderie to one of tension.

"You know what I mean. I have to be fully dressed with you here."

"Good grief, Jet," she scoffed, "you ain't got nothing I ain't seen before. Our mothers used to bathe us together."

Jet got up from the table and retorted sharply, "It doesn't look the way it used to, girl." Then he walked to his bedroom and slammed the door.

Astonished by his rudeness, Grace's mouth gaped open and she looked at Livingston.

He stared thoughtfully at Jet's closed door and, in his calm manner, said, "Until I move out, I think we should move our sleepovers to your place in order to stop us from cramping Jet's style." Then he lifted his newspaper and began reading again.

CHAPTER 6

Grace sat at her desk and with a weary sigh picked up the fourth pile of papers that she needed to grade. "This is the last stack before I call it a day," she muttered to herself. After grading the fifth test paper in a row with a score of less than fifty percent, she withdrew a paper clip from her desk drawer, bound the papers together, and put them in the inside flap of her gradebook to finish when she had more patience.

Her desk telephone rang. Picking up the receiver she said, "Grace Foxfire."

"Hello, Grace. This is James Thomas."

"How are you doing, Mr. Thomas?" Grace liked her principal. She found him easy to talk to, and in the two years since he had been at the school he had made a lot of improvements and instituted a lot of programs to help its students.

"I'm glad that I caught you in." Then he said in a somewhat chiding tone, "You should have been gone over an hour ago."

"I'm on my way out. I was just trying to finish up grading some papers, but I got disheartened by the results and set them aside. I don't know why these kids don't study for tests anymore."

"They're too consumed with other distractions. Video games have been the ruination of today's school system."

"There are computer educational programs out there for them also."

"I know. Too bad that's not what they're purchasing. This leads me to why I wanted to talk to you. How would you feel about going to the International Reading Conference? We need to send a representative, and I have a little extra money in my slush fund to pay for the trip."

"Really?" she said, surprised. "I thought that all of our funds were already depleted for the year."

"Well, I'm robbing Peter to pay Paul. The conference's subject is reading on the content level. It has mini-workshops that showcase how to integrate reading and computer programs in order to reach students performing beneath their grade area. Are you interested?"

"I sure am," she responded excitedly. "Where is the workshop being held?"

"In Manhattan. I'll go ahead and have my secretary make all the arrangements. Do your TDY paperwork for the week before Thanksgiving."

"Yes, sir," she replied enthusiastically. After she hung up the phone she said, "I can't wait to call Solange."

The wind whipping around the street corner sent a chill down her spine. Feeling a sneeze coming on, she covered her mouth with her hand and then reached in her pocketbook. Before she could withdraw a tissue, a man standing next to her handed her his handkerchief. She declined with a smile. "No, thanks," she said, "I got it."

"I don't usually do this," the man said nervously, "but if you're not married, would you like to go and have a cup of coffee?"

"Oh, I'm sorry," she said, nonplussed, "but I can't."

"You're already taken, huh? I'm not surprised, the beautiful ones always are."

Now she took a good look at him. At first glance he wasn't someone that you would give a second look, but on closer inspection Grace felt herself drawn to his eyes. There was something kind in them, as if life hadn't been so hard on him that he had soured. Smiling in response but without speaking, Grace crossed the street when the light changed. She deliberately put a little distance between herself and her admirer. She had been living in Atlanta for five years and had never had she been approached in such a forward way. Now that she had Livingston and was not looking for another man, she'd been approached quite a few times by men who looked presentable and professional. *Solange would have found him attractive.* Even though she spoke to her on the telephone and via e-mail a couple of times a week, she missed her friend dreadfully and couldn't wait until she got to see her next week.

When she let herself into her apartment, she kicked off her shoes and went to the refrigerator. After pouring herself a glass of wine, she walked, glass in hand, to her bedroom. Seeing the blinking light on the answering machine she pressed the control and grinned when she heard Livingston's voice. "Honey, call me when you get in." There was a short beep and then Jet's voice, "Hey, birthday girl. You're getting old. Call me." Then another beep and Solange's voice. "Why don't you have your cell phone on? Did you get anything in the mail from me?"

"I don't know because I didn't check the mail yet, Solange," she spoke to the answering machine.

Picking up the receiver, she quickly dialed Livingston's number.

"Livingston Lockhart."

"Hey, darling. What's cookin', good lookin'?"

"Not a thing but a chicken wing," he responded to her banter. "Are you ready for your birthday present?"

"Did you buy me anything?" she laughed.

"I have a present for you and then some," Livingston responded suggestively.

"Hmm, I wonder what that could be," she replied innocently.

"You'll just have to see, won't you? I made seven o'clock dinner arrangements for us at Morton's."

"Well, well, well. I know that I'm pickin' in high cotton now."

"Hang with me and there's more where that came from. I'll see you right after six."

"Will do," she answered before she hung up the telephone.

When Grace opened the door and saw Livingston she gasped. He would be handsome even dressed in overalls, but tonight he looked positively debonair in his black double-breasted suit and white shirt open at the collar. His face was clean except for the thick mustache that he always kept trimmed neatly.

She, too, had gone the extra mile with her appearance. Her red dress that stopped a couple of inches above her knees was the perfect contrast to her paper-sack tan complexion. In celebration of her birthday, she'd added eyelash extensions to frame her honey-colored oval eyes and dramatic red lipstick to match her nails. Her black square-toe pumps completed her outfit and made her look and feel chic.

Livingston devoured her with his eyes, and without regard to her lipstick gathered her in his arms and gave her a long, deep kiss.

Breathless when she finally came up for air she managed, "You just gave me the best birthday gift anyone could ask for."

"Don't be too sure of that," he replied suggestively. "Ready to go?"

"I sure am," she answered. "Just let me lock up."

As Livingston drove them to the restaurant, she felt an anticipation that she'd never felt before. Memories of the many lonely birthdays she'd had or the ones that would have been depressing if not for her female friends, felt light years away.

She was glad when Livingston interrupted her thoughts. "Have you heard from Jet today?"

"He left me a message on my answering machine wishing me a happy birthday. I was running late so I didn't get a chance to return his call. I'll do it before I leave for New York."

"What time does your plane leave Monday?"

"Not until twelve o'clock. The car service is going to pick me up at nine forty-five."

"Are you sure you don't want me to take you to the airport?"

"No, because you would have to leave work and you'd get caught in all that morning traffic on the interstate. That's about three of hours of driving."

"When are you going to see Solange?"

"She's going to pick me up from the airport. Also, since you and I didn't get around to seeing it when it was here, she got tickets for us to see *Wicked* and we're going to hang out whenever she can get away. All three days I'm done with my classes by three o'clock so I'm wide open after that."

"Good," he said with satisfaction. "That means you'll be so occupied that you won't have a chance to look for another man."

Grace knew by the glint in Livingston's eyes that he was teasing. "Like I could leave this." She dropped her hand between his legs and cupped him. "I don't know how I'm going to make it without your lovemaking as it is. Four days is a bit of a stretch for us."

"I'll make sure that I give you a good once-over the night before you leave."

"That's something I can get on board with."

Once they were seated at the restaurant, Grace looked around and then said to Livingston, "I'm surprised you accepted this table. You usually insist on something a little more secluded."

"I wanted you to be the center of attention. After all, you *are* the birthday girl."

Grinning at him, she looked at her menu. "I don't know what's good here. Order for me, please."

He nodded affirmatively and when the waitress came to the table he said without hesitation, "We'll start off with a bottle of your best champagne, then Caesar salad, broiled steak with sautéed onions, corn and garlic mashed potatoes."

"Yes, sir," she replied, leaving with their menus.

Once their food arrived, they attacked it with relish. Livingston always had a healthy appetite, and Grace hadn't had anything to eat since a bagel with cream cheese at breakfast because she didn't want to look bloated in her dress.

Once full of food, she sat sipping her wine. Livingston spoke after wiping his mouth. "I saw a house that you might be interested in seeing."

Grace's heart skipped a beat. "You did?"

"I saw it because it's one block over from the development my company's building. It's almost finished, but the people who put the deposit on it can't afford it. The husband lost his job because his company downsized."

"That's a tough break, but I don't know if I want to benefit from someone else's bad luck," she answered doubtfully.

"It's not your fault that this family is going through hard times. Blame the economy. They may be able to keep the one that they're in because the wife is still working. I think that we should look at it before you go to New York. It's perfect for you."

"It is?"

"You could even pick out your own colors and carpeting." His eyes scrutinized her face with an intensity that was somewhat disarming. "I listen to you talk, Grace. Whenever you look at building plans that I have lying around my place, you point out what you like and what you don't like."

"How much is it?'

When Livingston quoted her the price, her face immediately fell. "I could never afford that."

He said slowly, "You couldn't, but we could."

Livingston reached inside his coat and pulled out a blue velvet box. Opening it, he turned the box around to face her. "Grace Foxfire, I love you with all my heart. Will you marry me and make a life with me?"

Stunned, Grace stared at the large princess-cut diamond ring; the diamonds outshone the fire of the lit candles on the table. Tears of joy cascaded down her face.

"Yes, yes, Livingston. I would love to be your wife."

The couples at the nearby tables had been surreptitiously watching the drama unfold and when they saw Grace nod her head and stick her hand out, and as Livingston slipped the ring on her finger, they applauded.

Once they arrived back at her apartment, Grace locked the door and leaned back on it.

Livingston stood there watching her with a quizzical look on his face. "What?" he asked.

"It's like a dream that I don't want to end." She smiled softly. "I'm so happy that I'm afraid."

"Don't be afraid, Grace. We'll be together forever."

And then, as was his custom, he picked her up and carried her to the bedroom.

After being placed gently on the bed, she lay back, eyes to the ceiling. *There is a God.* Then she got up.

Impatiently she unfastened her bra and pulled down her underwear. Then she stepped out of her shoes and gently pushed Livingston's chest, making him sit on the bed.

Kneeling, she deftly removed his shoes. Then she stood and pulled off first his jacket, then his shirt and undershirt. She lovingly moved her hands across his chest, and then, naked, she sat in his lap and burst into tears.

Livingston put his arms comfortingly around her. "There, there, Grace. This is our engagement night. Why are you crying?" he asked in a wondering voice.

She tried to quell her tears. "I cry when I'm happy. I never thought I'd find the right man to love me the way I want to be loved."

"Grace, relax." His eyes held her captive. "I'll never leave you and we are going to have the type of love that people make romantic movies about." Then sliding her off his lap, he unbuckled his trousers and got naked.

Grace dropped to her knees, grasped his penis and slowly urged him towards her.

"Ouch," Livingston grunted so Grace relaxed her grip. Gently she took her forefinger and smoothed it across his tip. It was wet with moisture, and the discovery made her wet. Taking both of her hands, she cupped his testicles, lightly teasing them. Then she bent towards him and very slowly drew him into her mouth. First she took a little of him in, then let him back out. Then she took in more of him and then she let him back out, only holding onto his tip.

Livingston moaned and she knew that his eyes were closed because he took his right hand and placed it on her shoulder in order to steady himself to keep from falling.

Then she quit teasing him and took him fully into her mouth. Grace sucked him until she couldn't suck any more, and she knew Livingston had been fulfilled when he spilled into her mouth.

Quickly rising, she went into the bathroom, and rinsed her mouth. Once she returned, Livingston was lying in bed holding out the bedclothes. She slid in next to him.

Livingston slid into her eager body and began to furiously pump with long, aching motions. "Livingston, I love you," were the only words spoken before they peaked.

The next morning, she rolled over and looked at the clock. *I never sleep to ten o'clock in the morning.* The chiming of her doorbell made her hurriedly grab a robe and walk barefoot to look through the peephole. Immediate happiness enveloped her when she saw that it was Jet.

"Hey," she smiled.

"Hey to you, too," he responded, kissing her upturned cheek and handing her a box.

"Uh-oh, what's this?" she said in mock surprise.

"Don't even try it, Grace. You know it's your birthday present."

Joyfully, she skipped over to the couch and tore open the large box. Dumbfounded, she stared at what was inside. It was Jet's mother's mink coat.

Jet walked over to Grace's kitchen counter and flipped on the switch of the preset coffee maker, which immediately began to gurgle.

"Why?" she whispered.

"Because I know how much you loved it, and I think Mom would have wanted you to have it."

"This should be saved and given to your future wife."

He avoided her eyes and responded with, "She wouldn't have the emotional ties to it that you have."

"Are you sure?" Grace searched his eyes for reassurance.

"I'm sure," he said.

Grace walked into the living room to stand in front of the mirror mounted on the wall. Wrapping the coat around her, she felt a peace envelope her. *It feels right. If it didn't feel right, I wouldn't keep it.*

Loving the way she looked, she spun around to face Jet, who was smiling at the picture she made. "Thank you so much, Jet. You've have helped complete the best birthday I've ever had."

"Really?" He grinned at her ecstatic expression.

"Yep," she answered. "Have you talked to Livingston this morning?"

"No. I called his office, but he was out."

"Then you haven't heard the news. Wait right here."

She ran down the hallway and grabbed her ring out of the box on her nightstand. Gently sliding it on her finger, she ran back to the kitchen and proudly held her hand out. "Look, Livingston and I are engaged."

A myriad of emotions passed across Jet's face. Then he said, with an inscrutable expression, "Congratulations, Grace. I know that you'll be very happy."

After Jet left, Grace practically danced around the apartment as she packed for her trip. Glancing at her watch, she saw she'd better step on it if she wanted to finish before she met Livingston at the house he wanted her to see.

When Grace pulled her Jeep up to the address Livingston had given her, she gasped. The large two-story red-brick Colonial looked imposing with its newly paved driveway. As she stared in wonder, Livingston drove up in the company car.

He walked towards her as she rolled down the window and asked, "What do you think?"

"I haven't been inside, but if it's anywhere near as nice as the facade, I'll love it."

"Let's go and check it out." He grinned at her before he strode up the walkway.

Grace followed him, astonished when he produced a key.

"Because we're in the same business, the builder let me borrow it so you could get a real good look at it. It's a lot of money to spend for something if you're not completely satisfied."

"Tell me about it," she said, maneuvering around him to walk into a long foyer flanked by two sunken rooms.

"This one is the living room," he said, pointing to the left, "and the other is the dining room. And the door to the dining room opens up to a kitchen with an island."

With Livingston acting as tour guide, they journeyed through an oversized den, four bedrooms, four bathrooms and an upstairs game room and a loft.

Once they reached the screened-in porch with a Jacuzzi, she turned to her fiancé and said, "May I have this house, please?"

"Yes, ma'am, you may have it." He grinned.

CHAPTER 7

"Why are you leaving now? You're the best man in my wedding." Livingston leaned on the door jamb and watched Jet as he packed his belongings.

"I'll be back for that. You can count on it."

"It's unlike you to make rash decisions. Hell, it took you two years to decide that you wanted to move back to the Atlanta area, and now you want to pull up stakes and move to that small town?" Livingston looked appalled at the thought of a single man leaving Atlanta, with its bevy of beautiful women, for a country town.

Jet averted his eyes as he slammed the closet doors shut. "I think it's a good thing for me to move back to Lake City. I have ties there."

"You never seemed all that attached to it when we were in college. You hardly ever went home." Livingston carefully scrutinized Jet's face, but he couldn't get a read on what was really going on with him.

"I was too busy partying with the honeys back then. But my focus has changed. Besides, I don't have the dislike for the place that Grace does, and with the not-so-good memories, I'll make better ones."

"You don't even have a job there."

"I don't need a job right now. I'm going to be pretty busy building my new house on Red Hill. I'm going to do some of the work myself."

"Red Hill?"

"Yes, it's about an acre of land on the outskirts of town. I've already scoped out where I want to build my dream house." Jet gave him a slight smile. "So you see, I do have a plan."

"But why now? This is too all-of-a-sudden."

"Not really. I've been thinking for some time that Atlanta isn't where I want to make my permanent residence, and if I'm going to build a house, I need to invest in the right place."

Hours later, Jet walked into the den where Livingston sat quietly nursing a beer and sat in the easy chair across from him. Jet held his bottle out in Livingston's direction. "Cheers," he said, then took a swig.

Livingston asked quietly, "Why didn't you tell me?"

Jet's body froze but he didn't respond.

"Why didn't you tell me that you're in love with Grace?"

Jet sat there staring at the dark liquid in his bottle.

Finally he spoke, pain evident in every word. "Because she loves you and not me."

"Does she even know?" Livingston stared at his fraternity brother with compassion in his eyes.

"She doesn't have a clue, and you have to keep it on the down low," he muttered.

"I won't say anything." Livingston gave Jet an intense stare. "Did you ever make a move on her?"

Jet turned eyes bright with anger and he scowled at Livingston.

He hastily amended his words, "I mean before we got together."

"No, because I wasn't sure of what I was feeling. I always pushed thoughts like that to the back of my mind. I thought it might be a teenage crush. Even back in the day, on the sly my mother used to tease me about it. But when she came to my mother's funeral, even in the midst of my sorrow, all of the feelings that I've ever had for her resurfaced." He shot a look of anguish at Livingston. "But I could see that she only thought of me as her brother. So after we buried Mom, I ran, and it wasn't until I saw her at Sutra that I realized my love for her would never change."

"And then I met her and I, too, fell for her right away," Livingston said solemnly.

Jet nodded his head and said, "She can have that effect on people."

Guilt was written all over Livingston's face. "Why didn't you tell me? Maybe I would have . . ."

Jet interrupted him. Hoarsely, he asked, "Would have what? Not gone for it?"

Livingston mumbled, "You should have made your feelings known to her."

"What good would that have done?" Raw emotion was reflected in every word. "I saw the way she looked at you that night. She's never looked at me like that."

"I would have never come on to her, made love to her, or asked her to marry me had I known how you felt."

Jet looked at Livingston and stated with certainty, "I know that. And that's why it's okay. You love her and she loves you. I've made my peace with that."

"I don't want things to change between us."

The air in the room hung heavy. "It won't. I just need some time to adjust, and I can't do it here around the two of you."

After Jet was gone, Livingston sat in the easy chair of the almost-vacant apartment and stared with deep concentration at the now-lukewarm beer in his glass.

When Grace spied Solange waiting for her at the curb outside the arriving flights door with a huge smile spread across her face, she hurried towards her and was met halfway. Grace returned her warm bear hug and exclaimed, "Gee whiz, it's already freezing up here."

"No kidding." Solange gave an exaggerated shudder. "They say you get used to it, but so far I haven't."

"Give it time." She gave a wolf whistle as she threw her bags in the back seat of the new Cadillac STS Solange was driving. "You go, girl. You're really rolling now."

Solange gave her a look. "I was so depressed the first six months that I was here, no family, or no friends, I decided that I needed to reward myself with something big before I chucked it all away and hauled ass back to Atlanta."

"You're more than welcome to come back," Grace encouraged.

"No, I think I'll stay put for awhile. I'm starting to get my footing and things are developing quite nicely."

"Oh well. It was worth a try. By the way, thanks for picking me up, but I could've caught the train to the city."

"Oh, I don't mind. I didn't go back to work after lunch. You can do that when you're the boss."

"Sho' you right."

Once they reached the Marriott in Manhattan, Grace registered and handed the card key to the bellboy. "Please take these bags to room 813."

Looking over at the bar area, Grace offered, "How about me buying you a drink from the lounge?"

"That would hit the spot. I could really use one."

"I really could use one, too. Of course the school flew me coach and kids cried all the way here. I could've screamed from frustration, but I just ground my teeth and bore it because one day, it might be my kid."

They were now seated in lounge area waiting for their drinks.

"Speaking of having children, how's Livingston?" Solange teased.

The waiter put their drinks down and as Solange picked hers up from the table, Grace gushed, "He's great!" Then, unable to contain her news any longer, she reached into her handbag and pulled out her ring box.

Solange gasped when she saw the beautiful diamond winking at her in the subdued lighting.

"We have to have it sized, but I wanted to bring it and show it to you." Grace slid the ring on her finger and held her hand out to Solange. "We're getting married!"

Solange clapped her hands. "Congratulations! I'm so happy for you. Have you set a date yet?"

"The first day of spring. We're going to go to Jamaica for a few days for our honeymoon. Which brings me to something I wanted to ask you, Solange. I love you to death." She was swallowing hard because she felt so choked up. "You're the sister I never had. Will you be my maid of honor?"

Tears glistened in Solange's eyes. "I would be honored."

Grace sipped her glass of white wine and watched Solange over the rim of her glass. Noticing her healthy complexion and the look of contentment on her face she said, "Okay, what gives? You look awfully happy for somebody living in this cold-ass state."

"What?" Solange opened her eyes wide and responded with, "Whatever do you mean?"

Grace snapped her fingers. "You got a man," she exclaimed. "'Fess up, what's his name?"

Solange feigned insult. "I don't like the idea that you think that I need a man to make me happy. I'm a progressive woman. I don't need . . ."

"Blah, blah, blah, blah, blah," Grace interrupted her. "Don't even try to sidestep my question. I know that you don't need a man, but there's nothing wrong with having or wanting one. There's something going on with you, I can tell."

"Oh, all right." Solange leaned forward. "You know me too damn well for me to get away with anything. There may be someone." She hesitated. "He's perfect way in every way but one."

"Well, if he's perfect in every way but one, snatch him up." Grace ordered. "What's wrong with him?"

Grace's cell phone rang, interrupting their conversation. Her annoyed look was replaced with happiness when she saw that it was Livingston.

"Hey, babe," she breathed.

"Hey, Livingston," Solange hollered across the table.

"Livingston says 'Hey,' " she said to Solange. "What?" Grace's eyebrows furrowed in irritation. "Oh no, I don't care what you need to do to get it." Then there was another long silence before she said, "I can't come back for that."

Solange watched the love in Grace's eyes as she held the telephone receiver to her ear.

Then with a soft smile on her lips, Grace spoke softly, "I know. I love you, too. Talk to you tomorrow."

Solange eyed Grace with concern. "Is anything wrong?"

"Not now. I think the crisis has been averted." She absently chewed her bottom lip. "Before I left, Livingston showed me this house and we decided to buy it."

"Gee, you guys are moving fast."

"Well, we're tired of cramping Jet's style. He's still very much the playful bachelor."

"Go figure," Solange said without surprise.

"We thought we had the house in the bag, but there's another couple that also wants it and they are willing to pay the builder more, so if we want it we have to go up on the price."

"Is the house worth it? Why not look around for something else?"

"No, this is the one that I want. It's uncanny. When Jet and I were growing up, there was this beautiful house in Lake City that we used to ride by when we were on our school bus. We used to stare at it all the time. Of course,

I never went inside, but the house Livingston showed me very closely resembles it. It's almost as if he knew, but he couldn't have because I'd never spoken of it to him."

"What are you going to do?"

"Livingston will take care of it. It's nice to be taken care of for once. I've been doing it all for so long, I'm tired."

Solange nodded her head. "I hear you. It appears that Livingston really has turned out to be the man of your dreams."

"He has," she exhaled. "We're going up on our price to match the other guy's, and I told Livingston to go ahead and do a contract and the bank paperwork while I'm gone. I absolutely do not want to lose that house," she ended with authority.

The educational conference was held in the banquet room of the hotel. After three days of accelerated classes, Grace felt reinvented. Her mind was teeming with fresh ideas to take back to her coworkers. As she nibbled on a blueberry muffin from the continental breakfast that was provided, she smiled when she saw two teachers she'd been associating with since she'd entered the dining area.

Minutes later, Emily and Miles came over to her with paper plates full of donuts, pastry, and bagels. Emily sat down and said, "Thank God this is it. I'm ready to get back to Philly."

Grace gave her a piercing look. "I thought that you enjoyed all of the workshops and techniques that they introduced to us."

"I did. Too bad we can't use any of this stuff."

Looking at Emily from across the table, Miles broke in, "I know what you mean. Year after year I come to the conference and leave buoyed by ideas, thinking that I'm going to change the whole way I teach for the next school year. Then after I talk to my principal and tell him the new things that I want to institute, he tells me we don't have the funds for it."

"That's what I mean. It feels like I just wasted my time. And because I'm one of the newbies in the school, I'm lucky to have a job, so I don't want to make too many waves."

"Well, my principal's different," Grace said. "He has a real yearning to make a difference. He believes inner-city schools are the crux of the education crisis."

"They're the ones that get shafted the most." Emily spoke with anger. "They get cut on funding if their students don't measure up on standardized tests, when they are the very schools that need to be given even more money to institute the programs we've been introduced to this week."

"If my principal can get this for us, he will," Grace stated with conviction.

Miles said, "Mine would, too, if he could. Where's the money going to come from to have one computer per student in a class?"

Emily added, "That's what's needed to make it successful. And not just one computer per student, but one *working* computer per student."

Not wanting to feel too discouraged, Grace changed the subject. "What are you guys doing this evening?"

"The same thing I did the last two nights. Watch some television and call it a night."

"Me, too. The least they could have done was to have a mixer for us or something," Miles said.

"Didn't you go out and see the city at all?" Grace asked.

"Yes, but because I live so close, I spend a lot of time in New York, so there was really nothing new to see," replied Emily.

"Well, this has been a dream for me. My best friend and maid of honor for my wedding works in White Plains and she's come over every day and we've hung out. Tonight we're going to see *Wicked.* I would've invited you guys along had I thought about it."

"I've already seen it with my wife and kids," Miles said.

"That's okay. My district's textbooks are up for adoption and I brought along copies so I can get a look at the new crap they're trying to push down our throats."

Grace's jaw dropped as she saw the long queue of people in front of the theatre. "That's a true sign that a play is worth seeing when you see this many people standing in 45-degree weather."

"It better be worth it," Solange warned. "If it isn't I'm going to demand my money back."

"Or at least a free glass of wine," Grace added, rubbing her hands together to keep them warm.

Solange reached over and took Grace's hand in hers and warmed them between her gloved hands. "You should have told me to bring an extra pair of gloves," she lightly admonished.

"I totally forgot," Grace explained. "I always pack like a two-year-old when I travel and always forget something."

"Here." Solange took off her left glove and handed it to Grace, who tried to refuse it. Then taking in the stubborn look on Solange's face, she acquiesced. They each wore one glove and clasped each other's naked hand for warmth.

As they walked to the end of the line, they heard a male voice whisper, "Look at those two lesbians. Aren't they hot?"

Upon hearing this, Grace rolled her eyes and Solange sadly shook her head. "I would straighten them out," Grace said, "but who cares what they think? Women can't be close friends without people getting the wrong idea."

"You're right. It's so juvenile." Solange snapped her fingers and moved her head from side to side. "I got a man."

Grace complained, "Are you going to let me meet this Ali Marks or not?"

"He's a police officer and he's out of town for special training. If things continue the way they are, I'll bring him to the wedding."

"Promise?" Grace asked.

"Promise," Solange repeated.

The curtain slowly opened to show a set that was tinged in hues of green and gold. Darkness settled on the theatre and made the audience feel as if it was midnight everywhere in the world. Fascinated, Grace and Solange stared at the lithe actress with black hair to her waist as she swayed to center stage and began to sing a mournful song that shook the chandeliers.

For over an hour, the audience sat in silence as they watched in awe and fell in love with the new version of *The Wizard of Oz.* At intermission, Grace and Solange stood in line at the theatre's store and Grace purchased a pair of green sunglasses as souvenirs. "I'm going to save these as a keepsake for my little girl."

"Little girl," Solange said, astonished. Her eyes rested on Grace's stomach. "You're not pregnant, are you?"

"Of course not," Grace chuckled. "Livingston and I want to do this the old-fashioned way. We're not even going to live in the same house together until we get married."

"What are you going to do with that big house?"

"Livingston is going to move in. Remember my landlord talked me into a two-year lease agreement in order to keep my rent down. I have a little while to go on it before it's over. Livingston doesn't really have any furniture, so to speak, because he sold it all for a song when he moved from Chicago, so I'm going to start setting up house. It'll be fun, going around shopping for all new stuff."

The lights in the theatre blinked and a bell rang three times. Placing her sunglasses in her oversized pocketbook Grace said, "It's time to get back." Arm in arm, she and Solange hurried back to their seats.

Flabbergasted, Grace stared at Livingston. "Why is Jet leaving now?" She stood in the middle of the living room with her arms akimbo. "I'm going to call him and try to talk him out of leaving."

As Grace reached for the telephone, Livingston spoke in a tone that brooked no argument, "Leave him alone."

"But now we have to change all our plans."

"Not all of our plans, Grace, just our living arrangements. You'll move into our new house because I promised Jet that I would finish out his lease for him. It's the least I can do, and I have to live somewhere."

"How about my place? I hope the landlord will let me out of my lease."

"He will. I called him and talked to him before I told Jet that it was doable. Think about how much easier it will be for you to set up house."

"I think he's making a mistake."

"It's his life and he knows what he's doing."

"I don't think that he does," Grace retorted heatedly. "Jet has really gotten on my nerves since he moved back from Chicago. First, he goes from woman to woman. Also, he's riding a motorcycle and knows how dangerous that can be. If I remember correctly, as a teenager when he expressed an interest in getting one, his mother wouldn't let him. And now he's pulling up stakes and moving to that country town." Grace shuddered at the thought.

"Jet's a grown-ass man. He can live his life however he wants."

"But we need him here," she whined. "I need him here."

Livingston scrutinized her face for one whole minute. Then he asked curiously, "Why do you need him here?" Livingston pointed his index finger to his chest and said, "I'm your fiancé. Don't you think that I'm enough for you?"

"Of course you are, babe." Grace lightly tapped him three times on his bald head. "It's just that it doesn't make any sense for Jet to leave right now."

"He knows what he's doing," Livingston replied with certainty.

Grace again reached for the telephone. "I'm just going to ask him to stay until after the wedding. It won't kill him to put his moving plans off for a couple of months. He doesn't even have to work because he doesn't need the money."

"Grace," Livingston ordered. "Put the telephone down and leave him the hell alone."

Miffed, Grace did as she was told before she stomped into the kitchen to stack the dishwasher.

CHAPTER 8

The next day, Grace sat across from her principal, James Thomas. "I was impressed by what I saw. The Edge program has a proven track record of raising students' reading scores," she said.

Mr. Thomas sadly shook his head. "We can't possibly come up with funds for one computer per student. That's an outrageous amount of money."

Grace unsuccessfully tried to mask her disappointment. "I know that it would be hard, but that's what it would take to make the program successful. I'm willing to cut down on some of the overhead. I'll come in for free after school and on Saturdays to train the other teachers."

"Grace, thanks for offering to go the extra mile but that would be just a drop in the bucket," Mr. Thomas said.

"Maybe the county would purchase twenty-five computers and we could set up a computer lab. Then we could do a schedule and teachers would have specific times to go."

"That's an idea worth looking into farther on down the road. But while you were gone, budget cuts came down and each principal is supposed to cut their workforce by twenty percent."

Crestfallen, Grace asked her principal, "What is the government doing to the educational system?"

"They're killing it one budget at a time," he replied.

Exhausted, Grace let herself into Livingston's apartment with her key and threw her briefcase in a corner of the foyer. She sniffed appreciatively at the aroma of food. "Uh-oh, what did you do?" she walked up behind Livingston and slid her arms around his waist.

"What's the matter? Can't a man cook for his woman without having done something wrong?"

"Yes, a man can, but does he?" she teased, leaning around him to view the fajitas in a stir-fry pan.

"I do sort of have a favor to ask of you," he said as he portioned out food onto two plates and handed her one. "My mom called today and she and my sister and her kids want to come to the engagement party."

"That's a wonderful idea. I really ought to meet them before the wedding, don't you think?" She grinned a little sheepishly because she'd been too busy to even begin a dialogue with them via telephone.

He sat down across from where she'd already seated herself. "It's a little more than that. They've never been to Atlanta and would like to stay for a couple of days. Do a little sightseeing."

"Oh! That would be okay, but I don't know if I can take any more time off from work because I just got back from New York."

"I don't expect you to entertain them; just let them stay with you because you have the room. I'll do it and whatever I can't do, I'll give them a map."

Sounds like a plan," she agreed, quelling the butterflies in her stomach about meeting her future in-laws.

"I'm glad we got that settled. Now back to the more mundane matters. How was your day?"

Grace swallowed a mouthful of food. "Horrible. We didn't get funding for the reading program."

"Let me get this right! The county pays for you to go to New York, they put you up, and then they're not going to institute the program that you highly recommend?"

"That's the gist of it."

"Well, at least you got a free trip to New York and got to see Solange."

"That was good. By the way, did I tell you that she called yesterday and said that she's also flying down for the engagement party next week?"

Livingston wiped his mouth with a napkin. "You didn't, but I assumed she would want to be here for you the same way Jet is coming to be here for me."

"Humph! I'm still a little annoyed with him."

Livingston's eyes pinned hers and he said brusquely, "Leave him alone, Grace. By the way, Jet asked if it was okay for him to bring a date and I said that it was fine."

"Really?" Grace's eyes widened. "He's not brought a woman around since he and Asia split. This might be the beginning of something serious."

"All Jet needs is the right woman and he'll be as contented as I am." Livingston leaned over and kissed the mouth automatically turned up towards him. "And in the meantime, he promised to give me one hell of a bachelor party."

Grace walked down a long corridor. Fog swirled around her feet as she looked around wildly for someone to point her in the direction she was supposed to go. She tried to call out but no words were forthcoming. Slowly, she pushed one foot in front of the other and when she came abreast of a long mirror, she realized that she was naked. Grace took her hands and tried to cover her breasts to no avail. She dropped her hands to hang futilely by her sides. In front of her she saw an open door and when she walked through it, she saw that the room was vacant except for an empty hospital bed.

"Grace, Grace." In the deep recesses of her mind, she heard Livingston's voice and felt his hand shaking her shoulder. She desperately tried to pry herself from the dream but she couldn't. *She walked over to the bed, and climbing on it she pulled the sheet over her entire body, covering her face.*

Grace tried to focus on Livingston's face as he peered at her. She was bathed in sweat from head to toe. Still trembling and unable to speak, she reached for the glass of water Livingston held out to her. She gulped the liquid and sat up as she began to sputter.

Concern was etched on his face. He sat on the side of the bed and searched hers. "What's the matter?"

Grace couldn't answer.

"Grace," he prompted.

"I had a nightmare," she whispered.

"I know." He spoke in a soothing tone and took his hand and wiped the tears. "I'm used to you thrashing in your sleep at night, but you usually settle down after a while."

"I'm afraid," she whispered.

"It was just a dream." Livingston tried to console her and reached out to grab her but she pushed him away.

"The first time I had this dream, it was the night before my mother died."

"The first time?"

"Yes, and the second time was right before Jet's mother died."

He tried to soothe her. "Those are unfortunate coincidences. But that's what they are, Grace, just coincidences."

"No, they're not!" Grace's voice bordered on hysteria and her eyes looked maniacal. "I'm going to lose you, I just know it."

"Grace, nothing is going to happen to me." He gripped her shoulders, gently shaking her. "Look at me! We're getting married next week and nothing is going to go wrong." Then sliding back into bed next to her, he pulled her close. "You'll see," he murmured, his voice already husky as he drifted back to sleep. "We're going to grow old and cranky together, sitting on rocking chairs in our front porch."

For the rest of the night she lay awake with her eyes fixated on a spider web in the corner of the bedroom.

The engagement party was being held at the country club on Lakeshore Drive. Between the two of them, they had sent out over seventy-five invitations and made sure there was plenty of food so no one would go hungry. There was a buffet with hors d'oeuvres and a wine bar with a bartender graciously refilling glass after glass. Music played in the background, but so far no one seemed inclined to dance. Instead, they clustered in small groups socializing, and Grace moved from group to group to make sure everyone was having a good time.

At one point, she looked over her shoulder and spied Livingston in a corner, laughing with a group of men who were his frat brothers and coworkers. As if he sensed her eyes on him from across the room, he turned and gave her a wink, which she returned.

Then she turned her attention to some of her single female coworkers eyeing Livingston's entourage.

Madeline, one of her favorites from work, broke away from the group and sidled up next to her. She patted her red hair and said, "Gee, why didn't you tell me that your fiancé knew all these fine men? This place is like match.com or something."

"I know. Before I met Livingston, I never even knew these men existed in Atlanta."

"I think there must be some fine men's club they hang out at and we don't know the location."

"Must be," Grace agreed.

She looked at the door and said excitedly, "Excuse me, Madeline. I want to greet my maid of honor, who's just arrived with her cousin."

Grace practically ran over and enfolded them in a group hug. "I've been wondering where you were."

"It's my fault," Babs said. "I just couldn't find a thing to wear."

"It doesn't look that way to me." Grace gave Babs a quick perusal. It was true. Babs looked stunning in an apple-green dress that clung to her body and showed every curve of her five-foot, nine-inch frame. Still, she didn't outshine Solange, who was dressed in a subdued soft green shift dress and matching pumps. She said to Solange, "I can't put my finger on it, but something about you is different."

"That's for sure," Babs muttered. "Excuse me, but I hear the bar calling my name."

"What's going on?" Grace demanded.

"I brought Ali with me. He's taking our stuff to the hotel room."

"I hate that you won't stay with me while you're in town. There's enough room for you and Ali. Babs, too, if she wants."

"No thanks. I think you've got your hands full enough as it is. How's that going, by the way?"

"Quite well actually. Rose, Livingston's mother, is real sweet. I mean, she's kind of on the quiet side, but I like her." Grace laid her hand on her heart. "She calls me 'daughter.' His sister, on the other hand, is a real firebrand. Where I live, they're building a new house down the street, and you can hear them banging those hammers early in the morning. She went down there and asked them why they had to start working before seven o'clock in the morning when people were trying to sleep. It would have been funny if people didn't know that she's staying with me."

"So you like them?" Solange examined Grace's face.

"Yes, I do, thank God."

Solange, with a tinge of jealousy apparent in her voice, said, "Don't start liking them more than you like me."

Grace scoffed. "That would be impossible. I'm just relieved that we get along so well because I know how much Livingston loves his family, and it's hard when people don't like their in-laws. I have friends at work that hate when we have summer vacation because a lot of times their spouse's kin want to come and hang out in Atlanta."

"Did Delilah bring her kids?"

"Yeah, and they're adorable. Kendra is six, Justin four, and Nalani two. We all went to Six Flags and had a blast." Grace lowered her voice to a whisper. "Delilah is embroiled in a bitter divorce, so that day was the most fun they'd had in long time. Justin is a special needs child and Livingston is so patient with him, it almost brings tears to my eyes."

"Are they here?"

"So far, that's the only snafu." Grace expelled a long breath. "They're always late. Every time we go somewhere, they hold up progress."

"Good grief, I hate that black people stereotype."

Grace chuckled. "There's a reason why there are stereotypes, you know. But we have to give them a break. I guess under the circumstances it takes a lot to get them all ready to go somewhere."

Babs rejoined them with a full glass of wine and asked, "What'd I miss?"

"Nothing important," Grace demurred. "I was just telling your cousin how much I like my future relatives."

"Just be thankful that they don't live in Atlanta. I bet the bloom would fall off that rose in a hurry." She looked at her cousin, "Did Solange tell you yet?"

"Tell me what?" Grace looked from one to the other.

Solange cocked her head in the direction of the door. "Here comes Ali, so now you'll see what Babs is making snide comments about."

Grace stared at the tall brown-skinned man with coal-black eyes as he strutted towards the trio. His sleek black hair was combed back from his face and an air of confidence exuded from him. Grace gave a gasp of astonishment, but quickly recovered before he reached them. *Check out my girl Solange. She's gone and gotten herself an Arabian stallion.*

He held out his hand and spoke with a deep husky voice, "I'd know you anywhere from your pictures. You must be Grace. My name is Ali Marks."

Grace knew she was staring with her mouth agape. *He is the best-looking cop I've ever seen*!

Grace spoke and her voice sounded faint. "Hi, and thank you for coming to my engagement party."

Ali pulled Solange close to him. "I wouldn't have missed it. I know how close the two of you are and I wouldn't think of being anywhere else." Ali turned to Babs and gave her an uncompromising look. "Isn't that how you feel also, Babs?"

She drained her glass and asked sharply, glaring at Grace, "Is wine the strongest thing that you have?" Then she stomped off.

Ali smiled without rancor and said, "I don't think that she's a fan of this Middle Eastern brother. She's probably been watching too much Fox News."

Solange looked embarrassed by her cousin's behavior, but before she could reply, Grace said, "She would want you if you were interested in her."

Livingston had broken away from another crowd of people and approached the group. He gave Solange a warm hug and looked inquisitively at Ali.

Solange had nestled herself against Ali and introduced him proudly. "Livingston, this is Ali. Ali, this is Livingston."

They shook hands. "Nice to meet you," Ali said.

"Likewise," Livingston echoed. "Would you like a drink?"

"Sure," Ali agreed.

"I have some of the stronger stuff behind the bar." He gave him an intuitive look. "After hanging out with Babs, you might need it." Then he spoke to the women, "We'll be back after a while." Before he left, he leaned down and gave Grace a peck on the cheek and Ali did the same to Solange.

"When Livingston offered Ali alcohol, I tried to give him the eye, but he didn't see me. I know that Muslims don't drink alcohol."

To this Solange bust out laughing, "Girl, Ali's no more Muslim than Barack Obama."

"Oh, my bad. Well, he's absolutely gorgeous, and so well mannered," Grace whispered.

Solange chortled even louder. "Now you sound like white people when they talk about Colin Powell."

"I'm sorry, girl. That is sort of a reverse racism, isn't it?" she admitted grudgingly.

Solange decided to let her off the hook and whispered back, "I know what you mean. He's striking looking, isn't he? It's crazy because I've never been a fan of Middle Eastern men because I've heard tales of how they treat women like second-class citizens, but Ali was born and bred in Brooklyn. I mean, he's as American as they come, yet he treats me better than any American man I've ever had."

Grace gave Solange an appraising look. "Why didn't you tell me when I was in New York? I think that it's worth a mention."

Solange replied teasingly, "His complexion is so swarthy I thought that maybe I could pass him off as a brother."

Grace chuckled. "Not with that slick hair you couldn't. He looks like he could have played Billy Dee's younger brother in *Mahogany.* So I take it you hadn't given Babs prior notice either?"

"No. I didn't even know she was coming with us until last night. I think that she's hoping to see Jet and rekindle some kind of romance." She surveyed the room. "Where is he, anyhow?"

Just then they heard a bunch of barking sounds from Livingston's fraternity brothers and she and Solange turned to see the topic of their conversation enter the room. All female eyes turned on Jet and all male eyes turned on his companion. Jet had on a pair of skinny black jeans with a black silk shirt and his companion seemed to have gone to the trouble of matching by wearing a black silk dress. Vaguely, in the back of her mind, Grace thought, *I've seen her somewhere before.* As she and Jet made their way over to her, she knew. *She's a model. I've seen her in* Essence *and she does a fragrance commercial.*

Jet grinned at her and Solange, obviously pleased by the attention his entrance had made. "Tia, this is Solange." Then he turned to Grace. "And this is my sister."

"It's very nice to meet you." Tia spoke with a slight English accent.

Grace didn't much care for the upturned tilt of her nose, but she said, "It's nice to meet you, Tia." She gave Jet a hard look. "But I'm not really his sister."

Jet gave a start of surprise. "Is that so? Since when?"

Grace watched the possessive way Tia clung to Jet's arm and answered sweetly, "Since forever."

Livingston and Ali returned and Grace could tell by the color of their drinks they had beefed up the liquor content from wine to something one might call a man's drink.

Livingston clapped Jet on the back and asked, "How are you doing, buddy?"

An indecipherable look passed between them before Jet replied, "I'm fine." He nodded at them. "This is my girl, Tia. Tia, this is my frat brother, Livingston."

"It's nice to meet you."

The sound of her voice grated on Grace's nerves, but she tried to mask her irritation.

Livingston pointed at Ali. "This is Solange's friend, Ali."

Jet nodded. "Nice to meet you, too."

"Likewise," he answered.

Grace slid her arm into the crook of Livingston's. "It looks like we're one big happy family."

His annoyance obvious, he said, "Maybe we will be when you-know-who gets here. I'm going out into the lobby and see if I can find out what the holdup is." He briefly squeezed her hand before he strode off.

Babs came to join the group. Her eyes glittered when she saw Tia clinging possessively to Jet. Suddenly she announced, "I'm going to the ladies' room, and then I'm out of here."

"How are you doing, Babs?" Jet smiled at her.

Babs hesitated as if she was going to say something, but she stopped herself. "I'm fine, Jet. It was nice seeing you again."

"May I follow you to the ladies' room?" Tia asked Babs.

Babs again hesitated, but, shrugging her shoulders, said, "Sure, why not?"

After they left, Grace wryly asked Solange, "Do you think they'll be okay by themselves?"

"Sure, Babs knows not to misbehave in public. My family's not that ill bred."

"I don't get it," Jet innocently said. "What are you talking about?"

Grace turned accusatory eyes on him. "Why did you bring her? You should have known that Babs might be here."

"So what?" Jet answered. "That brief fling Babs and I had was over months ago. She can't be holding on to that anymore."

"Not everyone gets over people as easily as you do, Jet."

"You don't know anything about me, Grace," he replied roughly.

Ali gave a loud cough, breaking the tension.

Grace felt horrible. Too late she remembered Jet telling her and Livingston that he'd been in love with a woman who didn't love him back and she felt an attack of conscience.

The music had slowed and people who'd hooked up were moving to the dance floor. Ali turned to Solange and, silently grabbing her hand, pulled her onto the dance floor.

He's probably trying to get away, afraid that we're going to show out like we do in the movies.

"Would you dance with me, Jet?" she asked softly.

Jet ignored her.

"I'm sorry for what I said. It's not up to me to judge how you live your life. C'mon," she cajoled, tugging him to the middle of the dance floor. "We've never danced together."

Jet's voice was husky. "We've danced together. It's just never been to anything this slow."

"Well, in keeping with the theme of the evening, since we've decided we're not brother and sister anymore, it might not be too weird."

Still Jet hesitated, but Grace propelled him to the dance floor by him pushing him in the middle of his back. Jet didn't hold her flush to his body but kept quite a bit of space between them while they danced.

Grace hummed the lyrics to her favorite Musiq Soulchild song, though her mind was on Jet and their unfamiliar territory. *This doesn't feel weird. Instead I feel strangely comforted.* After they'd drifted into the third song, Grace opened her eyes and they connected with Livingston's in the doorway. Flanked by his family and Tia, he watched her and Jet.

CHAPTER 9

Grace called Livingston's work number. "I'm at Haverty's Furniture Store and finally found a bedroom set that I want."

"Good," he answered.

She could tell that he was preoccupied with a task that he was working on. "Can you meet me during your lunch break so you can see it?"

"I can't get away. I'm trying to tie up loose ends before we go to Jamaica. If you like it, get it."

"You haven't gotten to choose any furniture for our new home," she complained. "Everything is in my taste. What if you don't like this?"

"I doubt that'll happen. I've liked everything else you've bought so far."

"Okay, but don't complain if I make a mistake and every time you walk into our bedroom you think to yourself, 'I wish I had taken off the time to meet Grace at the furniture store. This furniture is hideous.' "

Livingston laughed. "I'll take my chances. Now I have to go because I have a meeting, Love ya!"

"Me, too," she responded.

Turning to the clerk who was trying to appear as if he weren't eavesdropping, she said, "I'll take it." Handing him her license she asked, "When can you have it delivered?"

"The earliest time we can get it to you is day after tomorrow."

"That'll be fine," she responded.

Grace was clearing her desk and putting the final touches on her substitute teacher plans when she heard knocking on her door. "Come in," she yelled. When she saw it was Madeline she smiled welcomingly.

"So are you ready for the big day?" Madeline grinned at her.

"Almost," Grace answered. "Solange is flying in later to help me put the finishing touches on everything."

"Nervous?"

"Pretty much. But the wedding is kind of small by most people's standards. You know I don't have any family, so I didn't want bridesmaids or anything."

"I think intimate weddings are better anyhow."

"I kind of felt a little sorry for Livingston because he had some frat brothers he would've asked to be his groomsmen, but then the bridal party would've been uneven."

"I doubt that he really cares. The man I met at your engagement party wants you to be happy for the rest of your life. I sensed that right away and I'm a pretty good judge of character."

Grace glanced at her watch and, standing, said, "I've got to go and meet Solange at my house."

"I'll walk you out," Madeline offered.

When they got to Grace's Jeep, they hugged briefly. "I'll see you at the wedding," Madeline promised.

After Madeline drove off, Grace sat in the empty parking lot and as she viewed her school, a feeling of infinite sadness ran through her. Cranking up her SUV she quickly drove off.

A couple of days later, Grace opened the door that led into the kitchen and breathed a deep sigh of annoyance at the chaos she was confronted with. She bent over and picked up a naked doll out of the middle of the floor, and stepping back, stubbed her toe on a plastic scooter. Picking that up, she went into the garage and placed it in a corner out of the way. Then reentering the house, she handed the doll to Nalani, who was now sitting in the middle of the floor banging one of Grace's pots with a large spoon.

Walking to the den, she grimaced when she saw the look on Solange's face as she sat on her couch in the middle of clothes that needed to be folded and put away out of sight. Grace walked over and kissed her on the cheek and then rolled her eyes.

Music was blaring, and crossing over to the stereo system, she punched the off button. Immediately, she heard Delilah yell down from upstairs, "Kendra, I'm not going to tell you again. Don't touch that stereo!"

Grace hollered back, "It wasn't her. It was me that turned it off."

Delilah walked over to the banister and said apologetically, "I'm sorry, Grace. I didn't hear you come in."

Solange muttered so only Grace could hear her, "I guess the hell not."

Grace tried to keep a straight face but felt compelled to say, "How can you even hear yourself think?"

Delilah laughed and said, "I know. Mother tells me the same thing. I'm cleaning up and I always work better to music."

Solange muttered again, "I can't tell."

"I guess it's that slave mentality. You know how the overseer had them singin' in the fields."

Solange couldn't help herself and whispered conspiratorially, "She must have seen that in a movie because I know she didn't read it in a history book."

Not able to stand it any longer, Grace burst into laughter.

"What?" Delilah asked.

"Nothing, Delilah." Grace played it off with some quick thinking. "Just the thought of you working in a field picking cotton is hilarious."

Delilah agreed. "I know. I would have to be a house negro, not a field hand. That's the way it would've worked out anyhow because they always put the light-complexioned slaves in the plantation house."

Distaste for the turn the conversation had taken made Grace responded curtly, "That's because they were usually illegitimate offspring of the master. I'd rather be a field hand." Then deciding it was best to change the subject she asked, "Where's your mother?"

"She's in her room lying down. I think that I'll go back to my room and do the same. I'm exhausted," she said before she walked out of view.

Grace surveyed the den. *Exhausted from what?*

Then she looked at Solange, who was lying on her side, holding her stomach, doubled over from laughter.

"Shush," Grace said. "She'll hear you."

Solange wiped her eyes with the back of her hands. "Okay, okay, I'll stop. I guess this time Babs was right. The bloom is certainly off this rose."

"I'm so over it," she said quietly, noticing Justin was staring blankly at them from his wheelchair.

Also seeing this, Solange asked, "Can he understand us?"

"I don't know how much." Grace tried to read Justin's expression but she didn't have a clue as to what he was thinking.

Motioning for Solange to follow her, Grace went into the master bedroom suite that was on the first floor. Sinking gratefully on the bed, she said, "They've been here over a week and they're driving me crazy. I'm constantly cleaning up after them."

Solange looked aghast. "She just walks off and leaves the kids unsupervised?"

"I guess you could say they're not unsupervised when I'm here. And his mother has arthritis real bad and pretty much stays in her room all of the time. At least until it's time for dinner."

"You should take the television out of there. That might bring her out."

"That's okay because then there'd be one more person in the den near me."

"Have you told Livingston?"

"Of course not. What could he do? You can't make people neat, and I don't want to embarrass him."

"Why don't you call Merry Maids or something?"

Grace gave Solange a disgruntled look. "I'm the maid, and believe me, I'm not so merry."

Solange snickered at Grace's pun.

"I can't call them because then he'll know. After all, I haven't needed to call them before, so why now?"

"Give Livingston a chance to understand, instead of holding all of this in."

"I'll think about it," Grace murmured.

"It'll only get worse if you don't do something about it," Grace advised. "Nip it in the bud right now or years from now when they come to visit, you'll wish that you had."

"I'll talk to Livingston," she promised. "Now, help me lift the mattress so I can put the bed skirt that matches my comforter set on. I want to fix up my new bedroom set."

Exhausted, Grace had Solange drive her home from the wedding rehearsal and dinner. She'd had her eyes closed and had almost drifted off to sleep when she heard Solange say, "Do you need to stop anywhere before we go back to the crazy house?"

Grace threaded her hand through her hair. She'd changed her hairstyle for the wedding by having her hair straightened and extensions added and her hair hung just below her shoulders. "No, I packed my suitcases yesterday to make sure that I had everything for the honeymoon so I wouldn't have to make a last-minute dash to the store for anything."

Solange continued to swiftly pass cars on the busy highway, dodging in and out of traffic.

"I think everything went off tonight without a hitch. I just wish I'd been here for your bridal shower."

"I didn't have a chance to give you any notice because I didn't know that I was even having one. Madeline threw me a surprise one after school one Friday. Besides, you've been down here twice in the last four months. I think that I'm costing you enough money as it is."

"The money's not a problem, but right before I left work something interesting came up. The company books are wrong. It appears that quite a bit of money is missing."

"That's not good."

"Yeah, I know. I told Ali and he told me to start looking into it without telling anyone."

"Do you think that the money disappeared before you took over?"

"I don't know yet. But if it did, that probably means that it was the last manager that was there."

"Speaking of Ali, I sure wish that he'd been able to make the wedding."

"He wanted to, but he also has drama going on at his job. Internal Affairs is afoot and they wouldn't give him any leave time."

"The country is in a recession and people are struggling. Whenever you have a lot of poor people, crime goes up because some people don't want to do without the things that they're used to."

"I know, and the people who are suffering are the consumers who have to pay more for the things that they want. That's really the trickle-down theory."

"You're right. The price of the dresses for the girls was outrageous. Livingston paid for them."

"But Kendra and Nalani are going to make beautiful flower girls."

"I know. They're not bad kids. They just lack discipline. Livingston does what he can when he's around, but it's their mom. She's pretty much checked out of motherhood ever since the divorce became final. She's having a hard time dealing with her own stuff."

"She probably needs to get some counseling. We black people are taught to keep our business to ourselves, that it's a sign of weakness to seek help. Parents have bad marriages and drag their kids through the muck and mire, then those kids repeat the behavior that is modeled for them, and their kids also have issues. The cycle continues generation after generation and that's why the family never strengthens."

"My pastor said that you don't need to go and pay someone $100 to $125 an hour to talk to someone about your problems. He said all you need is your bible and a conversation with God."

"He's wrong and shouldn't be telling his congregation that. A bible doesn't talk back to you, or ask you questions. My parents got therapy and it saved their marriage."

"Really?" Grace gave Solange a look of surprise. "I can't believe they ever needed counseling because they've always gotten along so well when I've been around."

"They're fine now, but they went through a really rough patch when I was in my teens. They were headed for divorce court and as a last-ditch effort they went for professional help. My dad had a lot of issues from his childhood that needed to be resolved."

A fleeting vision of her mother surfaced, but Grace hastily pushed those thoughts away.

"Marriage is no fairy-tale." She gave Grace a stern look. "No matter how much you and Livingston love each other, there may come a time when one of you wants out. If you get to that crossroads, don't be too proud to ask for help before you make your final decision."

A denial that such a situation could ever occur was stilled when she encountered the seriousness of Solange's expression.

"Promise me, Grace."

"Okay," she said to mollify her friend, "I promise."

When Solange pulled up in the driveway, Grace looked in her sideview mirror and saw that Livingston was right behind them with the kids.

"Your family's here," Solange said, chuckling.

"Yes, they are," Grace responded with mixed feelings. She looked up and saw Delilah standing in the front doorway.

Nalani and Kendra ran towards their mom and she grinned at them, giving them a playful swat on their behinds. "You girls go inside. Kendra, put Nalani's pajamas on her."

"Okay, Mommy," she said, tugging Nalani's hands and pulling her with her inside the house.

"How'd everything go?" Delilah said as she approached them.

"Not too bad," Livingston said as he lowered Justin's wheelchair ramp using the lever on the van.

Once he was lowered to the ground, Delilah bent towards Justin and said, "Did you have a good time with Uncle and your aunties?"

"It was fun."

Smiling at them, Delilah gripped the handles on the wheelchair. "I guess I'll go and get him ready for bed. Tomorrow's a big day for all of us."

Grace said, "The limousines are going to come and pick us up around ten o'clock, so be ready."

"I will. I set my clock for seven so I'll have plenty of time to get my brood straight." Delilah leaned over and kissed Grace, and then Solange on the cheek. "I've never had a sister, but I feel as if after tomorrow, I'm getting two."

Grace's eyes misted over and she gave her a big hug.

Even Solange turned her head, circumspectly blinking back tears.

Delilah stared at her brother and gulped before she said, "I'm so proud of you, Livingston. You couldn't have been nicer to me or my kids, and Mother hasn't felt this good in years. I'll always love you and never forget what you've done." She reached her hands out, and Livingston clasped them and gave her a kiss on the forehead.

"I love you too, Delilah," he said gruffly to her before she turned to leave. "Keep pressing on. It's always darkest before the dawn."

Solange followed closely at their heels and Grace knew she had left so that she and Livingston could have some time alone to say goodbye.

After they watched them disappear, Livingston pulled Grace to him. He tilted her chin up and lowered his lips to hers. His kiss was loving, and it tasted bittersweet. When he finally withdrew his mouth from hers he whispered, "Thank you for being so kind to my family. I know it hasn't been easy. Now I need to go home to shower and change before I go and meet Jet and the guys for my bachelor party."

She opened her eyes and stared into his. "I love you so much, Livingston."

"I love you too, Grace," he replied before he got in his car and backed it down the driveway.

Grace walked down a long corridor. Fog swirled around her feet as she wildly looked around for someone to point her in the direction she was supposed to go. She tried to call out,

but no words were forthcoming. Slowly, she pushed one foot in front of the other and when she came abreast of a long mirror, she realized that she was naked. Grace took her hands and tried to cover her breasts to no avail. She dropped them to hang by her sides. In front of her she saw an open door and when she walked through it, she saw that the room was vacant except for an empty hospital bed. She walked over to the bed, and climbing on it, she pulled the sheet over her entire body, covering her face.

When Grace woke she was soaked and her bed linen was wet. Turning her head, she realized that it wasn't yet nine o'clock. *The bachelor party. I have to find Livingston.* Hastily scrambling to her feet, she went to her closet and grabbed a pair of slides. Shoving her feet into them, she stumbled out into the living room.

The television was playing, but Delilah was asleep on the couch. She looked up the stairs and didn't see anyone, but she heard the water running in the upstairs bathroom and knew Solange must be in the shower. Grabbing her keys out of her pocketbook on the counter, she bolted out to her car and once inside hit the garage door opener, put the car in reverse, and gunned it down the driveway.

Grace drove as if the devil himself were sitting in the backseat egging her on. She screeched to a halt at the four-way intersection that led into Livingston's subdivision. Out of her peripheral vision she saw a police car, so she sat idling and watched him. When he didn't flash his lights to pull her over for reckless driving, she impatiently waited as the other three cars that were before her leisurely took their turns. Driving with more care, she turned onto Livingston's street and breathed a sigh of relief when she saw his car coming towards her. Frantically she stuck her hand out the window and waved him over. Before Livingston's car was at a complete stop, she put hers in park and ran across the street to him.

"Livingston, don't go, don't go," she pleaded, tears of anxiety coursing down her face.

Livingston took in Grace's disheveled appearance in her boxer shorts and one of his T-shirts he'd left at her house and got out of the car. "What's wrong? You're running around half naked."

"Don't go," she babbled. "Don't go to Jet's bachelor party."

Shocked, he asked, "Why on earth not?"

"I had my dream. I think something's going to happen to you, to us," she sobbed.

"Grace," he said in his calm, soothing voice, "nothing is going to happen. I don't know how many times I have to reassure you."

Grasping at straws, anything to make him listen, she blurted out, "The night I met you, there was this guy in the club for his bachelor party. He was getting married the next day. He was disgustingly drunk and he asked me for some sex. I know what you guys do at these things. I forbid you to go."

"Forbid me?" Livingston's eyes narrowed and he looked at her in a way she'd never seen before. "Woman, have you lost your mind?" Livingston turned to open his car door.

"Don't go," she shrieked.

Livingston shouted, "You're talking crazy. Jet and the boys are waiting for me and I'm not going to disappoint them because of your foolishness. Dammit. If you think I would cheat on you the night before we get married, then we shouldn't be getting married at all!"

"I don't think that!" she shouted back. "But I need you not to go tonight. Do this for me, please," she beseeched him.

"Are you serious? Do you think that I would let the guys down? What am I supposed to tell them? I can't come because my fiancée had a dream?" he added sarcastically.

"Call Jet. He would understand if you told him."

"I'm glad as hell he would because I damn sure don't." He glared at her and spoke harshly, "After we get back from our honeymoon, I think you need to get some therapy to find out what's at the bottom of these nightmares that you have."

"So you think I'm crazy?"

"Not crazy, at least I hope not, since we're getting married tomorrow. I just think that you need to talk to someone."

Grace took her arms and put them around Livingston's waist as if they were a vise. "I'm begging you, please don't go."

He pried her hands from around him, looked around and saw that a man and woman were standing on the sidewalk watching the soap opera scene. "Grace," he said with finality, "get in the car. Go home and get a good night's sleep."

When she started to say something, he took his finger and put it to her lips. "Your nerves are on edge and you're spoiling my party mood." He reiterated, "Go home. I'll see you at the church tomorrow. In fact, I'll even be early," he finished, trying to lighten the atmosphere. Then he took her hand in his and pulled him towards her.

Grace didn't close her eyes as he lowered his mouth to hers. Instead she devoured his face with her eyes. Livingston gave her a languid kiss of love and reassurance. Then he released her and turned her around, giving her a gentle push towards her car.

Livingston watched Grace solemnly get into her car. Then he got in his and drove off.

She sat there for a minute or two with her head resting on the steering wheel. Then she cranked her car and slowly drove home.

When she let herself back into her house, Delilah was at the refrigerator grabbing an ice cream bar. When she heard the door open behind her, she swung around, putting her hand on her heart. "Grace, where are you coming from? I didn't even hear you leave."

"You were asleep on the couch." Grace sank wearily onto a barstool at the breakfast bar and put her face in her hands.

"What's the matter with you?" Delilah said as she tore off the wrapper, placed it on the counter and at the same time bit off a large chunk of the bar. "You're not afraid of getting married tomorrow, are you?" Delilah stared at Grace's worried expression.

"Of course not," Grace responded in a dull tone. "I'm just too tired to sleep."

Delilah snapped her fingers. "Oh, I have something for that. Wait right here."

Delilah bounded up the stairs and quickly returned with a small bottle in her hand. "I take these when I've had a really rough day. You know, with the kids. Some days I just can't get them to settle down, and then later that night, I can't settle down myself. I'm like a wind-up toy."

Grace took the bottle and read the label.

"A friend of mine works at a doctor's office and she gets them for me. They're time release and are guaranteed to knock you out for at least eight hours."

"I don't know about taking someone else's medication," Grace said doubtfully.

"There's nothing wrong with them. I've been taking them for years."

"I do need a good night's rest," Grace murmured.

"Then go to your room, and I'll make you a cup of herbal tea," Delilah offered. "That will help the sleeping pill work faster and you'll feel like a new woman in the morning."

"Thanks, Delilah," she muttered gratefully and, with the bottle clenched in her hand, headed towards her bedroom.

The next morning when Grace awoke she felt unusually groggy. She glanced at the alarm clock and realized that it was almost nine o'clock. *This is my wedding day. I'm lazing around in bed and I need to be up getting ready. I've waited my whole life for this.* Hurriedly she swung her legs to the floor. When she stood she felt a little dizzy and grabbed the bedpost to steady herself. *Gee, I think that pill Delilah gave me is a little too strong for me. But at least I relaxed and slept through the night.*

Gathering her wits, she forced her legs into action, opened her bedroom door and stood in the aperture. Quietly, she observed the pandemonium that was once her peaceful home. It looked like a scene from the movie *The Color Purple.* Delilah sat on the couch and was in the process of raking through a screaming Kendra's hair with a comb. Nalani sat on the floor, clad only in a diaper, clutching her doll. Rose was pulling a shirt over Justin's head.

Then out of the corner of her eye, she saw Solange walking towards her. She was dressed only in a slip that went with the lilac dress she was going to wear for the wedding, but she'd already applied her makeup and she looked ethereal.

"I was just coming to wake you up, lazybones. I thought that you were going to sleep all day." When she reached Grace, she gave her a warm hug.

"I think that I could've," she admitted grudgingly.

"What? And miss the most important day of your life? I think not."

"I know," she agreed with a laugh. "Since I plan on only doing this one time, I would hate to miss it." Then Grace's attention was drawn to the continuing drama as she saw Delilah pick up the now-screaming Nalani and begin to comb her hair.

Solange gave Grace an "I know you want to get the hell out of Dodge look" and said, "I had an idea while you were sleeping. I called the limousine service and told them to come and get us early. I think that after you take your shower, you should finish getting dressed at the church. That way you'll have fewer opportunities to wrinkle your dress, and if I wait until the last minute to do your makeup, it'll be fresh and dewy."

"That's a wonderful idea," Grace gushed. "I don't know why I didn't think of that myself."

"That's what maids of honor are for. To second-guess the bride on the small but not unimportant details." She eyed the boxers and T-shirt Grace still wore and said, "Now scoot. Go take your shower." She discreetly nodded at the scene behind her and whispered, "I'll explain the change of plans to your out-laws." She paused to let Grace know that her phrase was deliberate and not a mere slip of the tongue. "And I'll get your dress and makeup case loaded into the limousine that should be arriving any minute."

Before Grace scurried back to the bedroom, she gave Solange a grateful high five.

Once in the bathroom, Grace stuffed her hair under a shower cap and stepped into hot pelting water and let the water do its job. Once she felt totally relaxed, she grabbed her loofah and poured a generous amount of sea salt scrub on it. *Grace Lockhart, Mrs. Livingston Lockhart. I love the sound of my new name. From the moment I saw him, I knew he was the one. You read about it in books, you see it in movies, but Livingston put a lock on my heart from the moment I stumbled into him outside the bathroom at Sutra. That's the way it's supposed to be. When you meet your soul mate, you should know it right away.* Picking up her razor, she shaved under her arms, her legs, and her bikini area and felt a sharp sting from the after-effects of the salt scrub she'd applied. She relished the feeling because she was readying her body for the coming night. For the first time she'd be making love as a married woman and she wanted everything to be perfect.

After leaving the shower, she gently toweled off, not totally drying her body, and reached for her sesame oil. She smoothed it on her body from her neck to her toes and then followed it with her favorite body cream. *It's going to be a long day, so I need a double dose of lotion before I retire to our hotel suite.* With a cotton ball, she applied her astringent. Just as Grace slipped into matching white lace lingerie and white hose and a sky blue garter belt, she heard a knock on the door.

"Are you almost ready? The limo is waiting."

Grace flung open the door, and Solange whistled at her.

With hand on hip Grace said, "All I need is an outfit to throw on to wear to the church."

Solange handed her a housecoat. "Wear this," she ordered. "It's easier and no one will be able to see you through the dark tint of the limo window."

CHAPTER 10

Once they arrived at the church, they observed cars already starting to fill the parking lot. "I guess they want the best seat," Solange said wryly. Tapping on the partition, she said to the chauffer, "George, please take us to the side entrance so we can slip unseen in the back door."

"Yes, ma'am," he replied.

An hour later, Grace stood in front of a full-length mirror and stared at her reflection. She placed her hand over her heart, trying to still the palpitations. Her off-the-shoulder white wedding dress was the perfect foil for her skin. The small pearl buttons on the fitted bodice drew attention to her ample cleavage, and, with her hair pinned on top of her head, she looked like a Grecian goddess.

Solange entered the room and gasped at the beautiful vision her friend made. She blinked back tears of joy. "In all the years I've known you, I've never seen you more beautiful or look any happier."

"Thank you, Solange." Grace turned to Solange and, after clearing her throat, she said, "Through the years, I've had my ups and downs, but I've always known that I had you to count on. I may not have parents, but I have you."

"Yes, you do," Solange answered softly. "Now don't say anything else, or you'll make me cry and ruin my makeup. I want to look nice for the wedding too, you know."

"Okay." Grace smiled, her bottom lip quivering. "Have you seen Livingston or Jet?"

"They haven't arrived yet." Solange took her finger and pushed a loose tendril out of Grace's face.

"Haven't arrived?" Grace exclaimed. "Traditionally the bride is late, not the groom."

"Don't worry," Solange gently scolded her, "he'll be here."

There was a knock on the door and Rose entered. "Oh, my Lord. My son is so lucky. Daughter, you look wonderful."

"Thank you, Momma Rose." Grace gave a grateful smile to her mother-in-law-to-be, well-turned-out in her canary-yellow suit.

"I'm thrilled that you're going to be my daughter. You've already been so generous and giving to me and Delilah and the kids. I know that we can be trying and we sort of stayed longer than we first said, but we wanted to spend as much time with Livingston as we could before he became a married man. Things change after that."

Rose smiled at Solange, who muttered her excuses and left the two of them alone.

"Nothing's going to change. Livingston's your son and he'll always be your son. I would never come in between the two of you."

"I know you wouldn't. But after people get married . . . Well, enough of that talk, I just wanted to say thanks again."

Understanding that Rose wanted to speak of lighter things, Grace asked, "Where are Delilah and the kids?"

"Out there in the other bathroom. Nalani spilled a little milk on her dress." She added when she saw the involuntary look of consternation cross Grace's face, "Not to worry, though, it'll wipe off easily. When you take pictures of the wedding party, no one will ever see the stain. You know what they say, there's no need to cry over spilt milk."

Grace had bent over to adjust her shoe. After slipping it back on her foot, she straightened up and gave a small yelp of surprise.

Noiselessly, Solange had reentered the vestibule and was silently watching her. She leaned on the far side wall as if she needed its support.

"You scared me half to death," Grace sputtered.

Solange didn't speak; instead she just stood there staring dumbly.

Grace knew by the look on her friend's face that something horrible had happened. She stood shakily and flatly stated, "Something's wrong."

Solange nodded her head.

"Livingston's not coming, is he?" She spoke with dread in her voice.

"No, he's not coming right now, Grace."

Solange's voice had a faraway sound, and Grace found it hard to focus.

"He stood me up. I should have known it was too good to be true."

Solange rushed over to her, gripped her shoulders, shook her slightly and explained, "Livingston did not stand you up. There's been an accident and he and Jet are at the hospital. You left your cell phone in the limousine, and the hospital staff called it looking for you."

"How bad is it?" she choked out.

"I don't know because they wouldn't tell me on the phone."

"I need to go to the hospital," Grace stammered. Hiking her dress up around her ankles, she ran to the limousine and she and Solange slid into the open door George already had waiting for them.

No words were exchanged on the drive to the hospital. Traffic was heavy and all the way to the hospital, Grace prayed as Solange held her hand tightly.

Grace didn't let the limousine come to a complete stop before opening the door and running, with Solange at her heels, to the information desk. Gasping for breath she squeaked, "I need some information. There's been an accident. My fiancé," she stammered.

Taking in Grace in her wedding dress and Solange in what was obviously a maid of honor's dress, the nurse gave her a look of pity and asked, "What is his name, ma'am?"

"Livingston Lockhart." Grace's bottom lip trembled from fear.

Quickly, the clerk typed on her keyboard. "He's in recovery. Dr. Kilburn is his doctor. I'll call Emergency and have him talk to you."

"How about my brother?" Grace barked out. "His name is Jethro Newman."

Again the receptionist typed some words. Keeping her head down, she picked up the phone and the intercom system in the hospital resounded in Grace's ears. "Dr. Kilburn, please report to the lounge area outside the Emergency Room." The receptionist, avoiding their prying eyes, said, "Will you please take a seat over there? The doctor is on his way."

Grace didn't budge. "What's his status?" she demanded.

"Ma'am," the clerk looked at her, willing her to understand, "I'm not at liberty to discuss any patient's condition." Then she shot her a look filled with pity. "Hospital rules."

Turning Grace around, Solange propelled her to one of the loveseats in the small area. Grace kept her head bent, silently praying, but she looked up when she heard voices. A man in a white coat started walking towards her after speaking to the receptionist.

Grace and Solange stood as he approached them and asked brusquely, "Are you Jethro Newman's sister?"

"Yes," she uttered so softly she could hardly be heard.

Now his eyes were filled with compassion as they met hers. "This morning about three o'clock, his car was hit by a tractor-trailer truck on I-20."

"Oh my God," Grace and Solange uttered at the same time.

The doctor sadly shook his head. "They were hit on the driver's side and the car was crushed and pushed into an embankment. The passenger seat belt broke during the collision and the passenger was thrown to a modicum of safety. He has a broken leg and a few minor injuries."

"Where are they? I need to see them," Grace croaked.

"I'm sorry." Again he shook his head sadly. "Mr. Newman didn't make it. He was DOA."

Grace slumped to the floor in a dead faint, hitting her head on the edge of the table in the waiting area.

When she awoke, she was lying on a bed in the Emergency Room and she met the eyes of Solange and Dr. Kilburn, who were intently watching her. Feeling something unfamiliar, she lifted her hand and felt a bandage wrapped around her head. *Damn!* she thought. *I'm still alive.*

Doctor Kilburn withdrew a small flashlight from his pocket and gently lifted her eyelids, shining the light into her pupils. He turned to Solange and said, "Physically, I think that she's going to be all right. I need another one of her relatives to come and identify the body."

"She's his only family. I'll go with you down to the morgue and identify the body."

Dr. Kilburn sadly shook his head and spoke quietly. "You can come also, but legally, I can't release the body to a funeral home unless a relative identifies it. Is there no one else?" he asked, concern etched on his features.

"No, it's just us." Grace spoke and didn't recognize her own voice. "I don't want my brother lying in the morgue any longer than he has to." She tried to sit up and the doctor and Solange steadied her.

Dr. Kilburn looked around and gave the head nurse who was watching them a nod, and she brought a wheelchair. Grace started to protest but he said gently, "I insist."

"So do I," Solange echoed.

The air in the elevator was so oppressive Grace had difficulty keeping her breathing even. She'd refused to take off her wedding gown and replace it with the hospital gown the doctor had offered her. The bottom of the wedding dress was filthy and the wheels of the chair rolled over it.

Once they reached the morgue, Dr. Kilburn squatted down in front of Grace. When he was eye level to her he said, compassion written all over his face, "Are you ready?"

Grace silently nodded and stood. Dr. Kilburn stepped aside, and side by side, she and Solange walked towards the body on the table the coroner had pulled out. Solange's mouth dropped and Grace spoke in a strangled voice, "It's not Jethro, it's Livingston." Then she slumped over the cold, lifeless body.

The next time Grace awoke, she was lying in a bed in a hospital room. When she stirred, she was immediately approached by Solange, who'd been sitting in a chair in the corner of the room.

She took in Solange's disheveled appearance. Her face was bloated from crying and the different hues of eye shadow she'd applied that morning had all run together. She looked like a sad clown. She'd changed out of her maid of honor dress and wore a pair of hospital scrubs and booties. Observing this, Grace tried to speak. When she finally did, her words were faint.

"Is it really true or is this another one of my horrible dreams?"

Solange took her hand and replied in a solemn tone, "It's true."

"Oh, my God." Grace turned over on her stomach and an avalanche of tears began to flow. She sobbed with her face in her pillow.

Solange patted her on the back consolingly. "Cry, Grace. Get it all out. Don't hold it in. Let the heavens cleanse you."

"Heavens!" Grace choked out. "There's no heaven, or God. That's all a fairy-tale to give people false hope that one day everyone is going to be happy. If there is a God, it's not the God I've been told about. No God would take that beautiful, perfect man from me or the world. It makes no sense."

Solange tried to sound soothing but doubt was also apparent in her voice. "We don't understand the ways of God, Grace. At least while we're here on earth. One day it will all be explained to us and then we'll understand."

"If you ever see Him," Grace spat out, "ask Him why every single person I love dies. First my father, then my mother, then Jet's mother, and now my fiancé on the day of my wedding. What curse has been put on me and anyone I love? Why won't God let me be happy?" she screamed.

Solange shook her head forlornly and said, "I don't know the reason this happened. I only know that you didn't deserve it."

Hearing the furor, the nurse entered the room. Looking at Grace in the hospital bed with eyes dilated and face flushed from panic, she said, "Doctor Kilburn is keeping you in the hospital for observation until tomorrow morning. He thinks that you may be suffering from shock. Would you like a sedative?" She gave her a look filled with mercy. "It should at least help you sleep through the night."

"Yes," she mumbled dully, holding out her open palm, "give me anything to make this pain go away."

Right before Grace slid into drug-induced unconsciousness, she heard Solange's exhausted voice in the hallway followed by Rose and Delilah's horrified screams.

Grace woke at one-thirty in the morning and realized she was alone. She turned her head and saw a note with Solange's familiar chicken scratch. *Honey, I went to your house to help Delilah and Rose get the kids settled. Hopefully, I'll be back in the morning before you wake and have a chance to read this note. Love always, Solange.*

After tossing and turning for the next several hours, Grace pressed the buzzer at the side of the bed and the nurse on duty appeared minutes later. "I can't sleep," Grace complained roughly. "Can you give me something to help me sleep?"

"I'm afraid I can't give you anything else, I looked at your chart when I came in and you've been given a hefty dose of sedatives already today."

"I need something," Grace stated flatly. "I'm sure you've heard by now that my fiancé was killed last night. I would think under the circumstances you'd be more understanding."

The nurse looked unrelenting. "Doctor's orders are that I can't give you anything else. It's for your own good. You don't want to get dependent on narcotics, do you? But I can get you a cup of herbal tea if you like."

"I don't like herbal tea," she said sullenly.

"Well, I'm sorry, but that's the best I can do."

Grace gave the nurse a cold look.

"If there isn't anything else, I have to go. Another patient called for me right after you did."

Grace's answer was to give her a look of disgust.

After the nurse from the land of insensitivity left, Grace gingerly climbed out of the bed. She crossed to the bathroom and, after using it, stared at her reflection. Someone had dressed her in a hospital gown. *I feel like shit, and I look like shit. Yesterday morning I woke and I thought the world was my oyster, and today I know that it's crap. If it wasn't for Solange, I'd kill myself, but I don't want to burden her with making my funeral arrangements.* Funeral arrangements. The thought of making them for Livingston made her feel squeamish and her knees began to buckle, so she held on to the wall to steady herself. *Jet. I need to see him and make sure nothing happened to him while I was asleep.*

Barefoot, Grace padded out into the hallway and saw that no one was sitting at the desk. She picked up the ledger and quickly scanned it. Jethro Newman was registered in one of the rooms down the hall. Not caring that her backside was exposed or who saw her, she walked to his room and pushed the door in. Jet was lying on the bed. His ebony skin was a stark contrast to the sheet that covered him. She tiptoed over to the bed and observed him.

As she placed her hand over his heart to make sure he was breathing, tears once again began to pour down her face. After wiping them away, she carefully pulled back the covers. The only obvious sign of injury was that one of his legs was bandaged in a soft cast. After breathing a sigh of relief, she stealthily slid into the bed next to him and fell into a deep slumber.

Before sunrise, her befuddled brain heard low voices around her.

"Thank God we found her," Solange whispered angrily.

"I didn't know she'd sneaked in here," the nurse replied, clearly ticked off by Solange's obvious insinuation that she was not correctly doing her job. "Last night she asked me for another sedative and I refused to give it to her."

Solange stared at the picture of Grace with her arm around Jet's waist and head on his shoulder and whispered, obviously relieved, "Well, she looks like she's sleeping peacefully now."

"But I can't let her stay here. It's against hospital policy. Besides, that's unnatural."

"What do you mean?" Solange turned antagonistic eyes on the nurse.

"I mean, it's icky. They're brother and sister, aren't they?"

Solange's ruffled feathers began to smooth out. "Oh, that's what you mean. No, they're not related. They've just known each other for a very long time." Then she turned imploring eyes on her. "Please don't disturb her. She's going to have enough to deal with when she wakes up, so I want her to rest as long as possible."

After a long steadying gaze at the couple in the bed, the nurse nodded her head in assent and turned to leave the room with Solange following her.

Jet lay on his back and stared at the ceiling. He looked down at Grace's sleeping form and sent up a silent prayer to God. *Please give her the strength to get through this.* And then the full enormity of what had happened hit him. *My best friend is dead and it's my fault. Maybe if I hadn't tried to drown my sorrow because the love of my life and my best friend were getting married, I would have been driving my own car and Livingston's life would've been*

spared. The only brother I've ever had, Grace's fiancé, would be alive. I've never known Grace to be as happy as she was with Livingston and now her dream has turned into a nightmare. I owe it to her to try to make things right, but only God can do that.

Grace stirred and Jet knew that she was waking. Clutching her close to his body, he waited.

Grace's eyes fluttered open and when they met the watchful ones of Jet, she breathed a sigh of relief. "Thank God, you're okay."

"Are you?" Jet softly asked her, taking her chin and lifting her face so he could look at her directly.

She sidestepped his question. "When I woke up last night, I was afraid that you weren't alive so I snuck in here."

"Are you okay?" Jet repeated his question.

"The doctor is releasing me this morning. He only kept me for observation." Then the burning question that needed to be asked was. "What happened?"

Jet took his hand and wearily passed it across his face. "I'm not too sure, exactly. All I remember is that we were driving down the road and a truck came out of nowhere. Livingston must have seen it coming out of the corner of his eye because he started blowing his horn and jerked the wheel, but we were hit. The next thing I remember was waking up. As I was being placed into an ambulance, I saw Livingston's body being placed in a body bag." Jet began to cry softly.

"The other driver was also killed."

"Better he die now than later," Jet retorted bitterly. "He killed my best friend."

"And the love of my life," Grace added with just as much bitterness in her voice as Jet. She felt Jet's body become stiff as a board when he heard her words.

The hospital door opened and Solange came in, followed by a policeman. Sympathy was written all over his face as he observed them. Obviously Solange had apprised him of all the particulars and told him of the intricate relationship she and Jet had, because he didn't bat an eye at the unusual scene confronting him.

"My name is Nathaniel Marsh," he said as he pulled some business cards out of his wallet and handed them to Solange. "I was the first officer to arrive at the scene of the accident." He coughed and continued, "I'm very sorry for your loss. We did a DUI test on Mr. Lockhart and he was not in any way near the legal limit or at fault for the accident. The skid marks on the road clearly showed that the driver of the truck was speeding and crossed from his lane to Mr. Lockhart's." He looked at Grace. "There was nothing your fiancé could have done."

Grace began to cry softly and, if it was possible, Jet held her even tighter.

"I never know what to say when tragedies like this happen, but I feel I should tell you. The person that hit you," and now his eyes were on Jet, "was a convicted child molester. He was out of his jurisdiction and hadn't notified the authorities that he was leaving town. In the back of his truck he had a double bed, refrigerator, boxes of Pampers and Depends, rope, and alcohol. You being exactly at the spot where you were may have saved one child or many children's lives from being destroyed. I don't know if that makes you feel any better, but maybe in time you'll feel that Livingston Lockhart didn't die in vain."

After the policeman left, no words were spoken for a very long time. Each of the trio was lost in their own private thoughts. Then Solange spoke. "There's something that I need to talk to you about."

Grace lifted her head and sat up in the bed next to Jet's still form. "Delilah and Rose are in the process of making funeral arrangements for Livingston," Solange said.

"I should do that." Grace threw back the covers and began to climb out of bed. She said harshly, "It's my responsibility."

Solange looked as if she would give anything in the world not to impart the next bit of information. "I don't think that it is. Did Livingston have a will?"

"Of course he didn't have a will!" Grace retorted bitterly. "We were supposed to be celebrating life, not death, remember?"

"I understand that, Grace," Solange answered patiently, "but what that means is if he didn't have a will, his next of kin is in charge of all the arrangements."

"Well, they don't have any money or taste and I don't want Livingston to have some crappy-ass funeral. He deserves more."

"I don't know if you can do anything about it," Solange said with deep sadness.

"They'll need my money, so that means I'll have some say-so over what happens." Jumping out of bed she said, "I need to go over to the house."

"Obviously I'll go with you, but I need to prepare you. They want to cremate him."

"Oh my God!" Grace pointed her finger toward her heart and proclaimed, "Over my dead body. Did you bring me any clothes?"

Solange produced a small duffel bag from behind a chair and handed it to her. Unmindful of Jet's watchful eyes, she quickly shed her hospital gown and pulled on shorts, a tank shirt and a pair of flip-flops Solange had brought her from home. Turning to Jet she asked, "When are you getting out of here?"

"I won't know until the doctor comes."

"I'll be back," she said before she stormed out.

CHAPTER 11

After Solange pulled up into the driveway of Grace's house she turned to her and instructed, "Be calm when you talk to them. If you want them to change their minds, you'll have to make them want to. Going after them like you have two loaded guns isn't going to help matters."

Silently, Grace nodded her head in assent. When she walked into her house, Delilah was frying pork chops and Rose sat on the couch watching television. Obvious surprise at her appearance crossed their faces. She walked over to the television and muted it. "Where are the kids?" she asked.

"Lying down. Why?" Delilah answered, placing her hands on her hips.

"Because I don't want them to hear this conversation. Obviously they're upset about the death of their uncle."

"Obviously," Delilah retorted as she turned back to the stove and turned the pork chops over in the pan.

Grace said without preamble, "I don't want to make matters worse, but I don't want Livingston cremated."

Delilah got a stubborn look on her face. "I'm sorry you feel that way, but it's a family tradition."

"Is that true?" she demanded and stared at Rose.

"Well, that's the way we buried my mother and Livingston's father," Rose said before her eyes slid away from Grace's.

"I mean no disrespect to you, Momma Rose, but usually when people cremate, it's because they don't have the funds for a decent funeral. That isn't our situation."

Delilah said, "I want to spare my children from the emotional drama of a funeral."

"Then they don't have to be there." Grace's voice broke, but she stifled her tears as she tried to control her emotions.

Up till then, Solange had been quiet, but now she glared at the two of them and heatedly asked, "Have you no feeling for her? She should have some say-so in this." She stressed the words, "She was going to be his wife."

"But she's isn't," Delilah retorted. "And she should have asked my brother before she agreed to marry him about how he felt about funerals. We've always handled our business like this."

"That's because you've always been as poor as church mice." Grace shot the words at her.

When she heard these words, Delilah's eyes narrowed and her lips pursed in anger.

Rose got up and walked over to Grace. Taking her hands in hers she said, "I think that Delilah is right. The arrangements have been already made and the memorial is tomorrow morning at eleven."

Pulling her hands from her, Grace stormed into her bedroom and threw herself down on the bed and sobbed uncontrollably until she was spent.

One o'clock, two o'clock, three o'clock. Grace lay in bed and listlessly pushed her hands through her hair. Finally she picked up the remote and turned on the television. *The Twilight Zone,* she thought derogatorily, *that's what's going on around me.* Rising from the bed, she went into the bathroom and withdrew the bottle of pills that Delilah had given her, turned on the tap water, filled her glass and downed one.

Grace woke feeling that the top of her head was being stroked. When she pried her eyes open, she saw Solange sitting on the bed next to her.

"It's ten o'clock. You need to get up to prepare for the memorial for Livingston."

"I can't go," she mumbled groggily and turned her face into the pillow.

"Grace, I know that this isn't the way you wanted it, but don't you think that you should say good-bye to him properly?" she asked in a stern voice.

There was a long silence in the room and, when Grace spoke, Solange could tell that she was lost in memories because her voice sounded childlike. "You know, when my father died, there was no corpse left, so to speak. Evidently the only way they could tell my dad from Jet's dad was by dental records, so they cremated what was left of them."

Solange gave a gasp. "Oh Grace, I didn't know."

"After the services, my mother was never the same. She turned to alcohol and drank herself into oblivion."

"But Grace, you're stronger than your mother. You always have been. You put yourself through college at

Howard and you never let your past color your future. You never gave up on life."

"Are you sure about that? Livingston is the only male relationship that I've sustained for any length of time through my whole life."

"You can't shoulder the blame for that. You've been cautious about who you let in your life. That's common sense in today's time. People are not always what they first seem." She pointed her thumb in the direction of the den. "The Gruesome Twosome is proof of that. It didn't take them long to show their true colors. When you live with people, you can't pretend to be something you're not." Now Solange's expression lightened. "But then there's Jet. I see that the two of you have a bond no person can sever."

There was a long pause and then Grace asked, "Where is Jet?"

"He called. They released him from the hospital, and he'll be at the services."

"Tell him I couldn't make it," Grace mumbled.

"Are you sure about this, Grace?"

She sniffed. "I can't bear the thought of someone cremating that beautiful, strong, comforting body that held me so many nights." Then she turned her face back into her pillow.

Solange knew for the time being she was dismissed, so after drawing in a heartfelt sigh she murmured, "I hope you don't live to regret it." Then she left.

Grace felt herself being watched. When she opened her eyes to the dimness of the room, she saw Jet standing in front of a window covered by vertical blinds. Had it not been for the slight crack of light that filtered between the panels, she wouldn't have been able to discern him at all.

"Jet," she breathed and pushed her body upright.

He was dressed in black from head to toe, and leaned heavily on a pair of crutches. His white cast showed from underneath his pants leg. His expression was grave and he shook his head sadly with disappointment. "You should have been there."

"I couldn't do it," she responded. "Déjà vu."

The silence in the room seemed interminable. Finally Jet said, "I understand."

"You always do."

"I'm going back to Lake City tonight."

"Don't go," she pleaded. "Stay here with me."

"I can't stay here, Grace."

"Why did you have to move there in the first place?" she wailed. "Why couldn't you have stayed in Atlanta near us? Things would be so much easier."

"Grace," he retorted, "things have never been easy when it comes to you."

She dropped her head, knowing he only spoke the truth.

"You could come with me," he offered. "I know that you took off time for your honeymoon."

"Go to Lake City? I think not. I would go anywhere with you but there," she muttered.

"I've made a life for myself here. You only remember the bad times from our childhood, but I also remember the good. How about our moms taking us to Myrtle Beach, or you singing in the church choir? Being able to walk a country road at night and not have to worry about being mugged. It's not necessarily a bad thing for everyone to know your name." He paused and stared straight at her. "Atlanta can be a cold place, Grace. Only a handful of people showed up today for Livingston besides his family, Solange, and me. You have nothing to keep you here."

"But why there?" she whined.

"It's my roots. Don't forget Lake City was the birthplace of Ronald McNair, and I want to help rebuild the area. The funds are there and the only thing needed is a champion. I'm on the zoning commission and on the board making decisions as to where tax dollars are being used. The little strip malls and everything with his name on it need to be a shining testimony to the hero he was."

"But anytime one of us is there, something happens to someone I love. Maybe if you had never . . ." She broke off, afraid to voice what she was thinking.

"Maybe if I had never what?" Jet's eyes bored into hers. "Maybe if I'd never moved there Livingston would still be alive? I can go you one better than that. Maybe if I had never thrown him a bachelor party, he wouldn't have died. Is that what you were going to say?"

"No, that's not what I was going to say." She averted her eyes from his.

"So you hold me responsible," Jet stated bitterly. "Join the club."

Jet started forward on his crutches and Grace bounded from the bed and threw her arms around his neck, almost toppling both of them. "I don't blame you, Jet. I just need you to stay and be here for me."

"I'll always be there for you, Grace. I'm just a phone call away." Planting a kiss on her cheek, he hobbled out.

Upstairs, Grace sat on the bed watching Solange put the last of her clothes in her carry-all.

"I hate to leave you, but I feel much better knowing the Gruesome Twosome and the rug rats are right behind me."

Solange's description of Delilah and Rose made Grace give a half smile for the first time in over a week. "I know. They're like fish. They stank after three days."

"How long were you planning to keep up the silent treatment to them?"

"As long as it took for them to get the message that I'll never forgive them for doing what they did to Livingston."

"When I heard Delilah making reservations for Southwest, I was glad that I was saved from having to tell them to get their junk and get to steppin'."

Grace traced the pattern on the bedspread with her finger. As Solange slid her bag closed, Grace said, "Jet said that there weren't a lot of people at Livingston's homecoming."

Solange sat down next to her and looked her squarely in the eyes. "But that doesn't mean that he wasn't loved, does it?"

Grace turned her head away in embarrassment.

"Most people have a hard time going to something like that, especially for someone as young and vibrant as Livingston was. It makes them fearful because it reminds them of their own mortality."

"I don't even have a gravesite to visit," Grace stated with deep bitterness. "I just hope they get the hell out of my house by tomorrow. Did you hear Delilah say what time flight is?"

"Noon, tomorrow," Solange smiled.

"Good," Grace muttered with satisfaction. "I'll come out of my room after they leave. I hope I never see them again."

Grace stood at on her front porch and waved at Solange as she backed down the driveway. When she turned around, she encountered the hostile gaze of Delilah, who was standing behind her, partially blocking her pathway into the house. Ignoring her, Grace brushed past. Then she stood in front of the clock on the wall and stared at it, saying loudly to no one in particular, "Two more hours. Then I'll certainly have to put in a call to Merry Maids." On her route back to the master suite, she caught Rose's apprehensive look as she handed Justin one of Grace's favorite dish towels to wipe the cereal that dripped from the corners of his mouth.

Once she was safely back in her haven, she went to the bathroom and grabbed for the bottle in the medicine chest. *Half of the bottle is gone, and Delilah can whistle "Dixie" if she wants what's left. We'll just call it even steven for three-plus weeks of free room and board.*

When Grace awoke it was after six o'clock in the evening. She heard a familiar blaring noise in the background and drew in a snort of annoyance. *They're so slack. They left my television on. I guess they feel, what they hell, it's not their bill so it's not their problem.*

Dragging herself out of bed, she felt a little shaky and she knew that it was from lack of food. Grace took a moment to stare at her reflection in the mirror and felt distaste for what she saw. She had deep hollows under her eyes, and she'd lost weight. Combined with the ten she'd lost for the wedding, she could be the winner, or at least runner-up, in a scarecrow contest. *But I don't give a damn anymore.*

When she walked into the den, she took a step back, stunned. Instead of finding an empty room, Rose and Justin sat staring transfixed at the television. Breaking her silent treatment, she demanded, "Why are you still here, and where is Delilah?"

Masking a look of trepidation, Rose said, "She had to go home on business, but she'll be back in a couple of days."

"Why is she coming back, and why the hell didn't you and the kids go with her?" Grace shouted.

Rose looked at Justin, "Please don't yell in front of my grandson."

"I'll do whatever the hell I want to do in my damn house! If you don't like it, get the hell out. As a matter of fact, get the hell out anyhow."

"Your behavior hasn't been rational since the death of my son, so I'll give you a little rope. Just don't hang yourself."

Grace's eyes bulged and she clenched her fists. She was so infuriated she was unable to speak.

Taking that as a sign that she was calming down, Rose said, "Delilah took Nalani and Kendra with her, but she left Justin because she didn't want to disrupt his schooling."

Schooling? How long have I been asleep?

"You know, it's really hard to get a place in special schools these days."

"Look, I don't know what's going on, but you're sadly mistaken if you think that you guys are moving in here. I need you to call Delilah right now," she demanded.

"She doesn't have a cell phone and she told me that she'd talk to you when she got back." Rose took her hand, placed it on the arm of the sofa and used it for balance as she struggled to her feet. "I'm going to take Justin and get him ready for bed."

Astonished, Grace watched Rose push the wheelchair past her. She fixed her eyes on the trail of tire tracks across her carpet. When Rose got to the foot of the stairs, she turned the chair around and began to haul the chair backwards up the stairs. Grace stared at Justin and saw a look of compassion in his eyes as they rested on her. One lone tear escaped from the corner of his left eye.

Grace was lying on the couch with an ice compress on her forehead when she heard Delilah's minivan. Earlier, she had picked up her checkbook representing her overdrawn account and hidden it between her mattress and box spring. Getting up, she flung the door open and saw a weary-looking Delilah carrying Nalani on her hip. Following was a sleepy-looking Kendra. The kids' faces beamed when they saw her. "Auntie Grace." Kendra ran to her and said, "I missed you."

It was all Grace could do to hold back the retort that formed on her lips. *If you think you miss me now, wait until tonight, girl.* Instead, she bent down and gave her a brief hug and ordered, "Take your sister to your grandmother because I need to talk to your mother."

Immediately Kendra grabbed Nalani and led her away.

Grace and Delilah faced each other like two boxers. "What the hell do you think you're doing?" Grace demanded in a nasty tone.

Delilah's response was just as venomous. "That's what I was about to ask you. How dare you be rude to my mother!"

"If she wasn't here, I couldn't be rude to her, could I? I want you to get your shit and get the hell out of my house."

"Funny, that's exactly what I was going to say to you."

"Excuse me?"

"I'm Livingston's next of kin. At least Mom and I are, and we were wondering when you were going to leave."

"You must be out of your damn mind!" Grace pointed her finger to her chest. "This is my house."

Delilah reached inside her shirt and pulled out a paper, which she tried to hand it to Grace. Grace automatically backed away in disgust. "Not according to this. I pulled the county records and your name isn't on this house. I went to see a lawyer. You have no rights here."

Grace screamed, "Livingston and I bought this house together."

She waved the sheet of paper around as if it were a banner. "Not according to this piece of paper, you didn't."

As quick as a cat, Grace's hand snaked out and she snatched the paper and tore it into little pieces that fluttered to the ground.

"That was your copy, Grace. I have another put away."

Grace's next-door neighbor, Quinnie, peeked her head out the door when she heard the ruckus. Delilah stormed past Grace to stand in the garage. "I don't want my neighbors hearing this mess. I don't want them to feel like they have a bunch of hood rats living next to them."

Grace leaned towards her. "That's what they would have if you were going to be living here, but you're not!" she spat out.

"We'll see," Delilah tossed over her shoulder as she stuck her head up in the air and stalked inside.

Grace stormed after her and just as Delilah reached the kitchen, she grabbed her by the arm, halting her. With her face only inches away from Delilah's, she said in a deadly tone, "Get out of my house."

"My brother's dead and I'm going to make sure you don't move some terrorist in here!"

Flabbergasted by this statement, Grace demanded, "What are you talking about?"

"I saw your homegirl Solange parading that Arab around at your engagement party. Birds of a feather flock together."

"They sure do," she said and turned to glare at Rose sitting there with dread written all over her face.

"I'm doing this for my brother's memory."

"You're doing this because you don't have shit!"

A look of triumph crossed Delilah's face and she said slowly, "I do now." Delilah looked over at her mother and ordered, "Mother, go to bed."

Evidently Rose had ventured downstairs when she heard the commotion outside, but now she scrambled as fast as she could out of the room. When she walked past her, Grace said malevolently, "I thought you said that you didn't have a way to contact her!"

Delilah turned to Grace and said, "Call your lawyer, and he'll tell you I'm right." She breezily walked past Grace and climbed the stairs after her mother.

CHAPTER 12

The sound of a school bus grinding to a halt in front of her house roused Grace and reminded her of the catastrophe her life had become. She'd only slept off and on all night, and even a sleeping pill every four hours hadn't helped her rest. *I've got to get these people out of my house. While I've been in mourning, they're been plotting. I can't let them win and take the only thing that I have left.* She picked up her cell phone from her nightstand and dialed Solange's cell.

"If I didn't hear from you today, I was going to give you a call when I got home."

"What do you know about Delilah enrolling Justin in school?" she demanded tersely.

"What?"

Grace repeated to Solange verbatim everything that had happened since she'd gone back to White Plains.

"They're squatters." Solange sounded appalled. "I didn't know where she was going every day with him. I just thought that she was taking him to some type of arts and crafts class or something," she stuttered. "I didn't know she'd enrolled the boy."

Grace could hear the sound of Solange tapping her pen on her desk. That meant she was doing some hard thinking.

"You need a lawyer." And she added almost under her breath, "In a hurry."

"I know. But I'm afraid to leave the house for fear they'll change the locks. The law might really be on their side."

"That's what you need to find out," Solange said.

"It's time for me to go back to work on Monday, but I e-mailed Mr. Thomas and told him that I needed the rest of the school year off; it's only another six weeks until summer vacation. It wouldn't be fair to my students to be their teacher, the kind of shape I'm in. They're better off with a permanent sub." Her voice cracked. "I know he thinks that it's for bereavement, so he won't question it." Grace mumbled, "Solange, everything I have is sunk into this place."

"Everything?" Solange sounded more appalled with every new bit of information.

"Yes. Don't you remember when Livingston called me in White Plains? I told him to do whatever it took to buy the house, and he did. We were going to add my name to the paperwork after I officially became his wife."

Solange made clucking sounds of disapproval with her tongue. "Do you need me to come down there?"

"No, because there's nothing you can do."

"Call Jet," Solange ordered.

"No," she whispered. "I need to learn to stand on my own two feet."

An hour later, Grace was on the floor of the bedroom cruising the Internet for a local lawyer when her cell phone rang. Looking at the caller ID, she felt fear and hope when she saw it was Jet's number. "Hello," she said dully

Jet was obviously pissed and his voice was authoritative. "Solange called me."

"I told her not to bother you."

"Don't be ridiculous. I'm glad one of you has some sense. What did my mother tell us about building our houses on sand?"

"Building our houses on sand?" Grace repeated dumbly.

"Yes," he responded curtly. "It means not taking care of business, not looking out for your own interests, not making sure you have a steady foundation to build on. In other words, sinking everything you have into a house without your name on it."

"But we were going to get married. If he hadn't been killed . . ."

"But he was," Jet cut in angrily.

"Livingston would've never done anything like this to me. He would've made sure that . . ."

"But Livingston is gone now and you have a big mess on your hands."

Grace didn't answer; instead she just hung her head and mumbled, "We would've lost our bid on the house if we'd waited."

"There are other houses, Grace, and it looks like you might lose it anyhow."

His voice softened with his next words. "I have a buddy on the other line who's going to talk to you."

"Hello, Grace. This is Attorney Levin." A deeply concerned voice that she'd never heard before resounded in her ear. "I've been apprised of the situation, but I need a few more facts. Did Livingston put the house in his family's name?"

"Not that I know of. No, of course he didn't because if he had, Delilah would have kicked me out the other night when she got home."

"Good, that means something. Did he leave a will?"

"Not that I know of."

"Did he leave any provisions for you?"

"Not that I'm aware of," she said doubtfully.

"Because you weren't yet married, all of his assets, including whatever he may have in IRAs and so forth, would automatically go to his next of kin."

"We had a joint checking and savings, but that money was withdrawn after he died and I didn't do it."

"Obviously it was his family. We could go after them for it because it was a joint account, but by the time we got them to court, the money would probably be gone so it would be a waste of time, unless we wanted whoever took it jailed."

"It had to have been Delilah because Rose doesn't even drive." She hesitated. "Even though she's a thief, I don't want to put Livingston's sister in jail because of his nieces and nephew." She added almost as an afterthought, "Once they grow up, they'll find out soon enough about her."

"We could go after the bank for illegally releasing the money to her, but if they used it on the expense of cremating him, that's kind of a moot point."

Jet made a sound that was a snort of derision and said, "Not on the ceremony I attended they didn't."

Attorney Levin said, "But once again, they're his next of kin. The one thing that you have going for you is that you've been staying there for a few months, right?"

"Yes," Grace said slowly.

"That means bills come there in your name, right?"

"Yes."

"Then they can't put you out. You have to agree to leave, so if you don't feel your life is in danger, wait them out. Maybe they'll change their minds."

Jet interjected, "I doubt that because they don't have anywhere to go. This is the best they've ever lived. I've been to Livingston's mother's house in Chicago and it's nothing to run back to."

"Well, I don't know what to tell you," Attorney Levin said with compassion. "You can't put them out, but they can't put you out either."

"It's like the movie *The War of the Roses*," Grace said caustically. Then she added gratefully, "I want to thank you for taking the time to talk with me, Mr. Levin."

"If there's anything I can do, call me," he ordered before he hung up.

"Jet," Grace whispered, "are you still there?"

"Of course I am, Grace." He paused. "What are you going to do?"

"I'm not giving up the last thing that I have of Livingston to them. They've taken enough."

A month later, after Grace heard the squeaking wheels of Delilah's minivan going down the street, she heard three tentative knocks on her bedroom door. "Go away!" she screamed.

Then she heard Rose speak in a sorrowful voice, "Grace, may I please come in?" Her bedroom door was slowly pushed open.

Grace had gotten up to turn the lock, but it was too late. She shot daggers at Rose as she stood there slightly shaking.

"I wanted to talk to you without Delilah around."

"That's hard to accomplish since she's always here." Her voice dripped sarcasm.

Rose sat down on the bed without Grace's permission and said, "I'm sorry about everything that's going on."

Grace moved her neck from side to side and put her hands on her hips. "If you were really sorry, you and your daughter would get those kids and get OUT OF MY HOUSE!"

"We have nowhere else to go. Now that Livingston is gone," her voice croaked, "this is the only chance that I have to make sure my grandchildren have a home." Rose began to sniffle.

Grace felt her heart melt a little, but then a vision of Delilah's face flashed in front of her and that fleeting piece of pity went away. "A home is defined by how you treat the people in it. Wherever you and Delilah live, it will always just be a house."

"You're still young." Rose averted her eyes and said shamefacedly, "You can rebuild. But Delilah, she just doesn't have what it takes."

Grace's temper exploded. "It's not my fault that she doesn't have anything. I put myself through college so that I wouldn't have to beg anyone for anything. Have you ever heard of student loans? Delilah could have done the same instead of relying on a man that obviously doesn't want her or her kids. Does he even call to check on his children? Not that I blame him because if I was ever married to Delilah, once I got rid of her, I would run, too."

"That's my daughter you're talking about!" Rose declared with an edge to her voice.

"Then you should have done a better job raising her," Grace retorted with a harsher edge than Rose's.

"How about Livingston? You don't seem to think I did too badly with him."

"Obviously he didn't want to be like the two of you, so he broke the mold."

"Why don't we have a family meeting when Delilah gets back and maybe we can work things out so we can all live together," Rose asked hopefully.

"I don't want to live with y'all after the way you disposed of Livingston without taking my feelings into account!"

"Daughter," Rose began.

"Don't call me daughter! You're no kin to me." Grace walked over and to her bedroom door and stood waiting for Rose to leave.

Rose got up from the bed. "I tried to reason with you, but you won't listen. It's out of my hands now."

Stomach growling, Grace went into the kitchen. Taking a potato out of a bin, she scoured it and dried it with a paper towel. Then she took a fork out of the drawer, stuck a few holes in it before placing it in the microwave and turned it on. She saw Delilah's reflection in the glass of the microwave and whirled around. "Move out my damn way." Grace's voice sounded eerie even to her.

"Make me," Delilah said. She then took her hand and swatted a glass duck that Livingston had bought Grace for Christmas. It fell to the kitchen floor and shattered when it hit the tile.

For a few seconds, everything went black. Then Grace lunged for Delilah and they fell, knocking over a bar stool. When they landed, Grace was on top.

Kendra saw them from the den and started screaming, "Grandma." Nalani began to moan from fear.

Grace had a vise-like chokehold around Delilah's neck and squeezed. When she saw Delilah's eyes start to bulge and roll back in her head, she came to her senses and let go. Wearily, she got up just as she saw Rose struggling down the stairs. Then her eyes caught sight of a bronze urn on the fireplace mantelpiece. She pointed at it and said to Delilah, "What's that?"

Delilah remained on the floor coughing with her hands to her neck, unable to speak.

Grace turned to Rose who was limping over to Delilah. "What's that?" she demanded hoarsely.

"It's my son, Livingston."

Grace's knees almost buckled, but pride made her pull herself together and, with a stoic look on her face, she went to her bedroom. She picked up her cell phone and speed-dialed Jet's number. When she heard his voice she said quietly, "Come get me."

There was a heavy silence on the other line and then he said, "Are you sure?"

"Yes," she croaked. "I'm done."

When Jet arrived the next day, he was driving a huge moving truck and had four men that looked like former wrestlers with him. He climbed out of the cab, reached back inside and pulled out a cane. Immediately, Grace felt ashamed. She'd been so gripped in her own personal drama that she hadn't been keeping in touch with him and didn't know how he'd been progressing since the accident.

Jet looked like a breath of fresh air. He was dressed in a pair of jeans, a T-shirt, and tennis sneakers. One of his fraternity caps shielded his eyes, but the uncompromising sternness of his jaw gave away how furious he was. Leaning slightly on his cane, he silently stared at the house.

Crossing to where he stood, she slid her arms around his neck, held him close and whispered, "I'm not going to cry in front of them because I don't want them to have the satisfaction."

"Good girl." He patted her on the back, then stepped back. He pointed at the four men who stared at her with kindness. "Meet Mark, Luke, Matthew, and John. They own a family moving company in Lake City and they're going to pack you up."

"I haven't even started. I didn't expect you until tomorrow."

"They're going to take care of it, Grace. That's what they're here for." He turned to them and said, "Strip the house bare except for the clothes upstairs. I want every dish, towel, and canned good taken." As each of the men grabbed bundles of bubble wrap, Jet said to Grace, "All you need to do is pack your personal belongings." Leaning on his cane, he started towards the house.

"Okay," she acquiesced.

Once inside, Jet felt immense satisfaction at the look of consternation on Delilah and Rose's faces when they saw him.

Because they always kept the television blaring, Grace knew they hadn't heard the moving truck.

When his eyes rested on the urn on the fireplace, they hardened like marbles. Then he surveyed the disarray and shook his head regretfully. When Jet walked into the middle of the room, Delilah recoiled and Rose flattened herself against the cushions in fear.

With barely suppressed anger, Jet picked up the remote and turned off the television. Sparks flew from his eyes. "I'm ashamed of you. Livingston wouldn't have wanted this. He loved Grace, and they purchased this house for them to begin a life together."

Grace stood behind Jet, half shielded by his body.

Delilah sputtered defiantly, "How do we know that she put any money in this house?"

"Because she said so. The legal system isn't always fair, but *you* could've been." His demeanor was unnerving and it jogged her memory to a time when as a boy, out of the blue, he'd hit a fellow classmate with a garden hoe for calling Grace's mother a drunk and making her cry.

Rose dropped her head and wept. The tears dripped from her drooping chin.

Jet focused his eyes back on Delilah. "I met your husband one time, and I knew that he was going to leave you." Jet took his cane and used it as if it were a golf club and swatted a sneaker that was in the middle of the floor into a corner of the room. It made a resounding thud when it hit the wall. "Maybe if you had cleaned up once in a while and had a hot meal waiting for him when he got home from work, he wouldn't have left you and you wouldn't be reduced to stealing other people's hard-earned possessions."

"You don't know nothing about me, Jet!" she shrieked.

"I've been single my whole life. I know women just like you."

Later, after Grace finished packing her clothes, she turned to Jet and asked in an exhausted voice, "What time are we going to leave in the morning?"

"The minute the guys wake up. But I want them to get a full night's sleep because they worked overtime to pack this huge house."

Jet turned to leave, and Grace was so close on his heels that she bumped into him when he stopped short.

"Where are you going?"

"To the hotel where the guys are."

"Don't leave," she beseeched him with her eyes. "Stay here with me until morning."

Jet rubbed the small scruff of hair under his bottom lip as he considered what she said. "I think that might be a good idea." He gave her a half smile. "I don't want to have to come back here later tonight and end up being brought up on domestic abuse charges."

That night as Jet lay on top of the covers fully clothed next to Grace, he wondered, *What next?*

Late the morning, Grace sat in the passenger side of her Jeep and watched Jet give the guys their last instructions. *Mark, Luke, Matthew, and John. Aptly named. Great apostles and great men.*

Jet walked towards her and after climbing inside, he shifted the SUV into gear and started to back out.

"Hold on," she said.

"Grace, leave it alone," Jet advised, scrutinizing her face.

Ignoring his advice, Grace climbed out and went back into the house. The bare walls and lack of furniture made the house seem tomblike. She saw Livingston's family sitting in the middle of the floor and, after giving them a cursory look, journeyed from room to room, mentally closing the door on her past. After going upstairs and returning, she stood at the doorway that divided the den from the rest of the house. She stared at Rose's averted head and said, "What did you gain?"

Delilah, still unrepentant, said, "A house."

"Big deal. Haven't you ever heard of ill-gotten gains?" She looked at the woebegone faces of the children and said, "I hate that your kids might suffer for your transgressions. They're good kids," she stated matter-of-factly.

"Don't worry about my kids," Delilah answered in a cruel tone. "I have a beautiful house to raise them in."

Grace looked around the bare walls and rooms devoid of furniture and said softly, "You can have this hull. But let's just see if you can keep it, because God isn't going to bless this mess." Then she blew the children a kiss before she turned on her heels and, with dignity and grace, left.

Once she reached the car, she slid into the door Jet had leaned over and opened for her and said, "Now I'm ready." He put the car in reverse and drove off in the same direction the moving truck had.

CHAPTER 13

They rode in silence for over an hour. Jet was obviously lost in his own thoughts, and the full enormity of what had occurred the last six weeks made Grace queasy. She took her hand and placed it on top of her stomach.

Jet looked over at her and asked, "Are you ready to get something to eat?"

"No," she said in a forlorn voice.

"I am," he said. "I'm going to pull off at the next exit."

"I haven't been very hungry lately."

"So I noticed." He eyed her gaunt features. "You not eating isn't going to change your situation. Have you decided what you're going to do?"

"I haven't thought that far ahead," she whispered.

"You have until school starts in August to try to regroup from everything that's happened."

"I hate to be a burden to you."

"You're not a burden, Grace. You're welcome to stay as long as you like. It's a give-and-take situation. You can be a great comfort to me. Livingston was like my brother, and I also have to try to deal with his passing."

"You appear to be doing okay, though," she said.

Jet slid his eyes away from hers, and when he looked back she could see real pain. "I keep busy," Jet replied.

"Instead of taking a position as a pharmacist as I had planned, I did some research and found out how easy it is to start a nonprofit organization."

"It is?" she asked, wide-eyed.

"Sure," he responded. "All you need is the proper paperwork and an I.D. number. Do you remember Jesse Gilliard, who was a senior when you were in the ninth grade?"

Grace squinted her eyes as she tried to bring up the image of a boy she'd seen in the halls of Carver High School. "Sort of," she responded slowly.

"Well, he's Dr. Gilliard now, and we've teamed up to get lower-cost medications to some of the people in the area that can't afford to buy the medicine that they need."

"How can you do that?" Grace asked. "I mean, I thought that the insurance companies had all of that sewn up and prices set."

"They do," he answered smugly. "But Canada offers the generic versions of many medicines that we have at less than forty percent of what people would pay if they had to go through their health insurance."

"I heard that medicine from Canada isn't safe."

"Some may not be," he said, "but the basic things that we're offering, for example, insulin, are as safe there as anywhere else. The other medicines that we have will eventually be offered in America ten years down the road. The FDA holds up progress, but there are pages of data that prove they're safe." He nodded with satisfaction. "A couple hours a day, I go to Jesse's office and when I get there a line has already formed. People bring in the prescriptions that their doctor gave them, and we provide the medicine at a lower cost than a regular pharmacy could or give them a generic. We have two volunteers that help people with the paperwork so we don't get shut down on a technicality. It's all perfectly legal," he ended with satisfaction, "and no one can do a thing about it."

"I'm so proud of you, Jet."

He smiled at the admiration he saw in her eyes. "I've been working hard to carve out a new life for myself."

"I think that you've accomplished it."

"All you need to do is find your niche, Grace, and then maybe you can find some kind of peace." He said almost as an afterthought, "But I know how much you hate Lake City."

"It's not the town, it's the memories."

"So replace bad memories with good ones."

"I feel as if I have to start all over again, and the prospect is daunting. When I was in college, there were a lot of days that I ate peanut and jelly sandwiches, but I never was destitute," she whispered in a forlorn voice.

"You're not destitute now," he corrected.

"All I have left is a houseful of furniture," she stated in a painful voice.

"Is it paid for?" he queried, lifting an eyebrow.

"Yes, because Livingston and I didn't want to start off our life with a lot of debt."

"Then you're not destitute. You have more than a lot of people, and you need to start seeing the glass as half full instead of half empty."

Feeling admonished, she hung her head and was relieved when he declared, "Let's stop at this Chili's and have lunch."

"Okay," she mumbled.

Once inside the restaurant, out of the corner of her eye, Grace noticed that Jet's entrance had drawn the attention of a group of women having lunch at a table. And then she saw them assess her.

She was casually dressed in sandals and a day dress that showed off her long legs. The problem was her hair. She hadn't been to a hairdresser since before the wedding, and the tracks of her extensions were noticeably loose.

Once the waiter took their order she mumbled, "Give me your hat."

What?" Jet asked surprised.

"My hair," she whispered, "my extensions are coming out and those women are snickering at me."

Jet looked over in the direction that Grace had been darting her eyes and smothered his laughter, handing her his hat. "Here you go, but I think when we get home maybe you should do something about it."

"I will," she said. With heartfelt relief, she grabbed the hat and plopped it on her head.

When their food arrived, Jet picked up his hamburger and took a huge bite.

Grace picked up a French fry and began to nibble on it.

Jet gave her a look, pointed at her untouched hamburger and said in an uncompromising tone, "Eat."

Grace picked up the hamburger, and once she started eating she felt better and smiled gratefully at Jet.

As Jet drained the last of his iced tea from his glass, she eyed him over the rim of hers and asked, "Are you still dating Tia?"

"No," he answered without emotion.

"Why not?" she asked. "She seemed nice."

Jet gave her a long look. "You couldn't stand her from the moment you met her, so why lie?"

Grace burst out laughing. It sounded good to her ears because she felt as if it had been ages since she'd enjoyed a good chuckle. "But she did seem to really like you."

"I know she did, but she's not the one and I wanted to let her off the hook before she got hurt. After my accident, as I lay in my hospital bed, I took a long, hard look at myself and decided that I wanted to be a new Jet Newman."

"I don't think the old one was so terrible," she murmured softly.

When the waiter came with the check, Jet withdrew some bills, folded them and handed the folder back to the waiter with a nod.

"I would help with that, but you know . . ." She tried to sound teasing, but instead the words came out flat.

"Money is the least of our issues," he said enigmatically before he stood up, indicating that he was ready to leave.

Once they entered the city limits, Jet slowed his speed. In the early evening, the small streets were brimming with people gathered in small groups and leisurely talking. Children ran after each other playing, and she saw old men playing checkers in front of a barber shop. "It's like a Spike Lee movie." She smiled.

"Life is a whole lot less complicated here," he said. "I hear they're getting a Starbucks soon," Jet grinned.

"Get out of here," she replied.

When they drove down Main Street, the heart of town, people stopped and stared at the unfamiliar SUV with a Georgia license plate. A couple of women pointed and she could see that they were craning their necks to see who was inside.

"Is there any way possible you can keep people from knowing I'm here?"

"Not if you leave the house. I always get a rundown from my customers when they come to get their medicine about everything going on in the community. I doubt that it'd be any different when it comes to you."

"Have you had any visitors since you moved back?"

"I get a lot of dinner invitations from the church mothers on Sundays." Jet moved his eyebrows up and down.

"Have you been taking them up on them?" she asked, glaring at him.

"Of course I have. A man's gotta eat, doesn't he?"

Once they left the city limits, Jet picked up speed again as he headed out to the country. As they rode, Grace spied small farms that hadn't yet been phased out by larger ones. Their fields were full of tobacco not yet ready to be picked. After a left and then a sharp right, the road narrowed considerably.

"Watch out for animals," Grace advised.

"I do, but country animals have a preservation instinct that city ones don't. You hardly ever see any road-kill around here."

Grace rolled her window down, looked at the fields and sniffed the air appreciatively. "The air has a good quality. The only time tobacco smells good to me is when it's in a field in its natural state."

"What?" he said mockingly. "I know you didn't say something positive about Lake City."

"I did, didn't I?" She gave him a lopsided grin. "Red clay," she exclaimed, pointing.

All of a sudden the grass on the embankments had turned from a lush green to red clay. Grace's memory was jogged to happy times when she'd played on the soft hills and had gone home covered with the dust from head to toe. Her mother would shoo her to the bathroom to take a bath and when she'd emerged, there was usually a glass of Kool-Aid and her favorite candy bar, a Baby Ruth, waiting for her as an afternoon snack. Her eyes misted over at the memory and she blinked back tears.

She turned her head and saw Jet's knowing look. Then he focused on an upcoming, curving turn. He slowed the truck and pulled into a long, winding driveway.

Grace's mouth dropped as she viewed the beautiful sage-colored Colonial. Large round columns flanked the ends of the front porch, which housed two rocking chairs. "You built on the Red Hill estate?"

"It wasn't much of an estate, but the land has historical value because it's an important linchpin in the civil rights movement," he said with satisfaction.

"But this isn't the house that used to be here," she corrected him. "This is a mansion by comparison."

"No, that place has been gone for a long time. After Reverend De Laine and his family left, no one dared to move out here because of the social climate of the town." He pointed across the manicured lawn. "That's the site where the Klan burned the church down." Then he pointed in the other direction. "And over there is where the house was that Mrs. De Laine ran to in order to hide from the Klan. And that wall, that's where Mr. De Laine shot his rifle at the men trying to intimidate him and his family. I had the rocks replaced and this brick wall built around the periphery of the property."

"I was supposed to visit the Courage Museum exhibit in Atlanta." As her voice trailed off she finished lamely, "With Livingston, but we ran out of time."

"I didn't know that." Jet added softly, "Grace, don't be afraid to talk about Livingston, and don't try to bury the memories of him. Remember the good times you shared. You'll always have that."

Jet hit the garage door opener he had placed in the console of the Jeep. When the door raised, she saw a white BMW, a motorcycle, and an ATV. "You finally bought a car? You are growing up," she teased.

"My physician asked me not to ride my motorcycle for a year, or at least until I can put the cane away."

"Do you know when that's going to be?" she asked as she automatically looked in the back seat at the object in question.

"No," he mumbled.

Grace could tell that by his expression that he hated having to use it at all. Trying to sound more upbeat, she said, "But I see that you bought yourself a replacement toy."

"I sure did. ATVs are great for this area. You can go as fast as you can and no one bothers you."

"You're really are still a teenager at heart, aren't you?"

Jet turned his head and their eyes locked for a long minute. He opened his mouth to say something, and then he closed it without uttering a sound. Then he grabbed his cane and opened his car door.

Grace slid her hand through the crook of Jet's arm and held on to him as he proudly showed her his house. Room after room they walked together. Grace slid him a sideways look and said, "I never knew a bachelor could have so much taste. Even a sunken bathtub and separate shower," she said admiringly.

"I tried to make the outside reminiscent of the old Colonial house we used to gawk at when we were riding the school bus as children, but I wanted the inside as upscale as possible. I asked Livingston for ideas and contractors that he had relationships with to make sure that the work was completed in a timely manner."

At the mention of Livingston's name, Grace's arm stiffened and she slid it out of Jet's and stared down at the floor. In order to distract her thoughts she said, "Hardwood floors. I've always wanted a house with that."

They heard the rumbling of the moving truck as it pulled into the driveway. "Your stuff is here. What do you want to do with it?"

Grace looked around the empty rooms and held her hands out. "I guess we should just go ahead and set it up. I have too much to put in a storage unit, and you need furniture."

"You're right about that. If that was the case you'd need to rent at least four."

"Your house is completely finished." She held her hands out wonderingly. "Why haven't you filled it with furniture?"

"I haven't gotten around to it. The clinic is taking up more time than I expected."

"I understand that," she said doubtfully, "but a mattress and box springs on the floor?"

"Yeah, I've been living like a real Neanderthal man. That just means that you have free rein to put your stuff out wherever you choose." He pinched her chin and went outside to greet Mark, Luke, Matthew, and John.

When the foursome entered through the garage, they looked apologetic. Luke spoke for the group. "I'm sorry you beat us here, but we had a flat tire right at the state line."

"That's no big deal. We just got here ourselves because we stopped and ate."

Matthew playfully slapped John on the shoulder and said, "I told John to stop, but he wouldn't and now I've got to go back into town and get something."

"You eat all the time, boy," Mark teased, looking at his brother's large frame.

"I think that we should start putting up the large furniture," Jet intervened. "Grace, please drive into town and get something to eat for these guys from the Kentucky Fried Chicken we passed on the boulevard." He looked at them as he reached in his wallet and handed Grace a wad of money. "All of you eat chicken, right?"

"Have you ever met a black man that didn't?" Matthew chortled.

"Not yet, I haven't," Jet laughed.

"Well, you won't today, either," Luke added as he went to start unloading the truck.

Giving Grace a look, Jet advised, "Get enough."

As Grace drove her Jeep back to town, she felt a peace start to invade her body. Dusk was setting in, so she put her headlights on low beam. Once she entered the city limits, she smiled at the sight of an unattended outdoor fruit and vegetable stand. *They would never leave that produce unattended in Atlanta. It would like that scene from in* Coming to America *when Eddie Murphy and Arsenio Hall arrive in Brooklyn and people steal all of their luggage when their backs are turned.*

Grace stood in line at Kentucky Fried Chicken and tried to pass unnoticed. *This is certainly a hub of activity,* she thought wryly. *I guess it's the meeting place for a Friday night.* When she finally reached the counter she looked at the cashier and said, "I would like two buckets of chicken, one original and the other crispy. Please make the fixins mashed potatoes with gravy, macaroni and cheese, baked beans and honey and butter to go with the biscuits."

"Yes, ma'am," the girl drawled.

Grace hid a smile. The people in Lake City had a unique accent no Oscar-rated actress could duplicate.

"Would you like something to drink to go with that?" the girl said as she punched keys on the register.

"Sure, two liters of regular Coke and one of diet Coke. The latter is for me," she smiled.

"I don't know why," the young girl smiled after giving her a speculative look. "Do you live here? I've never seen you before."

Before Grace could respond she heard, "I don't believe it. Is that my goddaughter under that purple hat?"

Oh, no! Grace plastered a smile on her lips as she turned in the direction of the strident voice.

"Gimme a hug here, chile."

Grace reached down to hug the small frame of Liza Taylor.

"What on earth are you doing here, and why didn't you let me know that you were coming to town?"

"I'm sorry, Godmomma, but I didn't know myself until recently."

"I should have known once that good-looking Jethro moved back here you'd be not far behind. You two always were inseparable."

The cashier called out for number 102 and Grace gratefully walked back up to the counter, handed her the number slip and began gathering the four bags off the counter.

"Let me help you with that," Liza offered. "I never remember you being so slight. You can't be more than a hundred pounds sopping wet."

Grace grimaced as she let her take two of the bags from her. "I think that you ought to add another thirty pounds to that. I'm tall, remember."

"Yeah, but you never did have anything on you but a butt," she said, tapping it lightly.

Grace bristled at the familiarity but held herself in check because she knew no harm was intended.

Once they reached her vehicle, Grace opened her car door and turned to say goodbye to Liza. She stopped at the look on her face.

It was a look of genuine concern as she looked at Grace. "What's wrong with your hair?"

"Nothing, I just haven't had a chance to fix it," Grace answered defensively. "I've been rather busy with other things."

"I know," Liza said bluntly. "Jet told me about you losing your fiancé the night before you were to get married, and that's a bad piece of luck, but you should never let yourself go like this. I mean, it didn't happen yesterday or I could understand."

"I'll take care of it," Grace said in a surly tone.

"My great-niece Naomi just finished beauty school and is trying to get some clients. Let me send her out to you to do your hair."

"I don't know," Grace said, "I don't like inexperienced people working on my head."

Liza wagged her finger at her. "Don't you worry about that, girl. Naomi, she does good work. In fact, she does mine."

Grace looked at Liza's hair and had to admit to herself that it did look pretty good.

"Okay," Grace agreed. "Does she know where Jet lives?"

"Does she?" Liza laughed. "Every single female from here to Florence is talking about that good-looking pharmacist who moved back here from Atlanta, built a mansion on Red Hill, and is helping people get medicine so they can feel better."

Grace shook her head because she knew that occurrence was probably the most interesting thing that had happened there in a while. Before she climbed into the truck and turned the key in the ignition she said, "Ask Naomi if she's coming tomorrow to arrive as early in the morning as possible, because I'd like to get it out of the way." She hesitated before she finished with, "I have a lot of unpacking to do."

Hours later, an exhausted Grace lay on the sofa and listened to the men's voices in the background as they talked in the garage. She was tired mentally and physically and didn't have the energy to find out where her sheets were packed, so she decided to make do on the couch until the morning. A few minutes later, as she was drifting off to sleep, she heard Jet's telephone ring.

"Hello," Jet whispered. "Yes, Solange, we made it."

There was a long pause and she knew that Jet was listening to what Solange was saying.

"I think she's asleep on the couch, but I can wake her. Are you sure?" There was another long pause and then, "She's here indefinitely. Okay, I'll tell her to call you tomorrow." Then there was still another long silence before he said, "She'll pull thorough this, I'll see to it."

Grace woke later that night and looked around the darkened room. *Where am I*?

Then she knew. In the darkness, tears began to trickle down her cheeks. She turned on her side and buried her head in her arm trying to muffle her sobs, not wanting to wake Jet. She cried for Livingston and his nieces and nephew. Then she thought of Jet and cried for him because of his loss and the repercussions he had to deal with because of the accident. The faces of everyone she'd loved and lost came to the forefront of her mind and she cried for her and Jet's fathers, though she couldn't even remember what they looked like. Then she wept for Esther and, last but not least, her mother.

After the deluge of tears stopped, feeling her way about in the darkness, she found her pocketbook and reached inside and located the medicine bottle. Stumbling over to the kitchen sink, she reached for a glass and ran tap water. She opened the pill bottle and after withdrawing one pill, then another, she took a knife and cut one in half. She placed the pills on her tongue and chased them down with water until she emptied the glass. Still not turning the light on, she lay back down on the couch and waited. About twenty minutes later, she felt her entire body relax and she slid gratefully into a deep sleep.

CHAPTER 14

The smell of coffee percolating roused Grace. Blearily she sat up and looked in the kitchen. Jet looked like a preppy in a pair of khakis and light-blue shirt. He was standing at the sink stacking dishes in the dishwasher. Grace's eyes focused at the clock on the wall. Blinking her eyes, she thought, *Eleven o'clock!*

When Jet saw that she was awake, he scrutinized her face and said, "I started to wake you up last night so you could go to your room, but I didn't want to disturb you. You never used to be such a late sleeper. What happened?"

"Nothing," she answered, swinging her legs to the floor. "I can do that," she said, pointing at the dishes.

"I got it," he replied.

"I should have remembered to get paper plates from Kentucky Fried Chicken."

"I'm glad you didn't. They're not good for the environment. If everyone used real plates, it would go a long way toward helping the planet go green."

Grace looked at him. "I don't remember you being so environmentally conscious when we were growing up."

"You don't really think about it when you live in a place like Lake City because of its fresh air, but once I started traveling and saw cities with skylines full of smog, I realized how real a problem it is."

Grace looked at Jet and said in a somewhat awed tone, "Jet, you've always had a good heart. But now you're older, the way you care about things," she placed her hand on her heart, "and what you do for others, it's amazing."

Jet hid his expression from Grace as he started the dishwasher. Straightening, he opened his mouth just as the doorbell rang. "I guess that's my clue to leave. I'm sure that's your hairdresser."

"Gee whiz, I totally forgot about that." Grace stood and caught Jet staring at her with a strange look on his face. She glanced down at her body. She'd slept in a pair of his boxers and one of his T-shirts and she knew she looked like she needed a makeover. "Will you let her in while I brush my teeth and put a bra on?"

"Sure," Jet answered without revealing what he was thinking. He walked towards the door.

Grace was in the bedroom shrugging into her bra when she heard a clanging sound from outside. "Do you mind helping me lift this chair up the steps?"

"Not at all," Jet answered smoothly.

A few minutes later, Grace heard, "You're so strong, Jet."

In the bedroom, Grace took her finger and acted as if she were sticking it down her throat to vomit. Then she hurried out to the den.

When she reentered the den, she was shocked to see a child that appeared to be around three or four years old in the woman's arms. *No, she didn't bring her child with her. That's so unprofessional. After how I've been run through the mill lately, I certainly don't feel like being bothered with other people's younguns. Well, to be fair, she did come to me and save me from being stared at in one of the local beauty parlors.*

Jet now had the girl in his arms. He was lifting her up and down, making her chuckle.

Grace stepped forward and said in a not-too-friendly voice, "Are you Naomi?"

"Yes, and you must be Grace." She eyed Grace's hair. "I'm sorry that I had to bring Ebony with me, but I couldn't find anyone to watch her."

How about your great aunt? She knew you were coming.

"I can't believe you left Atlanta for this country town." She smiled whimsically. "I'd like to live in a big city one day."

"Circumstances dictated that I relocate here for a while." Grace's tone was brisk.

"Okay, ladies." Jet looked at Grace and lifted the top of the cookie jar. Then he replaced it and gave her a look. "I have to meet with a city councilman about renovating the Ron McNair strip mall. I'll be back later this afternoon." He handed the toddler to Naomi, grabbed his cane that was leaning against the wall and said, "Nice to see you again, Naomi," before he departed.

Naomi's eyes followed Jet, and once he couldn't be seen anymore she turned her attention back to Grace. When she smiled, the corners of her eyes crinkled. "What do you want me to do to your hair?"

Grace hesitated for a moment and then said, "I want this weave out, and I need a perm."

"No problem." Naomi spoke confidently.

Hours later, a very pleased Grace stared at her reflection in the mirror. For the first time in what felt like an eternity, she liked what she saw.

Naomi had given her the Rhianna cut and Grace loved the light feeling. It was a benefit to have short hair since the weather was already getting hot, and she knew before long the days would be almost insufferable. *I feel ten times better.* She smiled her gratitude at Naomi. Grace took the lid off the cookie jar and withdrew money. "How much do I owe you?" she asked Naomi.

She could see her mentally tallying her price. She asked, "Is seventy-five dollars too much?"

"Seventy-five dollars! For all this? Here." She quickly shuffled through the bills and handed some to her. "I can't take advantage of you. My hairdresser in Atlanta would have charged me at least one hundred and fifty dollars."

Naomi looked at the cash and said doubtfully, "We don't charge that kind of money around here for our services."

"It's a hundred dollars. Buy Ebony a toy or something."

"Okay," she acquiesced. "Here's my number." She handed her a business card. "Call me if you want me to do your hair again."

"Let's just go ahead and set up a standing appointment. Every two weeks I'd like a wash and set and," she mused, "and I'll probably need a trim."

"That's great," Naomi said, obviously pleased.

"Same time, same place?" Grace asked.

"Yes, but can I bring my daughter? It's so much easier than trying to find her a babysitter."

Grace hesitated and looked at the pudgy baby's wide, innocent eyes and said, "Of course you can."

Naomi was in the process of packing up her belongings when she asked, a little too casually, "Is your brother seeing someone?"

Here it goes. For hours we've been chatting about everything under the sun. I wondered when she was going to start trying to get the lowdown on Jet. Her mind began working overtime. *I hate to lie but I don't want her dating Jet and bringing that baby over here all the time.* Her eyes rested on the sleeping form on her couch. *She's a good child, though. She's been here for hours and not had a tantrum.* Crossing her fingers behind her back she said, "Jet's dating a model named Tia."

Naomi's mouth drooped despondently and she said, "No wonder he's been living here all this time and no one knows of him having a steady girlfriend. Sometimes I cut hair at the barber shop and the guys down there said that he was gay, but I knew he wasn't. I can always tell. I have gaydar about that sort of thing."

"Jet gay?" In spite of the fact that she'd just told a bald-faced lie and felt her conscience tugging at her, she fell out laughing. "Pass the word. The boy is not gay!"

"As far as I'm concerned, he might as well be. I mean, if he's dating a model, what chance does a girl from Lake City have to get his attention?"

Feeling horrible but unable to extricate herself from the lie she'd fabricated, Grace said, "Models are just like other people. They just wear more makeup and don't eat."

When Jet got home, Grace was in the kitchen putting the finishing touches on dinner. He caught the whiff of meat loaf cooking in the oven. Walking over to the stove, he sniffed with exaggeration.

"It's not Wednesday. Do I smell rice and corn to go along with the meatloaf?"

"You sure do. It brings back memories, doesn't it?"

"Good ones." His eyes had a faraway look and she knew he was thinking about his mother and how that was one of his favorite meals as a child.

"Dinner will be ready in thirty minutes, so you have time for a quick shower."

"I'm starving, so I'll be out in twenty."

Grace was on her knees unpacking a box of her things when Jet reentered the room. He had donned a pair of shorts and a wife beater. She smiled at him. "You really have developed a sense of style. I don't remember you being so trendy."

He sat at the kitchen table. "It's easy to wear the latest when you have the funds to buy things. Sometimes I feel guilty to be so solvent when the economy is bad and so many people are losing everything."

Grace gave him a look. "You deserve your money. What that doctor did to your mother . . ." She shook her head.

"I believe in fighting back under the right circumstances."

Grace picked up Jet's plate and heaped generous portions of food on it before she put it down in front of him.

"What are you drinking?" She opened the refrigerator. "We don't have much of a choice, so it'll have to be iced tea or water or soda."

"I'll take some water, thanks."

Grace withdrew two mismatched glasses from the cabinet and filled them. Looking at them she said, "I'm going to unpack my kitchen stuff as soon as possible."

After placing them on the table she hurriedly fixed her plate and sat down.

"For the first time in a long time, I'm actually hungry." She attacked her plate of food with relish.

Without responding, Jet bent his head and prayed.

Grace's fork dropped with a clatter. "I'm sorry, I forgot to say grace," she said, chagrined.

Jet gave her a look. "It'll come back to you in time. Your soul is ingrained with faith, you've just lost a little of it for now. I went through the same thing after I lost my mom, but with time, you'll find joy instead of pain when you think of Livingston."

Grace turned her head and stared out the window.

Jet knew from years of knowing her that she wasn't ready to absorb what he was saying, so he changed the subject. "I added your name to my checking account at the Lake City Citizens bank. They're going to mail you a debit card in seven to ten days. Until then, you'll find what you need for incidentals in the cookie jar."

"Jet," she stammered, "I don't feel right spending your money because I messed up mine."

"As I said before, money's not an issue for us. I have plenty."

"Then what is our issue?"

The sound of the telephone ringing interrupted them and Jet reached for the cordless receiver. "Hello. I'll have to call you back because I'm in the middle of eating dinner."

"Who was that?" Grace asked.

"No one important," he answered, tackling the food on his plate. "Naomi did a good job on your hair."

"And she's cheap, too." Grace grinned.

"Good," Jet said. "Then you won't mind getting it messed up."

"Why would I get it messed up?" she asked, smoothing her hand over the shaven part at the base of her neck.

"I'm going to take you riding on the four-wheeler after dinner and show you the surrounding countryside."

"It sounds like fun," she replied, digging into her mountain of food.

Grace stood in the driveway as Jet slowly backed the vehicle out of the garage. Making a U-turn he sat on the seat and asked with a devilish smile, "Ready?"

"I guess so. So you really know what you're doing, right?"

"You can trust me," he answered.

"I know I can." She hopped on the seat behind him.

Jet slowly steered down the driveway and, after looking both ways to make sure no cars were coming, he revved the engine, turned onto the road and slowly picked up speed.

Grace slid her arms around his waist and buried her head between his shoulder blades. Every time the bike slowed she looked up. One time she saw Jet waving at a neighbor, and then another time a farmer on his tractor plowing his field. Eventually she felt her body relax and Jet picked up more speed. As the wind blew through her hair, she felt exhilarated and free from all of life's worries. They sped through the countryside and Grace smelled manure. She'd never known the smell to be so comforting. After a half an hour or so, Jet made a wide turn and pulled off the side of the road cut the engine, and pointed off in the distance, "Over there is a swimming hole. The water is so clear and blue it beats any pool I've ever been to."

"Let me see it."

Shutting off the engine, Jet took the key and began to limp through the underbrush. There was a path that was obviously man-made from the tramping of people on their way to the lake. When they got to the small clearing, Grace started to climb across the rocks that were used as stepping stones to descend to a lower level where the water was waist deep.

"Be careful in those sneakers," he instructed. "Those rocks are slippery."

"Then I'll just take them off." Sitting down on the marshy grass, she took her sneakers off and immersed her feet, splashing water as she kicked them around.

"In all my years of living here, I never even knew this was here," she breathed with wonder in her voice.

Jet sat next to her on a large boulder. "When you're a child, all you know in your world is your immediate surroundings. When you're an adult, you have a chance to see what else is out there."

"Thank God for that," Grace said.

"And then sometimes you end up going full circle and end up where you started from in the first place," he stated with an inscrutable expression on his face.

Birds chirped quietly in the background. No words were necessary as they listened to them and the trees rustling in the wind. Finally, Jet stood up and said, offering her a hand up, said, "We'd better get going because I want to get home before dark."

"And I have a sink of dishes waiting for me," she smiled.

"I can take care of that," he said without rancor.

"No, I'll do it. After all, you worked today, and I didn't."

Jet simply shrugged his shoulders.

One they got back to the ATV, Jet sat on the bike, put the key in the ignition, and cranked it, putting it in neutral. "Now it's your turn to drive."

"No," she said hastily, "I'd be too nervous."

"You'll be just fine." He got off the bike and motioned for her to slide to the front. "This is your gas pedal, ease on it slowly when you want to pick up speed and ease off it when you want to slow down." He squeezed the hand grip. "This is your brake. Squeeze it," he ordered.

Grace squeezed the grip.

"Get a feel for it. Any time you want to slow down, ease off the gas and gently squeeze the brake until you slow." Then he climbed to the back and put his arms around her.

Grace pressed on the gas and jumped when she heard the roar of the engine. After it idled down, she gripped the handlebars, put it in gear and slowly took off. Once she got the hang of it, she picked up speed. Grace loved the feeling of control and felt invigorated as she navigated the bike on the small country roads. Once they pulled up at Jet's house, she put the ATV in neutral and turned off the engine. She hadn't felt so free in years. After she jumped off the bike, she leaned over and planted a fat, sloppy kiss on Jet's cheek. "Thank you so much," she oozed, "I haven't had that much fun in years."

Later on, after finishing the dishes and wiping down the counters, Grace called out, "Jet?"

When he didn't answer her, she walked down the hallway and, hearing music, pushed open the bedroom door.

She stood in shock and stared.

Buck naked, Jet had his head bent and was securing a gold chain around his neck. Suddenly he looked up, and immediately surprise crossed his face, followed by something imperceptible.

Stunned, Grace felt her face grow red from embarrassment. She stammered apologetically, "I'm so sorry, Jet. I didn't know that you weren't dressed."

Grace backed out and slammed the door and leaned against it. *Damn! That bitch Babs lied on him. Jet is hung like a horse.*

As Grace tossed and turned that night, her thoughts were of Jet. After a while, he'd come back to the den. They didn't speak of the incident, and as they watched a *Lost* marathon on television, Grace kept sneaking peeks at Jet. He as he had stretched out his long legs on the ottoman in front of the couch. Several times, she felt his eyes turn to her as she sat in the chair perpendicular to where he sat, yet he said nothing.

Later in the room across the hall, Jet lay on his back, thinking about Grace. After the encounter in his bedroom, he'd felt her studying him and there had been a subtle shift in her body language that evening as they'd watched television.

The memory of the snugness of her body against him as she'd held him tightly on the ATV excited him. Fascinated, he watched the sheet that was covering his torso begin to lift to look like a teepee. Suddenly, thoughts of Livingston encompassed him and feelings of guilt flooded through him. He immediately lost his erection. Jet sat up and took a swig of water from the glass on the nightstand. Turning back to settle back into bed; instead he sat up straight and blinked. "Livingston?" he whispered. *My mind's playing tricks on me.*

"Your mind's not playing tricks on you," the vision said. "Grace has lost her way and I need you to help her come to terms with what has happened. She's mourned long enough."

Jet shook his head. "I'm trying, but she's lost her faith."

"She hasn't lost her faith in you. Use that to help her make her way back to the living."

"I don't know how to help her," Jet answered.

"It's okay for you to have her," Livingston said.

Jet dropped his eyes. "How do I really know that I'm not hallucinating this because it's how I would want you to feel?"

"Pinch yourself."

Jet took his hand, dug his fingers into his arm as hard as he could. The pain was real.

"Am I still here?" Livingston said

"Yes," he answered softly.

"Then you know this is for real. I love Grace and I want her to be happy. You've always loved her and you almost lost her to me. Don't lose her again. Grace has a depth of feeling for you that she doesn't understand. Make her look at you with new eyes."

"I don't know how to do that," Jet answered solemnly.

"Follow your instincts. Teach her how to love you, Jet. I'm depending on you to make the woman that I love happy." Livingston turned around and walked through the closed door of the bedroom and disappeared.

As Jet lay back on the bed, an inner peace that he'd never experienced before invaded his body.

The next morning Grace was unpacking another box of her things when Jet walked into the den. "Good morning," she said.

"Same to you," Jet answered. "I see you're up and about early."

"I can't stand the mess. I vow to have everything unpacked and the house fully decorated within the next two weeks."

"That's a tall order," he said, looking around.

"But it can be done if I put myself on a schedule. That's a good thing about teachers. We know how to plan our day and follow the plan to the smallest detail." She looked up at him. "I'm making a list for the grocery store. Do you have anything special in mind that you'd like to eat?"

"No, not really. Anything you cook is bound to be good."

"Well, I learned from the master. No one could make collard greens and sweet potato pie like your mother."

"You're going to make me fat." He grimaced.

"You could use a little meat on you," she retorted.

"If that isn't the pot calling the kettle black," Jet countered as he poured himself a cup of coffee.

"I've already eaten more in two days with you than I did in four days in Atlanta."

"Good," he replied with satisfaction. "I wondered if you wanted to go check out a movie tonight. There's a new Denzel flick out, and I know how you dig him."

"Sure, why not?"

"I have to go to Jesse's office, but I'll be home by five. The movie starts at seven forty-five."

"Dinner will be ready when you get here."

Jet deliberately walked over to Grace and kissed her on her forehead. "Have a good day," he said. Whistling, he walked out the door adjoining the garage.

Grace stared after him with her mouth hanging open. Then she touched the spot on her forehead that still felt warm from his lips.

The ringing telephone made Grace stop her frenzy of activity. Grabbing the receiver, she sank onto the leather couch and said, "Hello."

There was hesitation on the other end and then a woman said, "I think that I must've dialed the wrong number. I'm looking for Jet."

Grace corrected her. "You have the right number, but he's not here."

"Oh, will you please tell him that Lorna called?"

"I sure will."

Grace only gave her a chance to squeak out "Thank you" before she cut off the call.

Then she looked at the caller I.D. and saw a number two next to the number. *She's the same person that called him last night while we were eating. She needs to take an etiquette class. If you call a man and he says that he's busy, don't call him back because he'll return your call if he's interested.*

Standing and stretching, Grace slid into her flip-flops, grabbed her purse and some money and got in her car and drove to the corner store at the fork of the road. Once inside, she grabbed a small shopping cart and strolled up and down the aisles picking up various items.

Once she got to the counter, a teenager give her a welcoming smile and asked, "Did you find everything that you want, ma'am?"

There was something vaguely familiar about the teenager but Grace couldn't figure out what it was.

"I sure did."

A man in a white butcher apron emerged from the back and said, "I don't believe what I'm seeing! Grace Foxfire, what are you doing back here?"

Grace gave a genuine smile to her first boyfriend, Isaac. "I would give you a hug," he looked down at his apron and sighed reluctantly, "but I don't want blood all over you."

"Maybe another time," she laughed. "I have to admit I have an exceptionally queasy stomach when it comes to that stuff."

"Then you could never be a butcher's wife." He laughed, then hastily amended, "I don't usually do the butcher work. My helper called in today because his wife went into labor."

"Well, he has a good reason for not showing up then, doesn't he?" She gave him a quirky smile.

"The best reason in the world," Isaac agreed. "So, I see you met my boy."

"From the moment I saw him, I knew he looked familiar."

"That's me fifteen years ago. I think that's how old I was when we were an item."

"Do you think you should be bringing that up in front of him? I don't want some mom with her nose out of joint calling me." She smiled at the inquisitive look on the boy's face.

"Aw, he doesn't mind. His mother and I divorced a long time ago and he hardly ever sees her. In fact, I'm looking for another wife."

Handing the boy money for her purchases she gave Isaac a steady look and said, "But I'm not looking for a husband."

Isaac brushed that aside. "I heard you were staying at the palace with Jethro. How about me taking you out to dinner?"

"I'm afraid that I can't, I'm pretty well booked. And Jethro goes by the name Jet now." She began to push the cart out the door and Isaac came around the counter and took it from her.

He pushed it out to her Jeep and said, "I'll give you a little time to get settled and then maybe you'll change your mind. You know where I am."

Not wanting to hurt his feelings, she gently said, "I sure do."

That night as Grace and Jethro left the theatre, as usual she had her arm inside the crook of his. "Denzel is one fine actor," Grace stated.

Jet gave her a look. "Do you mean he's a fine actor or that he's fine?"

"Both," she chuckled. "Who was that chick playing opposite him?"

"I don't know. She's a newcomer on the acting scene."

"Well, she's really good. I heard that Denzel always coaches the new actors in his films because he knows that sometimes you only get one chance."

"I don't believe that people only get one chance. I kind of think that God is more lenient because he knows that we're all human beings and that means we make mistakes."

A silence fell on them before Grace abruptly changed the subject. "What time does Piggly Wiggly close?"

"Not till eleven. Do you need something?"

"I like to shop in bulk so I thought that if it wasn't too late, we could get groceries for the next two weeks."

Jet was giving her a speculative look and she shrugged her shoulders and explained, "When I went to the country store today, Isaac made like he was going to start trying to date me."

"You're a beautiful woman, Grace. Don't you expect to be come on to everywhere you go?"

"It's not so much that it's unexpected, but the attention is unwarranted. For the first time since Livingston's death I look forward to waking up in the morning. I don't want anything to upset the apple cart."

Jet gave a grunt of satisfaction. "Let's go to the grocery store and stock up on some things."

Piggly Wiggly was pretty much deserted at that time of night and Jet patiently pushed the cart as Grace went down aisle after aisle. Once they were at the conveyor belt and the cashier was ringing up their items, Grace heard someone say, "I've been calling you and you haven't returned my calls."

Grace turned and saw a petite woman dressed in a pair of blue jean shorts, striped polo shirt and wedge sandals.

Jet said, "I know that you called once."

"I called more than once," she pouted. "I spoke to her today."

"Oh, my manners. Grace, this is Lorna. Lorna, this is Grace."

The two women silently sized each other up.

Lorna gave Jet a look. "I left a CD in your car and my little cousin is harassing me for it back."

"Oh, I'm sorry, but I'm not driving my car. We have Grace's Jeep."

"Can you please bring it over to my house later tonight?" she whined. "I really need it."

Jet hesitated, looking at his watch. "Okay, I'll be over in about an hour."

With a smirk on his face, Jet watched Grace stalk to the car.

Sliding inside after he unlocked the car doors with the remote, she folded her arms in front of her and declared, "That's what I don't like about small towns. You can't help running into people you don't want to."

"I don't mind seeing Lorna. She can be a lot of fun," Jet replied smoothly.

There was a thick silence on the drive to Red Hill which neither one of them attempted to break.

After Jet helped Grace bring the mountains of grocery bags in the house and put them on the kitchen counter he asked, "Do you mind doing this by yourself while I take Lorna her CD?"

"Do I have a choice?" Grace answered mockingly.

Giving her a look, Jet left and Grace heard him cranking up his BMW and backing out of the driveway.

After unpacking all the groceries and taking a shower Grace looked up at the clock. *Almost two o'clock in the morning. Well, I'm not waiting up for him anymore.* She walked over to her pocketbook and withdrew one of Delilah's pills. *I'm almost out.*

Grace sat up in bed. Swinging her body around, she placed her feet on the floor. She tipped over a small object on her nightstand, yet she didn't awaken. Robot-like, she walked to her bedroom door and opened it. Slowly she walked across the hall and turned the knob to Jet's bedroom, entered it and walked over to the bed.

At the sound of his door opening, Jet sat up in bed. He watched Grace as she walked towards him in a trance-like state.

Grace reached down and pulled back the covers before sliding into the bed next to him. Then she turned over and minutes later, he heard her breathing deepen and she began to snore lightly. Jet lay back down, turned over on his side, careful not to disturb her, and went to sleep.

CHAPTER 15

The next morning, when Grace awoke she stretched and turning over on her side, she felt a hard body next to her. She smothered a yelp when she realized it was Jet and he was staring at her. Their eyes connected and time stood still. *He's in bed with me*!

Not moving, her eyes shifted around the room and she realized that instead of him being in her bed, she was in his. *Oh my God! I hope he's wearing underwear.* Grace raised the covers. *Nope, he isn't.*

"How, when?" she stuttered, chagrined at what she'd done.

"You were sleepwalking," Jet replied without emotion. "When I saw you coming in here, I was afraid to wake you."

Grace's brow furrowed as she tried to remember leaving her room in the middle of the night. She couldn't.

"Have you ever done this before?" Jet watched her closely.

"No," she denied with feeling. "I've never ended up in the bed of a man when I didn't want to."

Jet raised his eyebrows at her words.

"What I mean is," she amended, "I've never woken up somewhere and not known how I got there."

"Usually when people sleepwalk it's for various reasons. Having a lot on their mind is a major factor."

"I'm sorry if I disturbed your sleep," she apologized.

"Anytime," Jet said and threw back the covers. When he was on his feet, he turned to face her.

At first, Grace averted her eyes. Then unable to stop herself, she looked at Jet. For the first time in her adult life, she really looked at him. Her eyes started at his feet and slowly moved up his hairless legs to his thighs. He had thighs that looked like they should belong to a NBA basketball star. His shaft was nestled in a thatch of curly dark hair. It hung low, reaching the middle of his thighs. Grace felt a hot flash of desire ignite. *What am I thinking*? She moved her eyes up and stared at his six pack, then his chest. Suddenly she had a frivolous thought. *He's like a hairless cat everywhere except his manhood. Good, I absolutely can't stand a hairy man*! When Grace's eyes met Jet's she encountered a look of extreme satisfaction.

"Grace."

"Yes," she murmured softly.

"Get dressed," he ordered, "I'm taking you to breakfast."

The Huddle House was located on the busiest street in Lake City. When they walked into the restaurant all eyes turned on them. They seated themselves, and soon an older gentleman slid off the stool at the counter and ambled over to them. "Jethro, I went to the doctor today and he told me that my medication isn't covered by Medicare. I don't have $300 a month to pay for it!" the man complained.

"Calm down, Deacon Brown. What is the name of the medication?"

"I can't pronounce it. It's something I never heard of."

"Do you have the script?"

Deacon Brown took his wallet out of his back pocket and handed a piece of paper to Jet.

Jet read the script and smiled, putting it in his pocket. He crooked his finger at Deacon Brown, motioning for him to lean forward so that no one else would could hear and said conspiratorially, "I have a special stash of that at my house. This afternoon, come over and I'll give you a month's supply until we can figure something else out for you."

Deacon Brown's face beamed. "Thank you so much, boy. I knew when you were growing up that you were going to be something special." Then he looked at Grace before wagging his finger at the two of them. "I knew that the two of you were going to end up getting married, too."

Grace's eyes locked with Jet's and the memory of what had happened between the two of them flooded her face with heat.

Instead of saying that they were only friends, which, during their teenage years, had been her immediate response when people had tried to put the two of them together, Jet noticed a softening of Grace's expression at Deacon Brown's words.

Jet watched Grace devour a ham and cheese omelet, grits, coffee and toast. He had the same except instead of grits he'd opted for the pancakes. Once he'd cleaned his plate, he leaned back and patted his stomach. "That was tasty," he said. "I need to go by the clinic and check on things. Do you mind riding along?"

"Not at all, I'd love to go and see the place."

"Then let's go."

It was a short ride to Church Street and when Jet turned his BMW into the parking lot, Grace saw people entering the building. "It's already busy," she said.

"It's always busy," he replied.

Once inside, Grace saw two tables with women explaining procedures or writing things down as they spoke with the people seated across from them. A row of seats against the wall held people waiting. Following Jet to the back, she remained quiet as he picked a packet out of a hanging folder and, after reading its contents, went down a short hallway and knocked on the door.

Grace heard, "Come in," before Jet pushed open the door and went into the room.

Jesse Gilliard smiled at Jet and rose to his feet when he spied Grace behind him. "Welcome back to Lake City," he said with a grin, walking from around the desk to vigorously shake her hand.

"Thank you." She returned the handshake.

"How long are you going to be here with us?" he asked.

"Indefinitely, since I like it better than I did when I was a child," she replied, looking at Jet. His eyes smiled back at hers.

Jesse Gilliard saw the sparks that flew between them and pressed his lips together to keep from grinning like a Cheshire cat.

"I had a question about this chart I picked up from the mailbox. Why are we being levied an extra tax on the property?"

"Because we conduct business here, so it's not considered a residence but instead commercial."

"But we're not charging our customers, so that rule doesn't apply. I have to meet Thomas Garrett this afternoon, and I'll discuss the matter with him."

"Great!" Doctor Gilliard said. Then he looked at Grace. "I can always count on Jet to handle things."

"So can I," she agreed with shining eyes.

As they were getting ready to get in the car, Naomi, carrying Ebony, huffed and puffed as she hurried up the sidewalk.

Before she even reached them she asked, "Did either of you see my Aunt Liza in there?"

"No, she's not in there," Jet answered.

"What's wrong?" Grace asked, seeing the sweat on Naomi's forehead.

"She's supposed to watch Ebony and I can't find her. I have to go to work at Wal-Mart and if I'm late one more time, they'll fire me." Tears filled Naomi's eyes as she said, "I can't afford to lose my job." Then she looked at Grace. "Will you please keep her for me until I get off work at nine? I'll come get her when I'm done."

Grace started to say no and then she looked into Ebony's liquid brown eyes and her heart melted. "Okay,' she answered and held her hands out.

At once, Naomi handed Ebony to Grace and said to Jet, "I'll get you my car seat." She motioned to her car, which was blocking another one in.

"I'll get it," Jet offered.

Grace was trying to balance Ebony on one hip when Jet returned with the car seat. Grace watched Naomi drive off after saying, "Thank you so much, Grace and Jet. You're life savers."

Once Jet settled Ebony in the back seat, Grace slid in the car and as Jet cranked the car she said, "I know that I'm living in Lake City. No one in Atlanta would dare hand their child off to someone who's practically a stranger."

Without answering, Jet put the car in gear.

Jet sat playing on the floor with Ebony as Grace cooked dinner. "Do you need me to go and get some baby food for her?" he asked, looking up.

"No, she can eat what we eat if I mash it up."

"Well, what are we having?" he asked.

"Spaghetti and meatballs. I think Ebony would do better with that than pork chops or chicken."

Jet's cell phone rang and Grace handed it to him from the counter from where she was standing.

Smiling at her, he said into the receiver, "Is it an emergency?" He gave Grace a doubtful look. "I'll see if I can make it." He looked at Ebony rolling around on the floor and then he eyed Grace. "They need me to attend an emergency council session in town. Are you okay if I leave you alone with Ebony?"

Affronted, Grace said, "Have you forgotten that I'm a teacher?"

"I haven't forgotten. Have you?" Jet replied mysteriously.

Grace planted her hands on her hips, but decided not to follow up on Jet's statement. "How about dinner?" she asked.

"That's what microwaves are for. You guys go ahead and eat without me. By the way," Jet said as he grabbed his keys off the hook on the wall, "if Deacon Brown comes while I'm gone, I have a bag of medicine in the coat closet." Jet handed her Mr. Brown's prescription. "Give him what he needs." Then he hurried out the door.

Grace was sitting on the couch with Ebony on her lap laughing at Jethro as they watched *The Beverly Hillbillies.* She looked at Ebony and said, "He's fine, too, just like Uncle Jet."

Ebony cackled and repeated, "Uncle Jet."

The doorbell chimed. Putting Ebony on the floor so she didn't fall off the couch, Grace went to answer it.

"Come in, Deacon Brown."

Taking his hat off when he entered the house, he looked around at the way Grace had decorated and said admiringly, "You've turned this empty house into a home."

"I'm not done yet. I have more boxes in the corner of the garage that I need to go through." She opened the hall closet door and withdrew Jet's black leather medicine bag. Motioning for him to follow her, she opened it and started picking up bottles of medicine, reading their labels. When she saw a couple of bottles of the same sleeping pills that Delilah had given her, with relief she slipped one of them into the pocket of her dress. Then, after maneuvering some more bottles around, she dug deep and found what she was looking for. Triumphantly handing the medicine to Mr. Brown, she said, "I found them."

Deacon Brown looked at her intently and said, "Thank you," and then gave her a criticizing look. "What'd you put in your pocket?"

"Nothing," she stammered, caught off guard. "It's just something to help make me sleep."

"Peace of mind could do that for you instead of drugs," he said frankly.

Immediately Grace's feathers ruffled and she said shortly, "I see you're getting something to help yourself."

"If I could do without it, believe me I would. I don't believe in taking a whole mess of medicine because it's not good for you. But if this helps keep me alive so I can enjoy my grandchildren a little while longer, I'll take it."

"Thank you for your concern, Mr. Brown, but I'm doing just fine."

After Deacon Brown left, Grace sat on the couch, holding Ebony and seething.

Grace was standing on the front porch waving goodbye to Ebony and Naomi when Jet returned. As their cars passed, Grace saw Jet wave at Naomi before he pulled into the driveway. She walked down to greet him and said, "You took longer than I expected."

"I know," he said, casually placing an arm around Grace's shoulders and turning her towards the house. As they walked side by side he said, "Those people can be awfully long-winded when they really don't want to do something, but I think we worked out the kinks."

"What kinks?" she asked, reentering the house and walking to the sink to wash her hands.

Jet sat at the kitchen table. "The city wants to build a youth center and call it the Ron McNair Youth Center. I have no problem with that as long as they keep it up and don't short the funds for special programs to make it run smoothly."

"We really do need a youth center for those kids off Knight Street. When I went into town I saw everyone just hanging out. They have nowhere to go and just stand on the corner all day long."

"I know," Jet agreed. "It's a real problem when you have people of three generations partying together. The older crowd that has practically given up on life taints the younger crowd that still has a chance. That's why the youth center is so important. It'll separate some of that mess because winos won't be allowed on the premises," he finished.

"Good," Grace said as she put a plate of spaghetti in the microwave and turned it on.

"I noticed Naomi was late picking up Ebony."

"She said that she was delayed closing out her register. Supposedly there was a large sum of money missing and they made all the cashiers wait until it could be accounted for."

"Really?" Jet said. "Did they find the money?"

Grace hunched her shoulders. "She didn't say. I guess so. By the way, you got an invitation to something in the mail today."

"What was it?"

"I don't know," she said. "I don't read your mail."

Grinning at her, Jet picked up the envelope off the counter and, after looking at it, said, "It's my invitation to Jesse's get-together. He and his wife are celebrating their ten-year anniversary."

"Has it been ten years already?"

"It sure has. They got married in undergraduate school."

"Were you planning on taking a date?"

"I was, but it would seem kind of strange to take the woman I'd planned to."

Grace lowered her eyes, guilty because she'd disrupted Jet's life so much.

"How would you like to bail me out so I don't have to go alone?"

"When is it?" Grace asked.

"The last Saturday night of the month."

"Sure, I'm beginning to feel cabin fever so at least that will be something different."

"Good. Now I'm beat," Jet said, handing Grace his empty plate. "I'm going to take a shower and go to bed."

Disappointed, Grace looked at his retreating back and sat down on the couch.

Grace let the warm water cascade over her body and she thought about what Deacon Brown had said to her that afternoon. '*Too much medicine isn't good for you.' But I don't see how one pill a night can be that harmful. After all, it's doctor prescribed and I see commercials all the time saying that it's not addictive. Anyhow, I'm feeling better now so I'll see if I can sleep through the night without it.*

Hours later, Grace sat up, frustrated, and stared at the clock. Decisively she got out of bed and went to her dresser and pulled out the pill bottle she'd hidden beneath her lingerie. Placing two pills on her tongue, she threw her head back and swallowed them dry. Slamming the dresser drawer, she stomped back to the bed and lay down.

An hour later, slowly, Grace sat up in bed, then stood. She walked to her bedroom door and shuffled across the hall to Jet's bedroom. Turning the knob, she entered the room.

Jet lay watching Grace through hooded eyes as she approached him. He held back the sheet that covered him as she slid in beside him. Then he pulled her to him and she snuggled against him with her head on his chest and fell into a zombie-like sleep.

When Grace woke the next morning, her head felt fuzzy. She looked around hazily. *Oh no, I'm in Jet's room again, but this time I'm alone.* She screwed her face up as she tried to remember, but her head began to hurt so she stopped trying to bring back the memory of leaving her bed and getting into his.

Embarrassed, she hurriedly got up and walked towards the den.

Jet was sitting at the breakfast table eating a bowl of cereal.

Grace gave him a shy smile and tried to say nonchalantly, "You're up early."

Jet gave her a steady gaze and said, without beating around the bush, "You need counseling."

"What?" Grace said, suddenly fearful.

"You're sleepwalking, Grace, and that's not normal behavior."

"Two times," she said weakly. "It's not as if I need to be locked up in the looney bin or anything."

"I didn't say that." He hesitated, then added, "But you've been through a lot. There's nothing wrong with a little counseling."

"Look around you," she said, spreading her arms out. "I'm adjusting. I cook, I clean, we do things together and I don't cry anymore."

"Just because you're functional doesn't mean that everything is okay. Your problems are probably simmering just under the surface, and at night when your mind is supposed to be rejuvenating for the next day, it isn't."

"You just don't want me in bed with you," she said in a pitiful voice. "I'm sorry that you find it so distasteful. Just start locking your door at night."

"I would never lock you out, Grace, but you need some help." Jet walked over to the counter and picked up a piece of paper. "This is a list of some reputable psychologists in the area. Pick one and call for an appointment." Jet held the paper out to her, but instead of taking it she dropped her head in shame.

"I can't save you, Grace. You have to save yourself." Jet put the paper on the counter and left.

Grace sank on the couch and cried for the first time since she'd left Atlanta.

That afternoon, Grace pulled up at the office of Dr. Harold Griffin. She shut the car off and rested her head on the steering wheel, trying to drum up courage to go inside the building. All of a sudden someone started rapped on her window, startling her. *Good Lord, it's Liza.* Turning the key back on so she could roll down the window, she smiled weakly.

Liza said, "Hello, darlin', I thought that was your Jeep. What are you doing here?" She gave her a quizzical smile.

This is why I hate small towns. Everywhere you go, you run into someone you'd much rather avoid. Grace searched her mind for a plausible reason for her to be sitting in front of a psychologist's office and stuttered, "I was going to go inside for directions," she said lamely. "What are you doing here?"

Liza nodded at the building. "My cousin works here cleaning up and I brought her some lunch." Liza showed Grace a brown paper bag. "What are you trying to find?"

"I'm looking for the post office."

"Darlin', it's in front of the Piggly Wiggly where it's always been."

"Oh," Grace said, cranking up the vehicle. "I'd better hurry up and get there before it closes. It's nice seeing you again." Grace sped out of the parking lot.

Sunday morning, Jet emerged from his bedroom dressed in a black suit. "Check out Mr. Brooks Brothers," Grace said and followed her statement with a high whistle.

Jet looked at her still dressed in her housecoat and said, "So I take it you're not going?"

"Nope," she mumbled.

"Why not?"

"I don't want to," she said shortly. "I'm not ready for the prying eyes or the questions."

"I don't think that you'll get the questions, Grace. Livingston's death was on the news and everyone knows he was your fiancé."

"That makes it worse," she muttered.

Jet balled his fists and put them in his pants pocket. "I know that you're angry with God for taking Livingston from you, but he spared me. Doesn't that count for something? Do you really feel that you have nothing to be thankful for?" Jet glared at her harshly before he stalked out, saying, "Don't bother cooking for me. I'll take up one of the church mothers' dinner invitations."

Grace's mouth tightened as she tried to mask her annoyance.

After Jet left, Grace turned on the television and surfed the channels. Then without really thinking about what she was doing, she took a shower. Fifteen minutes later, she was sliding into stockings to match a white suit she'd withdrawn from her closet. Plopping a white hat on her head, she left the house and headed towards Deep River Holiness Pentecostal Church.

Once she was at the parking lot, she hesitated. No one was standing outside the church so she knew that she must really be late. Drawing a deep breath, she got out and quietly entered the foyer of the church. *I haven't been inside a church since my wedding day.* Peeking through the sanctuary window, she attracted the attention of an usher who opened the door.

The usher tried to lead her to an empty seat near the back of the church, but Grace gave a negative shake of her head, and proudly walked to the front where Jet sat. Muttering her apologies, she climbed over four people to reach him.

Once she settled down next to him, Jet turned his head. When their eyes met, his held a look of forgiveness. Then he squeezed her knee comfortingly.

Feeling the animosity and the heat of someone's eyes, she turned around and caught Lorna staring at her from a couple of pews behind. She deflected her hostile stare with a sweet smile and then turned back to listen to the minister.

When Pastor Greene was near the closing of his sermon, Grace heard one woman whisper to another, "I heard that Grace was back in town and is staying with Jethro."

"I know. My brother was going to buy some peas from the country store and saw them riding around on a four-wheeler like little kids."

"She's seems awfully happy to say that she lost her fiancé not too long ago."

"I heard that she goes with Jethro. Lorna says that he hasn't spent any time with her since Grace came back to town."

"She and Jethro were dating?" The woman lowered her voice.

"*Were* is the correct assumption. Look at how he's got his arm around Grace."

"That's unseemly," the other woman whispered.

Grace heard a snicker and then, "What's unseemly about it? They're not really related, you know?"

"But they were raised as brother and sister. I wouldn't cross the line with my play brother."

"I met your play brother, and he doesn't look like Jethro, or you might have second thoughts."

"Well, if they're sleeping together, they should get married," the voice said in a superior tone. "God condemns living in sin."

Grace heard a different voice say admonishingly, "Hush, y'all gossiping in church and that's just what Pastor finished preaching on. Didn't y'all hear one thing he said?"

Grace's eyes met Jet's and his lips twitched as he tried to hold back his laughter.

Then one of the women whispered, "Jethro's mother is turning over in her grave if they really are boyfriend and girlfriend and living together. She was a deaconess in the church and she'd think that was wrong."

Immediately, the smirk was wiped off of Jet's lips and his expression changed to one of deep meditation.

After services, Grace stood off to the side and cynically watched while some of the church mothers twittered around Jet. At one point, he threw his head back and laughed. As she watched him with arms folded, she tapped her foot impatiently.

She was beginning to feel ignored, but the next thing she knew, she saw Isaac making a beeline towards her. Feeling lonely as she watched people socializing, she felt relief to see someone from her past.

Isaac said, "How are you doing, Grace?"

"Good," she replied. "It's really nice to see you."

"How would you like to go and get that meal now?"

Grace hesitated. When she saw Lorna approaching Jet she answered, "Sure, why not?"

"Since you have your car, I'll meet you at The Railroad Station."

The Railroad Station? Isaac is really trying to impress me. That's the most expensive restaurant in town. I wish that I hadn't agreed to go. But not knowing what else to say at this point she said, "Sounds like a plan," and started to walk to her Jeep.

Finally breaking away from his crowd of admirers, Jet made his way back to her. "Are you ready to go home?"

With a small pout she said, "Actually, I'm going to meet Isaac at The Railroad Station for dinner. You seemed *so* busy that I made other plans."

Jet's eyebrows furrowed in irritation. "Do you need to have every minute of my attention, Grace?" He glared at her and in a stony voice said, "I don't think it's fair for you to bring other people into our little drama." Then he stalked off and got into his car and left.

Grace sped to The Railroad Station. When she got there, Isaac was outside waiting for her. She drove up to him and said apologetically, "I'm afraid that I'm going to have to cancel our plans."

"Why?" Isaac asked. "What happened in the last fifteen minutes?"

"I just don't think that I should give you false hope. What we had is in the past and I want it to stay there."

Isaac's eyes glittered angrily.

With real remorse Grace looked at him. "I'm sorry if I hurt your feelings, but I don't want to mislead you. Now I have to go because I, well, let's just say that I have to go."

CHAPTER 16

When she got home, Jet had already changed from his suit and wore his signature lounging outfit, a pair of basketball shorts and wifebeater and was seated on the couch staring blankly off into space. He was so deep in thought that he apparently didn't hear her open the door or the sound of her heels on the tile.

As she stared at his profile, she thought about what he'd said to her at the church before he'd left. *Did she demand every minute of his time and if so, why?* Grace didn't remember being so possessive of him when they were growing up. In fact, it'd been the opposite; but now, every time she saw him looking at another woman or another woman looking at him, she got an uneasy feeling in her gut.

Pulling off her shoes, she walked into the den. She sat down on the cushion next to him, and putting her hand on his thigh, she leaned her head back on his shoulder and spoke quietly, "You're right. I don't know why I'm so possessive of you. I just know that I am."

For a few seconds, Jet didn't move. Then he spoke and his voice deepened to a husky sound that made chills run down her back. "You don't know why, but I do."

Jet turned Grace's face to his and, leaning in, he touched her lips with his.

Surprise made her lips tighten, but Jet opened her mouth with his. Very slowly, he inserted his tongue into hers and gently explored the inside of her mouth.

Grace found herself being lowered to the couch with Jet sliding on top of her.

He took the two palms of his hands and gently held her face so she couldn't escape. Then he dropped them to caress her breasts through her dress, never once freeing her mouth.

Grace felt the zipper of her dress being slid down and next her breasts were freed from their bondage. She flung her head back as far as she could and when she felt Jet's mouth close around her nipple she emitted a moan that sounded like an animal being released to run wild.

Jet suckled her breasts for what seemed to be an eternity before he pulled himself up. "We do have a bed. Would you like to join me?"

As she mutely nodded her head, Grace dimly heard the doorbell being rung. Angry at the intrusion, she blocked out the noise. Then she heard a banging on the door.

Jet let out an epithet before he stood. Staring down at his body, he took his hands and grabbed his penis and tried to make it go down. After he adjusted his shorts with a wry smile, he looked at her.

Grace had opened her eyes, and with a dissatisfaction she didn't try to camouflage, she pulled her dress up and stormed to her bedroom, slamming the door. Once inside, she was tearing off her dress and sliding into a pair of shorts and blouse before she heard Jet's voice and that of a woman. Then she recognized Naomi's voice and white hot anger engulfed her. *I'm going to get a new hairdresser because Naomi is getting way too comfortable over here. Hasn't she heard of telephoning people's houses before showing up?*

Once she was dressed, Grace left the bedroom to stand beside Jet.

"I'm so sorry," Naomi said with tears trickling down her face, "but I didn't have nowhere else to go."

Grace's irritation disintegrated when she saw Ebony reaching for her.

Jet looked at Grace and his expression was unfathomable. "Liza is in the hospital and they're keeping her overnight. Naomi wants us to keep Ebony so she can stay at the hospital tonight."

"Oh." Grace felt a small cringe at her earlier thoughts and took Ebony, adjusting her to fit on her hip. "Of course we'll keep her."

Naomi held out a small bag. "Here are a couple of outfits for Ebony." She gave Grace and Jet shamefaced looks. "You know how dirty she gets."

After the door closed, Jet leaned against it and studied Ebony and Grace. "I heard that kids can ruin a couple's sex life. Now I know firsthand how true that is."

That night, Jet lay in bed across the hall, thinking. He wore a satisfied smirk. *Grace Foxfire. Mrs. Grace Newman.* It had a solid ring to it. If they hadn't been interrupted, he'd be inside Grace at that moment, making her cry out his name, making her want him all the more. Tattooing her body with his for life . . . Ebony was in bed with her, so he wouldn't interrupt, but after their petting session this afternoon, he knew that it was only a matter of time before Grace Foxfire was his. She was certainly worth the wait. He'd make sure to show her what Jet Newman was all about.

Grace was sitting on the front porch sipping a glass of lemonade and watching Jet cut the grass on the riding lawnmower. Ebony sat on his lap as he did so. Because Ebony had been staying with them longer than expected, they hadn't discussed the fact that they had almost made love, and, truth be told, Grace was somewhat relieved for the distraction.

From pure exhaustion, she wearily passed her hand across her face. She hadn't had a good night's sleep while Ebony was there, because she hadn't taken any of her pills, afraid Ebony would need her in the night and she wouldn't be any good to her if she was too groggy. Lying awake, she'd thought of Jet.

The memory of his mouth and hands made her squirm uncomfortably in the rocking chair. Grace searched her mind for a reason why she and Jet shouldn't become lovers, and the only plausible one she could find was Livingston. What would he have said?

Thankfully, her attention was diverted when she saw Naomi's car turn into the driveway. A feeling of loss consumed her because she knew that meant Ebony was leaving. She would miss her. Grace hadn't realized how much she missed teaching until Ebony had come. She'd filled Grace's days with activity and laughter as they played games together. Sometimes Ebony amused herself as she rode the big wheel Jet had bought for her, giving Grace time to do chores in the yard. Grace went into the house and grabbed Ebony's overnight bag, and she handed it to Naomi.

"Liza had a small blockage and they took it out, so she's back home now. Thank you so much for what you did, keeping my little munchkin and all," she said, looking at them.

"It was no trouble at all," Grace replied at once.

"And don't even think of thanking me. Grace is really the one who took care of Ebony."

Naomi looked at her gratefully. "I could tell from the moment I met you that you would be a great mother."

Grace's eyes misted over. She had a fleeting vision of Livingston, quickly replaced by Jet's face.

Naomi stared at Ebony in Jet's arms and said, "I think my daughter's put on weight just from staying with you for three days."

When Jet started to hand Ebony to her mother, she started kicking and screaming. "No," she yelled, "I want to stay with Aunt Grace and Uncle Jet."

Naomi stood stock-still as she watched her child cling to Jet. Then she said in a slightly disgruntled voice, "Hush your yelling. We'll be back on Saturday to do Aunt Grace's hair for the party."

Turning her head to avoid Jet noticing how painful it was to watch Ebony leave with Naomi, Grace said with a downcast expression, "I'm going to go and get the mail."

"I'll put the lawnmower away," he said, climbing back on its seat and driving to the garage.

Grace stood at the mailbox, sifting through the mail. She'd had her mail forwarded from Atlanta and almost everything was junk mail or credit card inquiries. The very last envelope was from her school. Hurriedly tearing it open, she skimmed the letter. It was from Mr. Thomas and stated that she would have to let him know if she was coming back the next school year or he couldn't hold her position. Inside the envelope there was an Intent to Return form. Grace absently tapped the paper. She looked up and saw Jet's back. He was cleaning the bottom of the lawnmower off with a rag. *I'll send it in tomorrow and let Mr. Thomas know that I won't be back. There's nothing left for me in Atlanta anymore.*

Grace started up the driveway, head bent as she contemplated whether she should also give Mr. Thomas a personal call along with her rejection letter. Suddenly she heard a rattling sound.

Coming to an abrupt stop, she lifted her head. In the middle of the driveway, a large rattlesnake was curled up like a rope. Paralyzed with fear, Grace couldn't move. Dryness invaded her throat as she was confronted with her worst fear. Though she couldn't move, she saw Jet out of the corner of her eye.

Motioning for Grace not to move, he picked up a garden hoe that was hanging on a nail in the garage and stealthily walked up behind the snake. Then he swung the hoe, catching and pulling the snake away from Grace. As it slithered on the driveway, he severed the snake's head. The snake's body continued to squirm on the driveway and he swung the hoe again and again until it was chopped into pieces. The rattles now lying on the driveway continued to squirm, and he next swung the hoe and chopped the rattles into pieces.

Motionless, Grace stood with her eyes transfixed on the pieces of the snake.

With relief, Jet dropped the hoe and walked to her. Without saying a word, he lifted her and carried her into the house.

Once inside, he carried her to her bedroom and gently placed her on the bed. He examined her body and then peered into her eyes for any signs of shock. "Are you okay?"

Mutely, she nodded and then in a bemused sort of voice said, "You didn't limp."

Surprise stole across Jet's face and he said, "I didn't notice. I guess my adrenalin kicked in when I saw you in danger." He lightly tapped her cheek and then said, "Now I'm going to run you a nice hot bath and while you relax in the tub, I'll go outside and clean up that mess. When I finish, you'll never even know a snake was there."

After Jet left, Grace lay on the bed and did some deep thinking. *Jet, you're my savior. I love you.* Shocked, she realized what she'd instinctively felt.

Once in the tub, Grace sank back in the bubbles and rested her head on a bath pillow. Because she was tall, she had to scoot down as far as she could to make sure the water rose all the way up to her neck. *Grace Newman. Mrs. Jet Newman. What am I thinking? All my life I've known this boy and now he wants me and I want him. Physical attraction is one thing, but it doesn't always lead to a long-lasting love. After all, we spend a lot of time together so no wonder Jet is attracted to me. But the same philosophy doesn't ring true for me. All my adult life I've worked and been around attractive men, but I've never spent every waking minute thinking about them like I do Jet. Except Livingston. This is too weird. We'd be run out of town on a rail if people knew what I was thinking. Grace Newman.*

Grace slid her wet hands over her body. First she kneaded her breasts, and then allowed her hands to drift down to her stomach, slick from bath oil. *Jet.* She closed her eyes and inserted her fingers into herself, gently pushing them in an upward angle. Then she stopped. *I don't want to pleasure myself, I want Jet to do it. Just one time and I'll get it out of my system.* Grace sat up and started to bathe in earnest. She buffed and rubbed every inch of her body, and then she shaved and got rid of hair every place except the place she wanted Jet to devour. *If he makes a move on me, I'm going to welcome it with open arms. Just this once.*

Grace stood in front of the full-length mirror and examined her naked body. She had lightly toweled, leaving her skin slightly wet so her body oil would easily dissolve into her skin. Picking up her favorite scent, Moonlight Path from Bath and Body Works, she rubbed the body butter on her skin from her toes to her neck and then lightly sprayed the matching mist in the air, walking through it so it would cling all over her body. Then she picked a cotton square up and poured astringent on it, wiping her face. Crossing over to her closet, she shrugged into a pair of black silk thong panties and matching wrap. Drawing in a deep breath, barefoot she went to find Jet.

Are you serious? She was shocked when she entered the den to find him asleep on the couch on his stomach, the remote control to the television in his hand.

Grace stared at the back of his head, willing him to wake up, yet he didn't stir.

Frustrated, she went into the kitchen and started clearing away the few glasses in the sink, hoping the noise would rouse him. When he still didn't budge, she wiped down the counter and cut off the kitchen light, then she stomped down the hallway into her bedroom, slamming the door.

Jet woke hours later and sat up. When he looked at the clock, he was surprised and swung his legs to the floor and stumbled towards his room. It had been a long day, and when he'd seen the snake, his heart had dropped, and petrified, his body had gone into automatic pilot. After the ordeal was over and he'd had a chance to think about what might have happened, he'd fallen into a deep sleep from mental exhaustion.

Before Jet entered his bedroom, he hesitated in the hallway, staring at Grace's closed door. But then he turned his back, went inside his bathroom, and took a long cold shower. *I wish I could wash my thoughts of her away as easily as this sweat. No I don't, because I really love her. I really, really, love her and it's the best feeling in the world.*

Grace had lain awake listening to the sound of Jet's steps on the hardwood floor. Disappointment flooded her when she heard his door close with a decisive click.

Hours later, Jet sat up in bed and watched Grace enter his room. *Oh no. Not tonight. I don't think that I have the willpower to withstand sleeping next to her without making wild, passionate love to her.*

Staring at some faraway place that no one else knew, Grace slid into bed with him.

It would be so easy to take her now. Then there would be no more waiting, no more guessing, no more lonely nights. But I don't want her like this. When I enter Grace, I want both of her eyes on me, begging me, pleading me not to stop.

After Grace fell into a deep untroubled sleep, Jet quietly slipped out of the bed and went to her room and got into bed. The scent of her perfume was imbedded in the sheets, pillowcases. *I can't let this go on. I'm no Forrest Gump. I'm going to get to the bottom of her sleepwalking tomorrow,* he vowed.

In the morning, Jet was at the table nursing a cup of coffee when Grace entered the kitchen. She gave him a sheepish smile and said, "Hey," as she reached in the cabinet, withdrew a coffee mug, and after adding a packet of Equal, and a teaspoon of Coffee-Mate, filled her cup to the brim. The aroma filled the air, and loving the smell she sat down across from Jet and took a swig.

Jet gave Grace an assessing look. After she put the mug down on the table he asked, "Did you ever make an appointment with any of those doctors on the list that I gave you?"

Grace's hackles rose and she replied sarcastically, "Yes, I did, Daddy!"

Jet persevered. "How many visits have you made?"

"Not that it's any of your business, but I didn't keep the appointment. Liza has a relative that works for Dr. Griffin and if Liza knows that I'm getting counseling, then all of Lake City will and I'll be humiliated."

"Then go to the doctor in Florence. It's only twenty-three miles away and no one will see you there."

"I don't need counseling. I need something else." She glared at him, remembering last night when he'd let her down.

He stared at her unblinkingly and said, "You have some things going on that you need to work on." Jet paused before adding, "Only a truly weak person doesn't ask for help when it's needed."

There was silence in the room except for the squeak of the kitchen chair as she fidgeted.

"I thought that you didn't want to be like your mother," he finally said.

She'd picked up her coffee mug and her hand stilled in midair. "Excuse me?"

"Your mother's drinking was only a small problem at first, but it snowballed to a larger one, one that she didn't think that she could overcome, so in the end, she just gave up."

"How dare you bring that up to me!" Grace said, her face mottled with rage.

Jet shook his head sadly. "I thought you wanted to be stronger than her." Then he got up and went to the hallway closet, withdrew his pharmaceutical bag and came back to the kitchen. He dropped it on the kitchen table with a loud thud. Next Jet took out an identical bottle of the pills to the ones she'd swiped. "When you moved in here, I had three bottles and now I only have one. I'm disappointed."

Grace dropped her head, avoiding his stare.

"I'm going to work now, and I think that I ought to take this with me for safekeeping," he added cynically.

The drive to Florence was one that needed deep concentration. She exorcised extreme caution because there were so many speed traps. For one mile of road, the speed limit was 35 mph. Then the next dropped down to fifteen, before suddenly turning into a 55-mph zone. Grace was carefully monitoring her speed because she had Jet's car. They had already planned that he was going to drop her Jeep off for an oil change. After the disagreement they had that morning, she didn't want to hear his mouth if she got a ticket.

Once she entered the city limits, the GPS began to beep. Following the directions on the monitor, she soon found herself in the parking lot of Martha Storey,

Psychologist. Apprehensively, Grace looked in her rear-view mirror, fearful that Liza or someone else she knew would suddenly leap out of the foliage and ask what was wrong with her. *What is wrong with me?* Even though she felt humiliated by the fact that Jet felt she needed counseling, deep in her heart she knew that he was right. *I thought that eventually I would adjust to the recent blows I've been dealt, but I can't sleep at night without the aid of a sedative.* An image of her mother came to the forefront of her mind. *I'm not like her. I'm functional.*

When Grace entered the doctor's small office, she drew in a huge sigh of relief to find the waiting area empty. A beaming woman smiled at her and said, "May I help you?"

"Yes," Grace whispered. "I'm Grace Foxfire and I have an appointment."

The young woman looked at her list and highlighted Grace's name. Then she handed her a clipboard with what looked to be about ten pages on it and said, "After you fill this out, please bring it back to me."

Despondently, Grace sat down in a chair and began to fill it out. Her eyes ran down the list and quickly checked off boxes. Have you ever been in rehab? *No.* Are you addicted to prescription painkillers? *No.* Do you have sugar diabetes? *No.* Have you ever taken amphetamines? *No.* Do you have a history of drug abuse? *No.* The list went on and on and on, but Grace's hand stilled when she got to the question, Have you ever had suicidal thoughts? After a very long hesitation she checked yes and as she did so, tears formed in her eyes and dribbled down her cheeks. Is there a history of alcohol abuse in your family? Yes. Discreetly wiping her tears away, she took the clipboard back to the clerk and, with averted eyes, handed it to her.

"Please take a seat. The doctor will be with you shortly."

Ten minutes later, the clerk slid the partition open and, smiling at Grace, she said, "The doctor will see you now." She got up from her chair and opened the door and said, "Follow me."

Feeling as if she were going to the guillotine to be beheaded, Grace did as she was told. When she entered the office, a Native American woman got up from her desk and walked around it and held out her hand to greet Grace. Grace shook it unenthusiastically.

"Thank you, Janet," Dr. Storey said. Motioning toward a small couch, she said, "Please take a seat. I tend to be more informal than most doctors."

Grace hesitated, not sure she wanted to sit in close proximity to a complete stranger. She felt a little better when the doctor pulled up a chair, giving her some personal space.

Dr. Storey smiled kindly at Grace and asked, "Why have you come in today?"

Grace avoided her eyes and said dramatically, "My friend thinks I'm crazy."

The doctor gave Grace a small smile before asking, "Who is your friend?"

"His name is Jet and I live with him."

"So he's your boyfriend?"

Grace's eyes again slid away from the doctor's. "No, we've known each other since childhood and he's looking out for me."

"Oh," Dr. Storey said. "Do you think that you're crazy?"

"No, I don't. And as for Jet," she admitted grudgingly, "he doesn't either. He's just concerned because I've been sleepwalking." Dr. Storey nodded her head, and jotted something down on the legal pad that had been in her lap.

"How long have you been sleepwalking?"

"Only the last month or so."

"Usually when people sleepwalk, it's because their mind is afraid to relax, so they continue to be active even when they're supposed to be asleep. Where do you find yourself when you wake up?"

"In Jet's bed," she whispered.

There was a long silence in the room before Dr. Storey asked, "How does that make you feel when you awake in your roommate's bed?"

Grace sat quietly contemplating Doctor Storey's question. "The first time, I was extremely embarrassed, but Jet didn't tease me about it or anything so I felt okay about it. The second time, I felt a sort of relief when I awoke and his arms were around me. It was comforting. But the last time was last night. When I woke up this morning Jet seemed very angry."

"I asked only how you feel when you wake in his bed," Dr. Storey said quietly. "Leave Jet out of the equation for now."

Grace's breathing became heavier. "When I woke this morning this morning in Jet's bed I felt happy, even though he wasn't lying next to me, because I knew that he'd been there."

Dr. Storey looked at Grace with understanding and said, "There are a few things going on here. Obviously there's a reason why you keep getting in bed with this man. Have you two ever been intimate?"

"No."

"Has anything traumatic occurred lately to cause your mind to be in chaos?"

Grace glared at Dr. Storey and blurted out, "You might be sleepwalking too if your fiancé was killed the night before you were to be married!"

Dr. Storey's mouth dropped open in shock. The next look she gave Grace was one of pity. "I heard about that. That happened a few months ago in Atlanta, right?"

"Yes." Then Grace gave Dr. Storey the details about how Livingston had died, how his family had cremated him against her wishes, and why she'd lost her house. As she spoke, tears gushed down her cheeks. She took the paper towels the doctor had retrieved from her adjoining bathroom since Kleenex couldn't handle the job.

Dr. Storey quietly watched Grace get control of her emotions and once the flow of tears had stopped, she watched her appraisingly as she said softly, "You've been through a horrible ordeal and the fact that you're up, dressed, and out of bed gives testimony as to how strong a person you really are. But that still doesn't explain why you keep getting into your roommate's bed."

"I don't even remember getting up out of mine. I'm exhausted when I go to bed, but I can't sleep. Then I take," Grace stammered, shifting her eyes away from the doctor's, "something and I fall into a deep sleep. The next thing I know, I wake up in Jet's bed and I don't know how I got there."

Dr. Storey held her hand out and said, "Hold on a minute. What do you take to help you sleep? Advil PM? Tylenol PM?"

"No," Grace mumbled and when she did tell her what it was, she kept her head bent, ashamed.

"How many do you take?"

"At first, one pill would keep me asleep for at least eight hours. Then it got to the place that I needed a pill and a half. Now I take one every four hours. I don't know how I got so dependent on them for a good night's rest. It just kind of sneaked up on me."

"That's the way prescription drugs work. You're hooked before you know it."

"I'm not hooked," Grace vehemently denied.

Dr. Storey continued as if Grace hadn't interrupted her. "It's kind of like alcohol. First a little gives you a buzz, and then you build up a resistance, and it takes more each time to get the same result."

Dr. Storey turned around and picked the questionnaire off her desk that Grace had filled out. She gave her a stern look and said, "Why did you check no where it asks if you've ever taken a narcotic?"

Grace sputtered angrily, "It's not an illegal drug. And as I said, I'm not hooked."

"I can't help you if you're dishonest with me or yourself," the doctor said chidingly. "When you're dealing with me, you need to put all your cards on the table. I don't know if you're hooked or not. But I do know that pill you're taking has a history of making people sleepwalk, even getting in their cars driving somewhere and then not knowing how they got there."

"I've never done that!" Grace denied vehemently.

"Not yet." Dr. Storey leaned towards Grace and gave her a no-nonsense look. "Test yourself and see if you can stop taking them."

"But I can't sleep through the night," Grace whined.

"We'll try some alternatives to help you. Are you exercising?"

"I used to all the time in Atlanta, but there isn't a Bally in Lake City."

"There are other things that you can do. Walking is excellent for stress. Take a warm bath before you go to bed and about twenty minutes before you want to go to sleep, drink a cup of hot herbal tea."

"Going to sleep isn't my problem. I usually sleep the first part of the night, but then I wake up early in the morning and can't get back to sleep."

"Then go make yourself another cup of herbal tea to get you through the rest of the night. Drink as many cups as it takes to get you through the night. You're in no danger from being hooked on herbal tea." She gave her a smile of encouragement.

"How long should it take me to stop needing the pills?"

"I don't know because everyone's different, but usually seven to ten days. Once we get you on a healthy sleep pattern, we'll deal with the other issues that you have to contend with. Obviously the loss of your fiancé has helped bring about this dependency on prescription drugs, but people lose loved ones all the time and that's not how they deal with their problems. There are some underlying issues that need to be thrashed out."

Grace looked at her watch and with relief noted that her hour was up.

Doctor Storey continued, "I'd like to see you once a week to try to help you work through some things. Is that okay with you?"

Grace hesitated for a second, then looked at the kindness in the doctor's eyes and said, "Okay."

CHAPTER 17

Grace was parking her car at Piggly Wiggly when her cell phone rang. Knowing it was Jet, she didn't answer it because she was still annoyed by their morning argument. Inside the store, she went down the cereal aisle until she found a sampler of Celestial Seasonings herbal teas. "I don't see how Herbal Tea can take the place of one of my magic pills," she muttered, "but it's worth a shot." She grabbed three sampler boxes and put them in her basket.

Grace was almost home when her cell phone rang again. Seeing that it was Jet again, she decided not to continue to be childish and answered the phone.

"What do you want?" She sounded peevish to her own ears.

"I'm just calling to see how your day went," he replied, sounding unruffled by her attitude.

"I think that you're checking up on me to see if I did what you told me to." When Jet laughed in his deep baritone way, Grace couldn't squash the smile that hovered around her mouth. "I went to see the psychologist in Florence."

"And?"

"She told me some things that I need to try so I can sleep without the pills."

"What else did she say?"

"She told me that I'm not crazy, that you are," she said snidely.

Jet replied without rancor, "She may be right, but we're not talking about me. What did she prescribe for you?"

"Have a long relaxing bath, drink herbal tea and walk for exercise."

"Gee," Jet teased, "it's not like you haven't heard that before."

Grace said nervously, "I'm not walking those country roads. If that rattler came that close to the house, what do you think could happen if I was out walking? What would have happened to me in my own yard if you weren't around? I was too afraid to even run."

"First of all, you run in a straight line, but that's beside the point. You're right about walking out there on Red Hill."

Grace turned into their driveway and hit the remote for the garage door. "What time are you going to be home?"

"I have one stop to make and then I'll be home directly."

"Okay, I'm going to start dinner."

"What are we having?"

"Broiled steak, salad, and baked potatoes."

"I can't wait," he said with satisfaction before he added, "see you soon."

Grace was putting the final touches on dinner when the house phone rang.

"Hello?"

"Hey, sweetie, how are you doing?"

"Solange," Grace said accusingly, "I called you the other night and you weren't home."

"I've been staying at Ali's house a lot lately."

"Do tell." Grace sat down and crossed her legs, ready for all the juicy details.

"There's not much to tell, except I love him."

"Congratulations, girlfriend. Love's a wonderful feeling, isn't it?"

"It sure is." As she said it, images of Livingston's and Jet's faces surfaced and seemed to blend together in Grace's mind. She redirected her focus back to Solange. "Do you know how he feels about you?"

"He hasn't told me that he loves me, but he acts as though he does, so I'm fine with that for now." Then she asked, "How about you? How's life in the big LC?"

"Not too shabby. Jet and I do everything together. He's been my rock."

Solange asked delicately, "How are you coping with Livingston's passing and that crap from his family?"

"I think about Livingston every day, but at least I don't burst into tears anymore at the mention of his name. And as for that family of his, they'll get it because God don't like ugly."

"Amen to that."

"I do have something to tell you though," Grace said, feeling the need to share. "I went to see a psychologist today."

"You did?" Solange asked, surprised. "I thought you just said that you're adjusting okay."

"I think I am, but I've been sleepwalking and getting into bed with Jet."

Instead of getting the reaction that she expected, which was Solange's signature, "Get out of town," she had to hold the receiver away from her ear because of her raucous laughter.

Once Solange controlled herself, Grace said, "Babs lied on Jet, girl, he's got it going on."

Solange stopped her laughter long enough to ask, "Have you two done it?"

"No, but we've been close to it. Solange, I want to ask you something and I need you to be really honest with me and think about what your answer is before you say it. Do you think it's disgusting that I want to sleep with my play brother?"

"No," Solange answered at once.

"Did you even think about my question before answering?"

"I've thought about it off and on ever since I saw you two in bed together in the hospital. It looked so natural. Mind you, I never saw you in bed with Livingston, but that's the past and you have to let it go and live the life that God has left you. Livingston would've wanted that."

Grace finally heard her SUV in the garage. Wiping her hands on a dish towel, she went to greet him and stared at the huge box he was sliding out from the open liftgate. Grace shook her head and said resignedly, "Only in Lake City could you drive like that and not get a ticket."

Jet was huffing and puffing as he tried to slide the box towards him. "Don't criticize me after all the trouble I went through bringing this to you."

"For me?" she asked curiously. "What is it?"

"If you get on the other side and push, maybe you'll find out."

Grace immediately walked over and started pushing on the box, working up a sweat. *Dr. Storey was right. I do need to work out.*

After the box was on the garage floor, Grace held the box sides, while Jet slowly pulled out its contents. Once he began to peel the plastic wrap off, she clapped her hands like an excited child on Christmas morning. "It's a treadmill!"

"Now you can exercise in the garage and not be in danger from nature's creatures."

Very deliberately, Grace walked over to Jet and slid her arms around his neck.

Her unexpected move made him tense up, but then he relaxed. *This is what I've waited for ever since I knew there was a difference between boys and girls.*

What Grace meant to be a thank-you kiss turned into something unexpected when her lips touched his. She let all her pent-up frustrations, longing, and waiting spill out of her as she devoured his mouth. Finally drawing hers away from his, she buried her head in his chest and whispered in a sensual voice, "I don't know why you're so good to me. I just know that I'm blessed."

After dinner, Grace walked on the treadmill as Jet sat in a lawn chair and put together a 24-inch fan to blow on her while she walked in the hot garage.

After he turned the fan on her, he grinned because the cool air made Grace's nipples harden. Through her T-shirt, they looked like doorknobs.

Leaving Grace alone, he went into the house and was clearing away the dinner dishes when she came back inside.

She looked flushed, sticky, and delicious. Jet took his hands and lifted her shirt to roll his hands across her mounds.

Grace started to stifle her gasp of pleasure, then decided not to bother. He lowered his lips and licked the midnight circle around each nipple. "If any man comes over here while you're exercising, come in the house and put a bra on," he ordered possessively.

"Okay," she breathed, her voice throaty from desire, "but they're not usually so prominent. My nipples only protrude like this when it's my time of the month."

Jet tweaked her nipple, and then let her shirt fall down into place. *Damn, it's her time of the month. I'll have to wait.*

Jet lay on his side on top of the covers in his boxer shorts with his back to Grace because he didn't want to frighten her by the constant woody he had whenever she was in the vicinity. No permission was needed when after her bath she'd drunk a hot cup of herbal tea and joined him in the bedroom. When he heard her light breathing deepen when she drifted into a natural sleep, he'd said to himself, *That's my girl*, and after sending up a thankful prayer to God, he drifted off to sleep.

In the wee morning hours, Jet was awakened when he heard a sound in the kitchen. Wearily, he sat up and, barefoot, padded into the kitchen.

When he entered the room Grace was standing over the stove in a pair of his boxers and one of his T-shirts waiting for the kettle of water to reach the boiling point. Motioning for her to sit, he withdrew a mug and after placing it next to hers, dropped inside it a tea bag from the box on the counter. Jet raised his eyebrow at Grace and said, "I can use something to help me relax, too."

She sat in a chair and cautiously sipped her cup of tea before she said, "Jet, I want to apologize for stealing your pills. I thought about it today, and what I did is a crime. Not to mention that I violated your trust."

Jet lowered his cup and said, "I knew you had them. I was just waiting for you to 'fess up."

"I didn't think that me needing those pills was the issue that it apparently is."

"Being totally dependent on anyone or anything is an issue, Grace."

"Then it's an issue that I'm staying here with you." She held her hands outward. "I have no income and I'm totally dependent on you for everything."

"Is that how you view our situation? I find it hard to believe that you don't think that you're contributing anything, Grace. You've totally taken over my household matters and freed up a lot of my time to pursue my ideas and help in the community."

Grace beamed from Jet's praise and she took her free hand and covered his. For the rest of the time, they sat silently at the table. Words were unnecessary.

Once they'd drained their mugs, Jet stood, placed them in the sink and filled them with water, then said, "Let's go back to bed." She slipped her hand into the hand he held out and he led her back into the bedroom.

"How are you feelin'?" Jet shouted above the music as he ran full speed on the treadmill.

"Better than I've felt for a while."

"You're not out of the woods yet," he cautioned. "You still probably have dependency in your system. But you should be okay in a couple of weeks." Jet pressed the dial on the face of the treadmill, and its tempo slowed to allow him to walk at a fast gait. Then it slowed to a crawl before stopping.

Once he got off the machine, Grace handed him a towel.

"What are you doing today?" he asked, wiping the sweat off his face.

"Nothing much. I thought that I'd start applying for a teaching position in the area."

"So you've decided not to go back to Atlanta?" Jet watched the myriad of emotions that crossed her face as she thought about her future.

"I never thought that I could be at peace in Lake City, but I think this is the best place for me right now."

"So do I," Jet replied and touched the tip of her nose with his finger before he went into the house with Grace walking behind him.

"I have to go to Summerton today on business. Do you feel like riding along? It won't take long."

"Sure," she replied.

The thirty-mile ride to rural Clarendon County didn't take long, as they virtually had the road to themselves.

Grace shook her head as she stared out the window at small farms whose houses could only be described as shanties. She stared at a dilapidated cotton gin and old grey buildings with wooden porches and outhouses behind them. Grace gave a shudder of distaste. "Can you imagine going to the bathroom in one of those places? The sight of them makes me realize how far mankind has come."

Jet looked at her. "We've come a long way, but not everyone has benefited. This is still considered one of the most economically depressed areas in the South. There are still people that don't have inside toilets. Progress has left them behind. The key to getting out of their stagnated lives is education. Without good schools and teachers there is no hope for some."

"It makes me realize how blessed I am. Whatever issues I had with my mom, she made sure that I went to school in order to arm me for a future."

Jet said, "It's nice to hear you say that, Grace." Then he announced, "We're here."

Grace spied a small building with a sign on the outside that read BDF. Turning to Jet she asked, "What is this place?"

He pointed at the sign. "That stands for Briggs, De Laine, Pearson, and it's a non profit organization that educates local children through volunteers and tutors."

"De Laine? That's the man from whom you bought the property and built our house in Lake City, isn't it?"

Grace didn't know it, but whenever she unconsciously referred to his house as theirs or asked him when he was going to be home, he felt in his heart that they were in it for the long haul and happiness flowed through him. But instead of voicing his feelings about this to her, he held them inside, not wanting to pressure her before she was ready to let go of her ghosts. So instead he said, "It sure is. It's named after him and was started by his offspring, along with other children of civil rights icons from the area. Before Rev. De Laine moved to Lake City, he lived here and was instrumental in helping to start the civil rights movement."

"I didn't know that."

"He was also a principal and wanted to get a school bus for the black children because they were having to walk sometimes over three miles to school while the white children rode past them on a bus."

"Was he successful?"

"Sort of. He got a parent named Pearson to file a federal lawsuit against the school district for not providing transportation, but it was thrown out on a technicality."

"What kind of technicality?"

"Apparently Pearson's land extended over into another county so they claimed it wasn't their responsibility and the case was thrown out."

"Bummer," she replied.

"Not really, because then other parents got involved and they signed a petition and met with Thurgood Marshall. At the time, he was a young lawyer in New York and he got involved with what's known as Briggs vs. Elliot, which was the basis for the later suit of *Brown vs. Board of Education.* Four other counties signed on and they took *Brown* to the Supreme Court."

"I can't believe I never knew all of this," she muttered, "and I call myself an educator."

"You can't know everything, honey."

"How did Rev. De Laine end up living in Lake City?"

"Once it became nationally known about the lawsuit, his house mysteriously caught fire. It burned down in front of him and his family while firefighters stood, watched, and wouldn't help, so and he and his family moved to Lake City. After the Brown decision that separate but equal is unconstitutional, they burned his church down in Lake City."

"I don't remember hearing any of this," Grace said in awe.

"It was before our time and it wasn't taught to us in school. After they burned his church down, a few days later they came back and drive-by gunmen attacked his home on Red Hill, but he fired back and wounded some of the men in the car. That night, for his safety he traveled to New York City and for years they tried to extradite him to face five charges of assault and battery with intent to kill."

Grace's voice was several decibels higher as she tried to fathom the injustices that Rev. De Laine and his family had faced. "He was trying to protect his family. How dare they try to jail him!"

"It didn't stop him. He led churches in Buffalo and he continued to be an active member of the NAACP till the day he died."

"Unbelievable. Now I see why you wanted to build our house there. It's an important part of history."

Jet nodded his head. "Rev. De Laine was pardoned posthumously in 2000 and federal lawmakers recently voted to award him the Congressional Gold Medal."

"And it all started in this small town," she said, utterly amazed.

"All you need to do is plant the seed of yearning and people will grow. Come on," Jet said, opening his car door. "I'm almost late for my meeting."

While Jet met behind closed doors with the supervisor on duty, Grace meandered around the learning rooms. She saw tutors sitting one on one with students, going over mathematics, and then in another room a volunteer had a group of kids in a circle around her as she read to them. Grace stood idly by watching a teenager in a corner working on an obviously out of date computer. Grace walked over to young man. "Hello."

He had been so intent on what he was doing he hadn't realized he was being watched. He was a tall, gangly youth with large eyes. When he smiled, he had a tooth missing in the front. The whiteness of his teeth, however, contrasted with his chocolate brown complexion made him look like someone Hollywood would like to call.

"I didn't hear you, ma'am," he said, his voice shy. "I'm trying to find out what I need to do to get into college."

"Any college in particular?" Grace asked, smiling at him.

"No, ma'am, I just know that I want to get away from here," he responded shyly.

"You need to go to a school in South Carolina because you won't have to pay out-of-state fees. That will save you a lot of money. Go to the Internet," she ordered, "and Google colleges in South Carolina."

The teenager did as she asked and over his shoulder, Grace looked at the monitor. "See, there's your list. With your mouse click on any college you think that you might be interested in."

"Thank you, ma'am."

"Don't you have anyone to show you how to do this? They seem pretty busy here, but how about your guidance counselor at school?"

"I graduated over a year ago, ma'am," he said, turning his head away, "but after working twelve hours a day and still not having any money, I think it's best I go to school."

"That's a smart thing to do. How about your mother? She might want to help you decide where you want to go."

"My mother passed three years ago, ma'am."

Grace's heart dropped and, embarrassed, she started to mutter her apologies. He stopped her.

"You couldn't have known, ma'am."

"Listen." Grace paused and then said, "I don't even know your name."

"It's Taft, ma'am."

"Well, if you need help figuring this out, I can come back one day next week and help you."

Taft's face brightened and then he said, "Tuesday is my only day off. Could you come then?"

Grace stuck out her hand and said, "I'm Grace, and I'll be here on Tuesday around eleven o'clock."

When Taft took her hand, she liked how firm his grip was.

As Grace stood in front of a wall looking at a gallery of pictures and reading the identity under them, she heard Jet say, "I'll be in touch."

Spying Grace, he waved her over. "Grace, this is Philip Monroe. Philip, this is Grace."

"I'm sorry I didn't get a chance to meet you when you came in but I was on the phone with B.B. De Laine, one of the founder's sons."

"That's quite all right." She looked around the beehive of activity in the room. "I'm in awe as to what you're doing here."

"Thank you. Jet tells me you're a certified teacher."

"Yes, high school English."

"We could always use tutors, if you have any free time." Philip Monroe smiled cajolingly.

"As a matter of fact, I was going to ask you what I needed to do to volunteer here one day a week."

Excitedly he said, "Just sign up. The center works in partnership with the local schools and we have a great need for teachers certified in reading. A large percentage of our students are reading below grade level."

"That's a real problem," Grace said, shaking her head sadly. "If a child doesn't read well, that spills over into all other aspects of their studies. They can't understand word problems in math, they have a hard time following instructions for all their classes, and you can forget science and social studies. Most of the time they don't complete their homework because out of frustration they give up."

"Anything you can do to help would be greatly appreciated."

"How about every Tuesday morning?"

As if by magic, he produced a paper out of nowhere and handed it to her. "Here's the sign-up sheet."

Before Grace sat down to fill out the volunteer information sheet, her eyes locked with Jet's. Warmth filled her at the look of pride that shone on his face as he talked to Philip Monroe but watched her.

Saturday night, Grace stood in front of the mirror and twirled around, inspecting herself from every angle. She had decided to go for a casual chic look, and the simple black dress was the perfect complement for the patent leather stilettos she wore. She'd added gold accent pieces. She thanked God that she'd been hooked up with

Naomi because she kept her hair looking nice even in the most humid weather. Nervously, she slid her hands down the sides of her dress, wiping away the moisture and peered at her reflection in the mirror. *There's no reason why I can't sleep with him. We're consenting adults and not hurting anyone. After Livingston, I never thought that I'd have a chance at happiness again, and I need to grab it if I can.*

"Grace!"

She heard herself being paged from another room in the house.

"Are you ready yet? I don't want to be late."

"I'm ready," she said as she swayed out to the den.

When Jet saw her he said, "You look fabulous."

"So do you," she replied as she drank in every detail of his blue pinstripe pants and matching shirt. "You look quite dashing, but how come you get to wear flats and I have to wear heels?"

"That's the curse of being a woman." His eyes danced as they continued to inspect her.

"You're right," she agreed. "I don't know how many times, Livingston and I . . ." Then she realized what she was staying and halted her flow of words.

"That you and Livingston went somewhere and he was comfortable in flats, while your feet hurt. That's what you were going to say, right?"

"Something like that," she muttered, suddenly feeling a rush of guilt that she was so happy.

There was a heavy silence in the room before Jet said, "Livingston probably felt like I do. You'll get your reward later on down the road for being such a sport."

Grace smiled gratefully. Jet wasn't going to let her slip of the tongue spoil their night.

On the drive to Jesse's house in the heart of town, which took about twenty minutes, they listened to the Big DM station. No matter the time of day or night it rocked with the most soulful music from over three decades. As they listened to the O'Jays, Grace eyed Jet in the darkness. "I didn't even ask you what your meeting with Philip Monroe was about."

"He wanted some contact information and advice as to the quickest and most efficient way to get some new computers in BDP. So many people in the area need them for daily use, but they don't have access to them."

"I bet," she agreed. "I met this kid trying to get college information off the one computer that they had and it was so slow, I could have dozed off waiting for it to pull up the website."

"I'm going to donate ten and they're going to run it like a library where people have to sign in and leave their driver's license or other identification while they use it. That way if any person goes on an inappropriate website, they'll lose the privilege to use them again."

Grace thoughtfully mulled over what Jet had said and treading carefully she said, "I know that you want to do good things for the people around you, but don't overextend yourself." She smiled gently when she felt the liquid pools of his eyes on her in the darkness. "I mean, you can't save the world."

"No, I can't save the world, but I can ease some of the financial burdens of some deserving people. I haven't put money in the stock market because of the way the economy is but instead I've put it in secure annuities that consistently pay a percentage every time I roll them over.

"BDF is a non-profit organization, which means that at the end of the year I get all of my donations back from the government in the form of a tax write-off. At least if I sink my money into the communities around me, I can see where it's going, unlike putting it in some huge foundation where I can't track it or it may get lost in the shuffle. Find out what it would cost to purchase that reading program you were trained for when you went to New York. I'd like to purchase it for the center. I'd rather give it to them than Uncle Sam."

Once they pulled up at the Gilliards', Grace silently counted the cars that were in the driveway. Five cars probably meant ten people at least. *I hope that no one I went to high school with is here because they always want to talk about days gone by, and I don't want to open that can of worms.*

As Grace sat in her seat musing, Jet jumped out of his side and walked around and opened her door for her. With dancing eyes he held out his hand and Grace grabbed it, glad to have something to hold on to as she tried to get out of the seat of the BMW without showing Jet all of her business. Once she was standing on firm ground, she said, "Your mother taught me how to get out of a car gracefully, but it's not always easy."

"I know," he said.

Side by side, they walked to the front door and Jet rang the bell. Immediately a uniformed maid flung open the door. When she saw Jet, she grinned at him, saying, "I wondered when you were going to get here." Then she said in a conspiratorial whisper, "They have a real snobville going on here."

Jet laughed and then asked, "Hannah, why are you dressed in that get-up?"

She made a derogatory snort before saying, "The missus asked me to wear it. It's a damn shame that no matter how much money Mr. Jesse makes, she can't overcome her Knight Street roots. She keeps trying to impress folks that ain't got as much as she does."

Then she took a good look at Grace and said in astonishment, "Why, you're Miss Abigail's daughter, Grace."

Grace stiffened and said, "Yes, ma'am."

"Don't 'yes ma'am' me. I went to school with your momma. It was so sad when . . ."

Jet interrupted her by saying, "I hope all the guests have arrived. I'm hungry and ready to eat."

This distracted Hannah. "The guests are in the parlor room socializing. Everything's catered, you know, so dinner will probably be any minute."

"Thanks," he said, grabbing Grace's hand and dragging her with him.

Grace held on tightly as she tried to keep up with his long strides. *I hope that's the only trip down memory lane I have to deal with tonight. As usual, Jet fixed it for me.*

Once they made their entrance, Grace did a quick perusal of the room and didn't recognize any of the other people except Jesse.

He saw them and whispered something in the ear of the woman at his side, who followed him over to where they stood. He gave a smile that included both of them and shook hands with Jet. "I'm glad the two of you could make it." Then he spoke directly to Grace. "I don't think you ever met my wife. Diana, this is Grace Foxfire."

"How do you do?" The woman gave Grace a friendly smile. "I've heard a lot about you."

"Really," Grace smoothly countered, "from whom?"

Clearly thrown by Grace's question, she responded with, "Oh, I don't know. Just around town, I think. You know how exciting it is in Lake City when people move back."

"Yes, I do," Grace answered honestly. "I'm sure when Jet returned it was a big splash."

"Oh, yes," she said, "all the single girls and their mommas were ready to have a party, but now that he's taken himself off the market, they ain't, I mean, aren't so happy."

"Hush, Diana," Jesse admonished his wife. "You talk too much. Your cousin is here. Why don't you go bug her while I check to make sure the caterers are ready to serve?"

"All right," Diana said. With an apologetic look at Grace, she touched her arm and then went over to greet Lorna.

"I didn't know Lorna would be here," Grace said with a slight edge to her voice.

"Me, either," Jet said "but I shouldn't be surprised since she and Diana are first cousins."

Oh, so that was the game. She mimicked Diana's voice and said, "Listen Lorna, this hot pharmacist came to town. He's single and he works with Jesse, so casually drop by the office and I'll be there at the same time and I'll hook you up. That way the two of you can get married, we'll be a foursome, and all live happily ever after."

Jet grinned at Grace before asking, "Did things work out that way?"

"No," she replied in a somewhat serious tone, "things don't always turn out the way you expect them to."

"I know," he agreed, sounding just as serious, "but when God closes a door, he always opens a window."

Seated at a long dinner table with eight other people, Grace was amused to see gold-embossed place cards with every guest's name on it. She was seated next to Jet, and across from him was Lorna.

As Grace dined on duck, yellow rice and asparagus, conversation flowed easily from one thing to another until the topic of health insurance was introduced.

A rather heavyset man reared back in his chair and said, "The health-care crisis is going to cripple the economy. If the United States goes to a health-care program like Canada, a bunch of lazy people will never get off their cans and get a job."

Jesse said rather sharply, "Uncle Jack, as a doctor I'd think that you of all people would want coverage for everyone."

"And I think you of all people would remember that I put myself through school and worked three jobs to get where I am. No one helped me."

"Unfortunately, your story is a common one for people of your generation. The depression was friend to few. Now, I think this country can do better by its citizens. I feel sorry for the people that have worked all their lives and can't afford to go to the doctor or buy their medicine."

Jesse's uncle wagged his forefinger at Jesse and Jet and said, "I know you two at your office are giving people free medicine. You better watch your step or you're going to get yourselves in some real trouble."

"I wouldn't worry about that if I were you," Jet said with a confident look on his face. "Don't you think that I thoroughly checked things out before I started my little clinic? It's perfectly legal to give samples to patients out of a doctor's office."

Uncle Jack blustered a little before saying, "How can you afford to do all that and not have a job?"

"Uncle," Jesse said.

"That's okay, Jesse. I don't mind answering. My mother had breast cancer and her doctor didn't care and she died. So the only way I could reconcile myself to her death was to sue the doctor and put him out of business, then help others with the money. It's for her memory."

An uncomfortable silence descended on the table while the other guests looked down at their plates, determined not to get involved.

Suddenly Diana announced in a shrill voice, "It's time for dessert. Anyone for some red velvet cake?"

Grace was patiently standing in the foyer waiting for Jet to finish conducting some business with Jesse in his study so they could leave. Off to the right was an open set of French doors. The cool breeze beckoned her to the veranda. Once outside, she heard two voices from the other side of the porch that wrapped around the house.

"I don't know about that, Lorna. Jet seems pretty into her. Did you see how attentive he was to her at dinner, filling her wine glass and all?"

"He was getting into me, too, before she got here, so that means we could've had something had she not shown up."

"She didn't just show up." Diana said, "he went and got her."

"Well, if he went and got her," Lorna said sarcastically, "he can also take her back. She's got to leave town for one thing or another and when she does, I'll be back in Jet's bed, and this time if he strays, I'll have a reason for him to come back to me."

"I know you don't mean trying the oldest trick in the book, do you?" Diana said in a disgusted voice. "That doesn't work nowadays."

"It worked for you. That's how you got Jesse to marry you," Lorna snapped.

Diana sputtered, "Angelique was a surprise. Besides, Jesse and I were in love and it was only a matter of time before we got married anyhow."

"But you made sure that you did marry, didn't you? That baby sealed the deal."

"Jet doesn't love you. He loves Grace. So how do you like that?" she ended in a pay-you-back voice.

"How do you know that?" Lorna asked in a disbelieving tone. "You don't talk to Jet about things like that."

"No," she dragged out the word, "but Jet told Jesse that he's in love with her and always has been. He's just giving her time to finish grieving over her dead fiancé."

"Well, while she's grieving over some man that she can't have, I'll be doing what I need to do in order to have the man that I can have."

Grace hovered in the shadows until after Diana and Lorna grew silent. Then, afraid they were on their way back into the house, she scurried back to the foyer just in time to see Jet emerging from the study with Jesse.

As they drove home, Grace was silent, mulling over the conversation she'd eavesdropped on before Jet interrupted her musings.

"Did you enjoy yourself tonight?"

"I sure did. The Van Fleets were very engaging, as were the Austins. How many times did you have sex with Lorna?" she suddenly asked in a demanding voice.

"What?" The car jerked on the narrow road and Jet had to straighten it.

"I asked you how many times you screwed Lorna before 'you came and got me?' " She mimicked Lorna's southern drawl.

Jet smothered the laugh he wanted to let out and spoke chidingly to Grace. "I don't kiss and tell. By the way, how much *did* you have to drink tonight?"

"You should know," Grace retorted, "you were watching me hard enough."

Jet responded wryly, "I don't know what's gotten into you. Lorna and I, well, she's a nice girl but not for me. After my accident, I needed someone and she was a good friend to me."

Jet pulled up in the driveway and Grace barely let the car skid to a halt before she opened her car door and sneered, "Don't screw her again or she'll stick a baby on you." Then she slammed the door and stomped in the house, slamming the garage door.

Grace heard the garage door closing and after grabbing a bottle of wine, grabbed a glass and filled it before she went into the den and slammed the bottle down on the table.

Jet walked into the room and sat down on the couch. "Alcohol? If you drink it late at night, it will make you wake up later and mess with your sleep pattern. Why don't you let me make you a cup of herbal tea instead?"

"I'm not ready to go to bed." Then she held her glass out to him.

At first he hesitated, then took it, and after putting his mouth on the part that had her lipstick print, drank the liquid, and gave the glass back to her.

Without speaking, she added more wine to the glass.

Jet leaned back and watched Grace carefully before he said, "I don't know why you dislike Lorna so much, but you have nothing to feel threatened about when it comes to her. Whatever we had is in the past."

"I don't like her. You can do so much better."

Jet held her eyes captive with his. "Then Grace, who do you see me with?"

She deliberately put her glass down on the coffee table. "Me," she answered softly and reached for him. Grace began to slowly unbutton Jet's shirt and, once she was done, she peeled it off him before sliding next to him so closely that there was no space between them. She lifted the glass again and held it to his lips and he drank.

Next Grace finished the rest, putting her lips on the exact spot he'd drunk from.

"I'm ready, Jet," she whispered.

"Ready for what?" His voice was husky with desire.

"For you, for us. Make love to me tonight. I can't hold out any longer."

Jet stood and searched Grace's face. In the pants he was wearing, his penis looked like a coiled snake ready to strike at any moment. Instead of running from it, she wanted to run to it. Jet looked down at his manhood and then back at her. Sexuality oozed out from his body as he slightly spread his stance in order to ease his discomfort.

"Are you sure?" he asked before walking to the bedroom, leaving her to follow him if she wanted to.

Grace stood from the couch, shrugged out of her dress, letting it fall to a heap on the floor on top of Jet's shirt, then followed the path he'd just taken.

She walked over to the bed and stood staring down at him as he lay on his back.

"If we do this," he said, sensuality oozing from every fiber of his being, "there's no turning back."

"I don't want to turn back," she said and slid in bed next to him.

Immediately Jet took control. He lightly touched her face, letting his fingers linger on her lips. Then he kissed her cheek before he moved his mouth to hers. Jet's mouth was firm, insistent, and probing as his hands began to explore her. Then he pressed his lips to her breasts and licked each, nibbling lightly on each nipple. Not moving away from her body, Jet tugged at her panties until they broke away.

Teasingly she breathed, "You ripped my thong. How is that possible?"

"I don't know," he murmured, "but I'll buy you another pair tomorrow."

Grace held his head cradled between her hands and then she pushed it down to where she wanted him to go.

Jet gently took Grace's thighs and lifted them to fall across his shoulders. When she felt the light pressure of his tongue she arched her hips upwards. When she did, his tongue probed her center. He kept his tongue dead center and licked her as if she were an ice cream cone. When she spilled her desire into his mouth, Jet reached into the nightstand. She sensed that he was struggling to fit the almost-too-small rubber over his manhood, but after what felt like an eternity, he grunted in satisfaction.

Grace lay back, waiting, hopeful. Somewhere in the darkness she heard him gently command her, "Open your eyes."

When she did, he reared above her and entered her in one fluid movement, all the while staring into her eyes. Jet began to thrust inside her. He didn't move slowly, but instead kept a steady rhythm that she could keep up with.

Grace moaned and called out his name intermittently. She didn't know how long he moved inside her. Only the squishing sound her body made as he moved let her know that she was sopping wet. He brought her to her peak, and she screamed "finally" when she climaxed with him. She slept soundly for the rest of the night.

Late the next morning, Grace's eyes fluttered open to see Jet staring at her. Her body lay across his, with her arm across his chest hugging him. Feeling a little shy, she lowered her eyes and said, "I'd kiss you, but I have morning breath."

In one swift movement, Jet rolled her over and pinned her to the mattress with him on top. Not closing his eyes, he slowly lowered his mouth to hers, opened his lips to hers and explored her mouth. "I never even noticed," he answered, his voice husky with desire.

Grace gasped, "Jet, you take my breath away."

He smiled devilishly and said, "It's about time."

Feeling a little discomfited by his statement, she looked away. "Sometimes something is standing right in front of you and you don't see it or appreciate it, but when you finally do, oh my God!" she breathed.

Jet positioned himself on his back and pulled Grace close.

She took her hand and pulled the sheet down, exposing Jet's naked body. Grace stared at his erect manhood and murmured, obviously impressed by the sight, "You're right, Jet. It doesn't look the way it used to."

"Thank God for that!" he responded proudly.

"No, thank you for last night," she breathed. "I really needed it."

"Don't thank me," he responded in a sexy voice laced with desire, "thank us."

As they cuddled, she picked up Jet's left hand, stared at its nakedness and asked softly, "What woman could you have ever loved and she not have loved you back?"

There was quiet in the room except for the sweet melody of birds chirping outside their bedroom window, and Jet answered in a serious tone, "You."

"Me?" Grace leaned back so she could look Jet in his face and said, "Are you trying to tell me that the woman you were referring to that morning when you talked to me and Livingston was me?"

"Yes," Jet replied, "it's always been you, Grace."

CHAPTER 18

In early afternoon, Grace woke, and going to the closet, grabbed one of Jet's shirts, buttoning it as she left the bedroom. She was startled to see him sitting on the couch watching television. "I'm surprised to find you here. Didn't you need to go into town today?"

"I've been and now I'm back." He patted the couch cushion next to him and said, "Sit."

Instead of doing what he said, she slid onto his lap and twined her arms around his neck. Without displacing her, he reached behind one of the couch pillows and handed her a Victoria's Secret bag. "Jet, you're always giving me stuff, you really shouldn't."

"Why not?" he asked and then quipped, "and if not you, then who should I buy presents for?"

Grace opened the bag and pulled out a handful of thong underwear.

Jet's eyes danced with merriment. "Those should last you for about a week. Seven pairs for seven nights."

"I think I'll just stop wearing panties to bed at all," she replied cheekily. "It'll be easier in the long run." Then her attention was distracted by something in the bottom of the bag. "What's this?"

Jet watched her closely, gauging her reaction.

A little stunned she stammered as she looked at the paper. "I don't know quite what to say when your lover gives you as a present the results of his AIDS test."

"What does it say?"

Grace gave Jet an "Are you kidding me?" look. "It says negative, of course. I wouldn't expect anything else."

"But you didn't know." Jet's tone and his expression were serious. "I've always practiced safe sex, but I have been with a lot of women in the past. I want you to feel comfortable sleeping with me."

She stared earnestly at him. "I am comfortable sleeping with you, Jet."

"Grace," Jet looked deeply into her honey-colored eyes and said, "I'm done experimenting. I want to be with you and only you. I wanted you to feel comfortable making love to me without a condom, so I went to see Jesse this morning and he did the blood test for me."

Grace handed the paper to him and said, "You've been very thoughtful, Jet."

He paused, locking his eyes with hers before he continued. "I think that we have something very special and I want to continue our relationship as if it's just you and me and the rest of the world's lovers don't exist. I want love for more than one season with you."

"That's what I want, too," she said softly. "Do you want me to take a test?"

"Hell no," Jet said. He didn't say anything for a moment before he stated the obvious. "Didn't you have to take a test before you and Livingston got a marriage license?"

"Yes," she answered softly.

"Then I know you're safe, because you haven't been with anyone else but me. So I think that we've got things under control."

"I think that we do," she murmured.

That night as Jet moved inside her, she climaxed over and over again, loving the feel of his hardness as he made her feel as special as a securely married woman.

Grace was sitting at the breakfast table making a grocery list when Jet got home. When she looked up to greet him, he kissed her in a way that made her heart melt and then ruffled the little bit of hair she had on her head.

"Now I have to go and comb my hair," she grinned. "You have it sticking up all over my head like I'm a newborn chick."

"Don't bother. I mean, who are you trying to impress, since it's just the two of us? We could walk around naked all the time and who'd care?"

"I would," Grace said. "I think half naked is better than whole naked."

"Maybe I can change your mind about that."

"What do you mean?"

"I figured we could ride the ATV this evening and go swimming in our spot."

"Swimming?" she asked suspiciously.

"Well, naked swimming, also commonly known as skinny dipping."

"I don't think so," Grace scoffed. "I'm not that much of an exhibitionist."

"Why not? You have a beautiful body and I've already seen every inch of it."

That was true. Ever since the first time they'd made love, she and Jet had been spending their nights enjoying each other's bodies and learning new things about each other.

"Why do we have to go swimming outside naked?" Grace whined.

"It's my fantasy," Jet answered quietly.

"What kind of fantasy is that?" she replied, aghast. "I can take you into the bedroom and do any other fantasy you want without having to expose myself to anyone that may happen to walk by."

"Ever since I was a little boy, I've wanted to swim naked in that pool with the woman that I love." Cajoling, Jet said, "Come on, Grace, do this for me and I'll do something for you."

"Someone might see us," she whispered.

"Have you ever seen anyone out there the times that we've been?"

"No but there's a first time for everything," she said dubiously.

Grace looked at the way Jet stuck his mouth out. It was so reminiscent of how he used to pout as a little boy that she didn't attempt to smother her laughter. "All right," she said reluctantly, "we can go skinny dipping."

"Hot diggity!" Jet grinned, pleased that he'd coerced her into doing something that was not in her nature.

In his haste to get Grace swimming naked before she changed her mind, Jet drove at full speed down the country road. Once they walked down the now-familiar path, Grace gasped at the blanket and cooler waiting for them under a tree.

She turned to Jet slightly affronted. "How did you know that you'd get me to do this?"

Jet kicked off his flip-flops and stripped naked in thirty seconds. Standing proudly in front of her, he said, tickling her chin, "You've always been a team player." Jet walked to the side of the pond, drew in a deep breath, and dove in, making a big splash. When he resurfaced, he wiped his hand across his face and treaded water. "The water is perfect."

Grace looked around and saw a tall tree. She went behind it and took off her clothes. It didn't take long since she hadn't worn any undergarments. She procrastinated and when she emerged from behind the tree, she wished that she had gotten into the water before Jet because he was staring at her bush as if he'd never seen it before.

"Grace," he said teasingly, "I think you're the hairiest woman I've ever seen."

His remark propelled her into action. "I'm going to kill you," she threatened, diving into the water next to him. She swam underwater to him and yanked his penis.

"Ow," Jet yelled, "it's on now!"

When Grace surfaced next to Jet, he went under, and, after gripping her waist to hold her still, he slipped his finger inside and started fingering her.

"You dog," she screamed, trying to squirm away from him. Then she stopped. *Hell, I'm enjoying this, so if I stop him I'll be the loser.*

They cavorted in the water, with Jet picking Grace up several times at times and throwing her slick, naked body into the water, only to grab her again and let her ride on his back. After Grace, more so than Jet, was exhausted, they climbed up the small embankment to rest on the blanket. She lifted the cooler lid and pulled out two bottles of beer. After twisting one open, she handed it to Jet. He'd been lying on his stomach but sat up and quaffed the liquid. Grace had the urge to pick on Jet the way she did when they were teenagers, so she pointed between his legs. "I thought water was supposed to make that thang shrink."

"Not mine," he boasted. "I'm a stallion."

"I think you need to lay off the Viagra. Too much of those pills can't be good for your heart," she said playfully before she took a swig of her beer.

"Viagra be damned," Jet bragged. "This is all me. Mind you, if there ever comes a time that I need it, I wouldn't be too proud to get some. But right now," he said, "I don't think you have anything to worry about, dear, so stop fretting. I got you."

Grace leaned over and playfully pinched him on the inside of his thigh because he'd had the upper hand all afternoon.

Jet put his beer bottle down and deliberately took Grace's out of her hand. Easing her gently on her back, he lowered his head to one breast and began to suckle while he molded the other with his hand. Then he lowered his mouth to her midsection and inserted his tongue into her navel.

Grace emitted a gasp of pure pleasure before suddenly moving from underneath him. She pushed Jet onto his back and straddled him, then leaned over and pinned him to the blanket by placing her hands on his shoulders. She sat astride him as if he were a horse and began to move slowly up and then down, clenching her clitoris every time she slid up or down on his joystick. A combined wet pleasure from the both of them made Jet so slick that he almost slipped out of her. Grace stared down at Jet and felt a surge of power as she viewed the ecstatic expression on his face with each and every thrust that he returned. When she felt him shudder inside her, with satisfaction she came and, exhausted, let him slide out of her. "Jet, I love you," she murmured before she stretched her body on the long length of him.

"I love you, too, Grace." Jet slid his arms around her waist and they soon fell asleep with her on top.

That night, Grace lay in bed reading. As she waited for Jet to finish showering, she heard the doorbell ring and noticing the lateness of the night, pulled on her robe at the foot of the bed. "Who is it?" Grace hollered as she walked down the foyer to the front door.

"It's Liza."

Oh no! Grace hurriedly ran into her old bedroom and pulled back the comforter, messing up the covers so the bed looked as if she'd been lying in it. Pulling her wrapper closer around her, she opened the door. Trying to hide her discomfort she said breezily, "Hi, Liza. What are you doing here this time of night?"

Liza's eyes darted speculatively behind Grace. She noticed Jet's bed was unmade, but he was nowhere in sight and said, "I need Mr. Jet. My arthritis is killing me and I don't have anything to take."

Grace pretended to think. "I think he's taking a shower, but . . ."

Jet had quietly walked up behind her and said in a somber tone, "I'm right here, Liza." He glared at her, knowing that her motive for showing up at his house at that time of night was not innocent. "You should take some Extra Strength Tylenol."

"I don't have any at home and no money to get any."

"You spent money in gas coming all the way out here," Grace snapped.

To this Liza said, "Goddaughter, I'm sorry if I'm interrupting anything."

Grace hastily denied, "You're not interrupting anything. Nothing's going on." Then she mouthed the words, "I'm sorry," at Jet from behind Liza's back.

Without speaking, Jet walked to the hall closet and withdrew his medical bag. After rummaging around in it, he withdrew a bottle of Aleve and handed it to Liza. "Go home and take two of these. That should get you through the night. If you come by the office tomorrow Dr. Jesse will probably have something stronger for you."

After Grace shut the door behind Liza, she turned around and leaned on the door. "She's a pain in the ass."

Jet stood in his shorts giving Grace a level look of anger. Then he pointedly stared past her to Grace's bedroom and the bed she'd deliberately undone.

"What?" she asked, stunned by the hostility.

"Are you ashamed of our relationship?"

"No," she stammered. "I mean, you know how Liza is. I don't want our business all in the street."

"What difference does it make if people know about us?" he retorted angrily.

"I just don't want people asking me a lot of questions."

"I know what you mean. After all, I would hate for someone to ask me why I would want you when you were going to marry my best friend," Jet said cruelly.

Grace blanched in horror before she said in a hurt voice, "You know, Liza *is* my godmother."

"And what has she ever done for you, Grace? All the time your mother was sick, she never looked out for you. I mean, she didn't even show up for the funeral and her excuse was she had to babysit her nephew's twins."

Grace bowed her head, shamed from the memory.

"I'm sorry, Jethro," she said and walked up to him and slid her arms around his neck.

He took his hands and pulled her arms from around him. "I'm Jet, not Jethro anymore. You'd best remember that in your dealings with me. Now, I'm going to bed." He ordered in a disgusted voice, "Make yourself a cup of herbal tea." Then he deliberately added, "Drink it in your room."

Grace felt her heart drop to her feet as she watched Jet go to his room. Once inside, he turned to face her and kicked the door shut.

Grace tossed and turned all night and in the wee morning hours, exhausted from lack of sleep, she sat up and crept to her dresser drawer and withdrew her bottle of pills. She opened it and placed one on her tongue, then spit it out into her hand. Grabbing a tissue she placed the pill inside it before stuffing it back into the bottle and tucking the bottle in the drawer. Naked, Grace walked out into the kitchen and turned the kettle on to boil. She stared at Jet's door, and when she saw no light from underneath, she willed him to hear her and come out. After Grace slowly sipped the tea, she got up and put the mug in the sink and, with leaden steps, she went back to her bedroom.

Jet lay in the darkness and heard Grace's movements. Once he heard her return to her room, he turned over, punched his pillow and went back to sleep.

The next morning when she dragged herself out of bed, Jet was gone. She looked at the clock and realized that if she didn't get a move on, she'd be late for her appointment with Dr. Storey. *I don't need to miss my appointment. I've never seen Jet so angry with me. When we were kids we used to fight all the time, but this is different. I have a different kind of emotional involvement with him. It really stung when he brought Livingston's name up in our*

fight. That was uncalled for and he should apologize for that. Maybe not, since he has a point. Why does he want me? I have issues.

Grace sat across from Dr. Storey with a downcast expression. Jet hadn't called the house before she left, or her cell phone. She fidgeted as she tried to find a comfortable position on the small loveseat.

"Is there anything in particular that you want to talk about today?"

"Not really," Grace replied in a monotone.

"Are you still relying on sleeping pills to sleep?"

"No, I haven't had any in weeks, but I was so stressed out last night I almost took one."

"What made you almost take one?"

"Jet and I had a fight and I woke up and couldn't get back to sleep."

"If you're living with someone who could drive you to the act of self-medicating, then that's an unhealthy relationship for you."

Stunned by the doctor's statement, Grace said irritably, "Jet's the best thing that's happened to me since . . ." She didn't finish.

"Since what?" asked Dr. Storey. "Since the death of Livingston?"

Still angry at the doctor's assumption that she and Jet had an unhealthy relationship she glared at her and said, "Yes, that's exactly what I mean."

"Then why did you almost revert to your behavior of taking a sleeping pill to get through the night?"

"Jet got angry with me," she gave the doctor a hard look, "and rightfully so because I tried to hide our relationship from my godmother. He thinks that I'm ashamed of him and I'm not."

"I'm not quite sure what you're getting at."

"Jet and I are lovers," she said flatly. When she saw the look on Dr. Storey's face she said defensively, "We're not kin."

"I know that, and I sort of suspected that things had progressed to that during your last visit. It's not uncommon for two, healthy, single people that live together to begin a sexual relationship. I'm just a little concerned as to how you will handle this if things end badly. Last night, he almost drove you to revert to an unhealthy behavior."

"I did that to myself. Jet kicked me out of his bed last night." She amended her words at the look of horror that crossed the doctor's face. "I mean figuratively he kicked me out. I wasn't in bed with him when he banished me to my old bedroom, but anyhow, after that I was so upset that I let him down, I couldn't sleep." She drew in a deep breath. "My godmother stopped by and I pretended that I was sleeping in the other bedroom."

"I see." Dr. Storey watched Grace with a contemplative look and asked, "If you feel so strongly about him, why did you try to pretend that the two of you are only roommates?"

"I dunno," Grace whispered. "I guess it's that I'm tired of being the talk of town. My mother's antics made me miserable throughout most of my childhood. She drank a lot, and sometimes she'd show up soused at the strangest places and people would snicker and whisper. And then the way I lost Livingston. I mean, it's not a common occurrence for a man to be killed after his bachelor party. I'm just tired of my business on people's lips."

"Every reason you just gave me for people talking about you was out of your control. Worry about the things that you can do something about. Decide whether you want this man short or long term. Also, think about whether this is the real thing, or whether he's a crutch like prescription drugs to help you get through a rough time."

"I love Jet," Grace said. Stunned by the realization of the depth of her love for him, she had a sort of bemused look on her face.

"Love him how?" Dr. Storey stared thoughtfully at Grace.

"I love Jet the way a woman loves a man. But I'm confused because I also love him the way a sister loves her brother. Is that sick?"

"Not at all, Grace, considering the history. I've noticed in the African-American community there are a lot of unwritten rules that people feel obligated to abide by. As far as I'm concerned, there are too many don'ts and not enough do's. It clips the wings and narrows the choices that men and women have as they search for real love. But I want you to make sure that you're not confusing love for gratefulness."

A memory of Jet making love to her surfaced, and she said with authority, "I'm sure that I'm not. But I do wonder. I mean, I've known Jet practically my whole life. Why would I now have this kind of love for him?"

"You said that he's different than he used to be."

"He is," Grace replied. "He's always been a good guy, but as my man he's one of a kind. Jet's so strong and confident. When we were young, sometimes I would have to step in when some of the older boys picked on him. Now he's the one protecting me."

"And you have a problem with that? Being protected and cared for is what women crave. That's one of the things that attracts us to certain men. Not that we necessarily need it, but we need to feel secure that it's there for us as a safeguard."

"I'm a little worried because it's taken so long to develop. The minute I saw Livingston, I knew he was the one."

Doctor Storey put down her notepad. "People love in different ways, levels and manners. That doesn't mean one love is better than the other. It just means it's different in the way it came to you. The way I see it, you're blessed. Many women go through their whole lives never having a great love that is returned, yet you've been lucky enough to have two. Rarely does lightning strike in the same place twice. Instead of doubting it, you should embrace it."

After she left the doctor's office, Grace hurried home so she could make an extra-nice dinner for Jet. Once inside the house, she reached in the freezer and withdrew the collard greens she'd cut up and cleaned weeks earlier and saved for a special meal. She took a ham hock out of the refrigerator and, after rinsing it under the faucet, put it in a large pot of water to boil. Then she withdrew a box of cornbread mix and set it on the counter. The chicken she'd taken out earlier was already thawed and after washing it, she seasoned it for frying.

Hours later, everything was almost done and she was turning the last pieces of chicken in the pan. Grace dialed Jesse Gilliard's office number.

"Dr. Gilliard's office." Grace recognized the voice of Hazel, the office secretary.

"Hello," she said, "this is Grace. Is Jet there?"

"No, ma'am," the friendly voice said. "He left over thirty minutes ago."

"Good," Grace said. "That means he should be home any minute. Talk to you later." Then she put the cornbread in the oven.

An hour later, Grace dialed Jet's cell phone number and it went straight to voice mail. Unsure of what to do, Grace hung up without leaving a message.

After nine o'clock that night, Grace heard the garage door open and close. Her unfinished plate of food and the empty place setting for Jet looked pathetic as it sat unused.

When Jet came inside, he was surprised to see Grace at the table, but he quickly masked his expression before he briefly nodded his head in her direction. He didn't break his stride as he headed towards his bedroom.

Watching his retreating back, Grace stood and said, "I made dinner for you."

"I already ate." Jet stopped and turned around, his face devoid of expression.

She waved her hand in annoyance. "You could have called. I wouldn't have bothered to cook all of this."

Jet didn't respond.

"I tried to call you. Why did you have your phone off?"

Jet didn't answer.

Grace drew in a deep breath. "I'm sorry about last night," she said beseechingly.

"So am I," he said before he turned on his heel and started to go into his bedroom.

"Were you with Lorna?" Her voice sounded like that of a jealous fishwife. "Is that who you ate dinner with?"

Once Jet got to his bedroom, he turned around and, without speaking, kicked the door shut.

Then she heard the lock turn.

After the third morning of the Mexican standoff, Grace knew when she woke up that Jet would be gone. Tears welled in the corner of her eyes, but she blinked them back. She dialed Solange's cell phone and when it went straight to voice mail she waited for the beep so she could leave a message. "Help!" was all she left because she knew that Solange would know that it came from her.

Not long after, Grace's phone rang. When she picked it up, Solange, clearly rattled, asked, "What's wrong?"

"Jet stopped sleeping with me," Grace declared dramatically.

"Good grief, Grace, so he's going through a dry spell." Solange continued in a droll tone, "Believe me, we've all been there. I thought it was something serious."

"That's not it. He's mad and he's not speaking to me either." Then she recounted what happened the night Liza made her unannounced visit.

"I'm with Jet. You don't even like that woman. In fact, you never really talked about her that much before."

"But she's the mouth of the south and I don't want her telling everyone my business."

"You must be out of your mind if you think tongues aren't already wagging. I mean, two single people living together out there in the country all by themselves? Trust me, anyone who has a brain in their head already knows the deal."

"Guessing and knowing for sure are two different things."

"Well, you're different from me," Solange said. "When I'm getting laid, I tell everyone. I obliquely introduce it into the conversation like, 'Gee, I'm exhausted because my man kept me up all night.' Or I'll stretch and say, 'My body aches from all the different positions my man had me in last night. You know what I mean.' "

Grace laughed out loud for the first time in days as she pictured Solange's antics.

When Grace's laughter subsided, Solange said, "And then with glee, I watch the facial expressions of the people I say that to. You know, Grace, not everyone's having great sex, and Jet is one nice piece of man flesh."

"I don't know how to fix it," Grace said slowly.

"Yes, you do, and if I were you, I'd hurry up. If you let him stew too long, it'll be harder to make nice. Now I have a meeting and I have to go. Call me after you hash things out."

"Okay," Grace said before she and Solange disconnected.

Grace took a shower, dressed in a pair of short shorts, a tank top and wedge heels. She looked like a model from an Old Navy commercial. After applying her makeup and smoothing her hair, she drove to town.

I know Liza hangs out in the men's barbershop in an effort to satisfy her quest for dirt on anybody and everybody. That nosy buzzard was kicked out of beauty parlors when I was a teenager because she never got her hair done, she'd just go inside and sit gathering gossip to spread about town. Peering out the car window, she saw Liza walking slowly towards the men's barbershop in the 96-degree heat. Pulling up alongside her, Grace rolled down her window and said sweetly, "You look mighty hot out there, Miss Liza."

She stopped and gave her a look. "You right, darlin'. It must be a hundred degrees."

"Ninety-six," Grace corrected her. "How would you like me to treat you to some ice cream at Sonic?"

Liza's face beamed. "That would be so nice."

Grace unlocked the passenger side door from her master control and said, "Hop in."

Once Liza was settled back against the seat, Grace gave her a look through her sunglasses and said, "We have to make one stop on the way."

"I don't care. I'm just glad you got me out of that heat."

Grace was at Dr. Gilliard's office in five minutes. Once she parked the Jeep, she jumped out, letting the engine idle. "That ought to keep you cool," Grace said sweetly and strutted up the walkway to the entrance. Just as she started to open the door, Jet came out.

Surprise registered on his face before he masked it. "What are you doing here?"

"Jet, I've been so lonely without you. Please let me take you for an ice cream," she said with a pleading voice.

Jet placed his hands in the pocket of his pants and rocked back on his heels.

"Don't be as childish as I am," she whispered.

After a minute, his expression softened but his voice gave no clue as to what he was really thinking. "Okay, but I don't have long because I have a meeting with the mayor."

Once Jet got to the passenger side, once again his face registered shock at seeing Liza sitting there. His eyes locked with Grace's across the top of the SUV. She opened the car door and climbed in.

"I'll get in the back, Jet," Liza offered before she scrambled to the back seat.

Sonic was the meeting place for all ages in Lake City. Loud music boomed from teenagers' cars, and children played tag as they waited for their mothers to call them for their treat. After Grace ordered a banana split for Liza, a cookies and cream flurry for Jet and a banana milkshake for herself, she deliberately talked about nonsensical things as she sat close to Jet on the concrete bench.

When Liza saw Grace pick up her napkin and wipe the corner of Jet's mouth and then plant a lingering kiss on the area she'd just cleaned, she hurriedly gulped down the remainder of her ice cream, eager to leave so she could spread the news.

Jet watched Grace's antics with an unreadable look and said very little, only answering a question if he was asked.

His aloofness made Grace apprehensive, but she persevered, giving him every bit of attention that he deserved. Once they were done with their ice cream, Grace drove Jet back to the doctor's office, and giving Liza a look she said, "I'll be right back. I want to see Jet to his car."

In silence they walked to where Jet's BMW was parked, and once there, Grace moved so close to Jet that she could feel his breath on her face. She took her hands and lowered his head to her and kissed him. She didn't grope him, but instead gave him the kind of kiss a woman gives a man when she has a deep love for him and is not afraid to show it to the world.

Jet returned her kiss but when she opened her eyes, it was unclear as to what he was thinking.

"See you later."

Jet didn't answer, simply nodded his head and got in the car after waving good-bye to Liza, whose eyes were practically bulging out of her head.

It was late that night, and Jet wasn't home yet. She'd showered and changed and was getting ready to make a cup of tea when she heard Jet pull up.

When Jet entered, she had her lips to her cup and Jet saw her sober expression. "Our meeting ran real late," Jet said quietly.

Grace just nodded her head to let him know that she heard him.

"I'm beat and going straight to bed."

Disappointed, Grace kept her head bent, swallowing the lump in her throat.

Jet put his medicine bag in the closet and headed for his room. Once he got to the doorway, he stopped and looked at her. "Are you coming to bed?"

Grace's heart did a somersault and she asked, "Are you talking to me?"

Jet leaned his heard forward, then surveyed the empty room.

Her heart pounded as she practically skipped toward the bedroom. As Grace passed him, Jet slapped her bare bottom before he closed the door.

CHAPTER 19

"How are you doing, Taft?" Grace asked the lanky teenager as he settled himself in front of one of the center's new computers.

"I'm really happy, Miss Grace. I got my acceptance letter from State."

"Congratulations," she said and patted him on the shoulder. "When do you start?"

"As soon as I can come up with the tuition. I'm here trying to find out if there is any grant money available."

"Go to the search engine and type in FAFSA. Sometimes they run out of money, so the earlier you apply, the better off you are."

As they waited for the site to come up, Taft said, "The school campus has furnished housing, so all I have to do is come up with the money and everything should be cool."

"So I gather that you're not going to try to live in a separate apartment?"

"I think that would be too hard for me since I've been out of school for a while." His facial expression was tinged with embarrassment. "I know that I'll be older than a lot of the other students in the dorm, but I don't want the headache of trying to pay all the bills that go along with having your own place. I'm going full time because I want to get in and out as fast as possible."

"Have you decided on a major?"

Taft gave Grace a sheepish look. "I was going to try for a business major, but since Mr. Jet had all these computers installed, I just can't seem to get enough of them. I think maybe computer engineering or something in that field."

Grace beamed. "That's what I call job security. Computers are here to stay."

The site came up just as a horde of students entered the center, throwing their book bags in a corner and running to the line of computers on the other side of the room. "There are my kids. Let me know if you need any help filling that out."

"Thank you, Miss Grace." Taft stared after Grace with something akin to hero worship.

She looked around the center and only then did she fully realize how much she'd missed teaching. She walked to the other side of the room where eager students waited for her to join them so they could log onto their reading programs. "How's everyone doing today?" Grace cheerfully asked.

A mixture of good, great and one horrible was forthcoming from the group of students.

"Uh oh, who had a bad day?" Grace asked.

"Jonathan got in trouble for looking on another girl's paper."

Grace looked at Monica. She could count on her to always drop the dime on someone else's bad news. "Is that true, Jonathan?"

"Yes'm," ten-year-old Jonathan answered, looking down at the keyboard of his computer.

"Didn't you study last night for your test?"

"I didn't have time because I had to babysit my little sister, put her to bed and wash dishes."

Frustration ignited in Grace's stomach, but she knew not to comment on a child's family situation. "Well, anytime you need to study for any test, you can do it here before you go home. I'll set up a quiet spot for you in my office."

"You will?" Jonathan's face brightened at the thought of getting such special treatment.

"I sure will," she said. She moved on, not wanting to prolong attention to Jonathan's home life. "Boot up your computers, and put in your usernames and passwords. Once you do that, the reading program should bring you to where you were the last time you were here. Don't forget to print your scores before you leave so I can place them in your folders."

Once they were quietly working, Grace went to her office to check her messages. Philip Monroe entered and said, "I just wanted to come by and see how you were settling in." He smiled at her.

"Everything's going great. I appreciate you giving me an office."

"It's the least I can do since you bumped up your time from one morning to two days. I've already seen a difference in the kids when they get here. They used to go home and play their video games and be totally unsupervised for hours until their parents got home from work. At least here we can keep an eye on them."

"I see how close-knit community is, so I'm sure the parents appreciate it."

Philip gave her a dry look. "Then maybe they should support it a little more financially. It costs a lot to babysit nowadays. I used to get twenty-five cents an hour. My son's babysitter charges me five dollars an hour. She said that's cheap."

Grace chuckled, "That's only a gallon of gas."

Philip joined her and said, laughing, "Don't I know it."

On the way home, Grace's cell phone rang and she saw that it was Naomi. "Hello," she said.

"Hello, Miss Grace," she stuttered. "I need a favor from you."

Grace rolled her eyes and withheld a sigh of tiredness. "What is it that you need, Naomi?"

There was an obvious hesitation and then Naomi nervously said, "I have to go to New York. My cousin Neesha has a beauty parlor and she said that I can rent one of her chairs there."

Appalled, Grace said, "You're thinking about moving to New York with Ebony?"

"I don't have no choice. There's not enough work here and I'm tired of subsidizing my income with Wal-Mart. I want to do hair full time," Naomi said. "That's what I wanted to talk to you about. I don't want to take Ebony until I have a nice place and have found a good person to watch her during the day. I hoped that you would keep her for me while I'm gone. You know how crazy she is about you and Mr. Jet."

"When are you going?" Grace asked.

"In about a week. I need to make plane reservations, but I can't do that until I find someone to keep Ebony. She don't really like Miss Liza, and my stepmother already has her hands full with my other brothers and sisters."

"I'll talk to Jet about it and let you know, but just for the record, I don't think that you should be taking Ebony to New York City. It can be dangerous for people if they don't know their way around."

"My cousin Neesha promised that she'd look out for us. Anyhow, I'm just going to check it out and see. When will you let me know if you can keep Ebony? Otherwise I'll have to take her with me."

"I'll talk to Jet tonight and I'll let you know soon," Grace promised before she abruptly hung up the phone.

As they ate dinner, Jet observed the petulant look on Grace's face and said softly, "There's nothing you can do about Naomi moving to New York with Ebony. She's her mother."

"And as her mother, she's *supposed* to look out for the best interests of her child. Naomi doesn't know anything about New York City. She's a sweet girl, but she's really not that bright."

"Has she ever told you who Ebony's father is?"

"No, Liza did. She said he's some military guy over in Iraq who doesn't even know about her."

"Well, if he ever finds out about her and how he wasn't told, if he's half a man he's going to be real pissed. Ebony is a delightful child. Any man would be lucky to have that little charmer as a daughter."

Grace looked at Jet to see if there was some hidden meaning in what he said but she couldn't decipher his expression. "So I guess it's okay with you if she stays with us?"

"I don't see that we really have a choice. It appears that Naomi will go regardless and who knows, maybe she'll back out of her intention of moving there. New York can be frightening to some people and one visit is more than enough to do it, especially for someone who's never really been in a big city."

"Maybe," Grace hopefully echoed Jet's sentiments.

Early Saturday morning, Grace sat next to Jet as he navigated his BMW in the fast lane of I-95. "Why are we going to Atlanta?" Grace asked as she looked at the heat waves already shimmering off the road.

Jet momentarily took his eyes off the highway. "I have something I need to check out, and I figured that you might be a little tired of the country life. You used to hate it when we were growing up."

"That was then, this is now," she said and patted his knee.

Jet gave her a dark look. "If you don't want to end up staying the night in a hotel, I suggest you stop touching me, woman."

"Yes, sir." She settled back into the soft leather. "I want to get back in time to get our clothes ready for church tomorrow."

"What am I wearing?" Jet teased.

"I bought you a black pinstripe suit and a cobalt blue shirt from one of those small shops on Main Street. It amazes me the shopping that they have in Lake City. I actually found a Vera Wang. Albeit it was last season's dress, it still was a designer dress."

"Did you buy it?" Jet asked raising one eyebrow at Grace.

"Do black people like chicken wings?" she asked with a grin.

"I guess that means I'll be seeing it soon."

"Tomorrow at the latest."

Jet smiled his satisfaction. Then he grabbed her knee and rubbed her bare leg. "I think that tomorrow's going to be a good day."

"I think every day with you is a good day." Grace leaned over and gave Jet a peck on the cheek.

"We should be there in about an hour," Jet observed.

"Good, I'm getting hungry."

"We can stop now if you want."

"No, I'll wait because you promised me Morelli's if I came with you."

"So I did, and I try to never break a promise."

The motion of the car lulled Grace to sleep. When the car drew to a halt, she sat up and looked around in a daze. First her eyes focused on the familiar house to the left, and then the right. Her face drained of all color as she stared at the house she and Livingston had bought. Angrily she looked at Jet and spat, "The last people in the world that I want to see are Delilah and Rose. I don't appreciate you springing this on me, Jethro!"

"It's Jet," he corrected her softly, "and they're not here. They lost the house."

"Already?" Grace asked, flabbergasted.

"It's been more than seven months. I had my frat brother in real estate keep an eye on the foreclosure list. I knew it was inevitable that they'd lose it. It's bank owned and I can purchase it back for you. I wanted to see what you thought and check it for damage before I made a bid on it."

"Delilah and Rose are so stupid. Livingston left the insurance from his job to his mother. They didn't have enough sense to pay the mortgage?"

"They didn't have enough money to pay it until they inherited. Most people don't realize that if a person dies without a will everything has to go through probate, and that can take up to a year. Banks repossess in three months."

"I didn't know that either."

Jet gave Grace a searching look. "Are you ready to go inside and put your demons to rest?"

"Yes," she whispered but didn't move.

Jet got out of the car and went around and opened Grace's door. He held out his hand.

She slid her hand in his and together they walked up to the front door. Jet reached down and took a key out of a planter with a withered plant inside. He looked at Grace and said, "I got people."

The inside of the house was empty. Without speaking, Grace pointed to the dirty tire marks left by Justin's wheelchair. There were holes in the wall that looked as if someone had kicked them out of anger and it needed a paint job to cover fingerprints and crayon on the walls.

Jet cocked an eyebrow at Grace as he observed the minimal damage that could be fixed with one week of a handyman's time. Climbing the stairs, Grace clutched on to him with her hand buried in the back pocket of his jeans. They went from bedroom to bedroom and when they entered the one that she'd shared nights with Livingston in, Jet walked away in order to give her time alone.

Grace walked to the empty closet and peered inside. Then she went to the adjoining bathroom. She stared at the sunken tub that she and Livingston had bathed in together and, as an image of his face blurred her vision, she could swear she heard the words, "It's okay to love him, Grace. It's okay to have a life with him."

"What?" Grace whispered in awe. Turning on her heel, she flew down the steps as if the devil himself was at her heels and flung herself into Jet's waiting arms, burying her head in his chest.

"What?" he murmured as he smoothed her hair. "You're shaking."

Thinking he wouldn't believe her, she said, "Nothing, I'm just ready to go."

"Okay." Jet pushed her away. "You don't have to decide right now, but I need to make a bid on it no later than Monday if we want to be in the running."

"I've decided. I don't want the house sold at auction because that's a disgrace to Livingston's memory. But I don't want to live here either. This life is over for me. I have a new life with you and I'm happy."

Grace felt Jet's body relax. It wasn't until that moment that she realized he had been all tensed up waiting for what she was going to say.

"Then I'll buy the house and have it fixed up. We'll take our time and sell it. I'll do a very careful screening process of the prospective buyers."

"We want to sell it to newlyweds just starting out together."

"That might be hard, the way the economy is. If we can't find a couple like that, maybe an older couple that want a big beautiful place for their children and grand-kids to visit."

"I think that's perfect," she breathed.

Once they were outside and Jet was locking the front door, Grace saw that their presence had attracted two of her neighbors, Quinnie and Meredith.

When they saw it was her, they hurried over. Quinnie was talking before they even reached them. "Are you moving back here?"

"No, I'm afraid not." Grace shook her head. "We're just sort of checking things out."

Quinnie said plaintively, "That's too bad. You were such a good neighbor. Those last people were horrible. They had parties late at night and barbequed every Sunday in the front yard."

"They were very unfriendly, too. On the day of my son's bar mitzvah, I asked them to turn their music down and was cursed out," Meredith complained. "If I hadn't been expecting the rabbi any minute I would have given it right back to her."

"And the way she treated her mother!" Quinnie said, "One day I heard a lot of screaming and then I saw her put her mother and a suitcase outside. When the mother saw me looking, she went to the back porch and sat there."

"She let her back in eventually, though," Meredith added dryly. "And that poor child in the wheelchair. I felt kind of sorry for him, trying to roll that heavy thing, but then they bought him a motorized one and he ran over my flowers and demolished my plants. They didn't even apologize for that either. I went to the homeowner's association and complained, but they wouldn't do anything about it."

"Well, I'm going to buy the house, fix it up and I promise I'll do my best to get you good neighbors," Jet promised.

"Thank you," they exhaled gratefully in unison.

Once Jet and Grace had driven off and turned off the street, Jet pulled his car over, shifted into park and looked at Grace. Not being able to hold it in any longer, they both doubled over in laughter until suddenly Jet stopped and a sober expression settled on his face. "We shouldn't laugh. I feel sorry for the kids."

Immediately, the smile was wiped off Grace's face and she said with in a voice filled with pity, "I hate that

Livingston's nieces and nephew have to go through this. To lose your home."

Jet said hopefully, "Maybe once they get the insurance money, they'll put the money to good use and buy a condominium, something they can afford." Then he shifted the car into gear and drove off.

The line at Morelli's Gourmet Ice Cream on Moreland Avenue led out the door to the sidewalk. As they waited their turn to be waited on, Jet skeptically looked at the sign. "I don't see anything here that I want to eat."

"Stop being so stodgy. You never want to try anything new. Whenever we go out to eat, you always order the same thing."

"When I like something, I stick to it." He gave her an assessing look and said, "You need to be glad that I'm like that."

She slid her arm in the crook of his. "I am when it comes to me, but not when it involves food. Solange and I used to eat here every weekend." Grace looked back up at the menu and said, "I'll order for you. I'll pick two of my favorites and you can have a taste of each and then have the one you prefer."

"Okay," Jet acquiesced. "While you order, I'm going to use the restroom and wash my hands. Here," he said, reaching for his wallet.

"Put your money away," she ordered, "it's my treat."

"Well, well, well, a woman that knows how to treat her man," Jet said with a teasing glint. "I can get on board with that."

Grace gave Jet a whimsical smile. "I haven't worked forever. It really is your money, you know."

"And you know my money is your money," he said before he slapped her on her fanny and walked off.

Grace felt warmness flush through her body and she was distracted, thinking about what would probably be another night of sexual bliss in his arms. When it was turn she said to the pretty girl standing behind the counter, "I'll have two scoops of sweet corn ice cream and two scoops of coconut jalepeno, both in cups and with plenty of napkins, for here."

Once she'd gotten their order, a table for two opened up in the corner of the restaurant and she made a beeline for it. She'd just sat down when she saw Babs enter the ice cream shop.

Grace automatically slid a little lower in her chair, hoping the crowd of people would camouflage her.

Then Jet walked out of the restroom, and when Babs saw him, she screeched and ran up to him, threw her arms around his neck and gave him a long, aggressive kiss on the mouth.

Caught off-kilter, Jet stood stock-still with his arms hanging down the sides of his body.

When Grace saw Babs's behavior, supreme jealousy and white hot anger surged through her body. She accidentally dropped her spoon and it clattered to the floor. She picked it up, and deciding to kill two birds with one stone, she walked over to Jet and said, "I knocked my spoon off the table. Will you please go and get me another?"

Jet hovered for a moment, looking at Grace's face and the way her eyes snapped angrily, not quite sure that he wanted to leave Babs and Grace alone.

Grace touched his arm lightly and said, "We're fine, it's just girl talk."

Then he shrugged his shoulders and went to the counter.

From the moment Grace had walked up to her and Jet, Babs's mouth had hung open in surprise as if she were catching flies. "I didn't see you in here, Grace. How are you doing?"

Real concern was etched on Babs's face, making Grace check her temper. "I'm doing much better, Babs."

"Are you moving back to Atlanta? I'm looking for a roommate."

"No, Jet and I just had to come to town on business. We're going back to Lake City tonight."

Then Babs leaned in and with a quick look at Jet, who was now heading over to his and Grace's table said, "Does Jet have a girlfriend?"

"Yes. Me," Grace answered with an edge to her voice.

"You!" Babs answered, stunned.

Grace folded her arms trying to figure out if Babs really did know and was yanking her chain. "I'm surprised Solange hasn't told you. She's known for months."

"She didn't," Babs declared. "Gee, Grace, I know that there may not be many choices in the podunk town you've run to, but you can't be so bored that you sleep with kin. I think kissin' cousins would be better than this."

"Lake City actually has quite a bit going on. I'm keeping busy."

"Can't you find a man that you're not related to?" Babs asked condescendingly.

"You know very well that Jet and I aren't kin."

"I think it's disgusting, shagging your brother." Babs made a sound as if she were vomiting.

"He's not my brother, but he is my lover." Grace said this with a cockiness Babs had never heard from her before.

"But you were raised as brother and sister!" Babs said, raising her voice and attracting the attention of people in the line.

"That was our mothers' choice, not ours. We don't have to abide by that. And frankly, it's nobody else's business but ours." She looked over at Jet, who was watching the scene with intense interest. "I have to go now, Babs. I don't want my ice cream to melt in this hostile environment."

"I think that you're one desperate female," Babs hurled at Grace as she walked off, attracting the attention of the patrons in the restaurant.

Very calmly, Grace turned and walked back to her, then said disdainfully, "I went through a desperate time, but now that Jet and I are a couple, I'm on the right track again."

"Don't forget, Grace, I had him first," Babs sneered.

"Bite me," Grace said, then turned around and sashayed over to Jet. She sat down and began eating some sweet corn ice cream. She didn't see Babs leave the restaurant, but she knew that she didn't remain in line and order because she would've seen her out of the corner of her eye. When she looked up, Jet was scrutinizing her and she asked, "So I take it that you prefer the coconut jalepeno?"

"I like both of them." His demeanor did not give away what his thoughts were.

"Good, then we'll share." Grace took one of the scoops of her ice cream, put it in Jet's bowl and then took one of his and plopped it down into hers. Then she attacked her ice cream with relish. When she couldn't stand the silence at the table any more she looked up at Jet and said, "What?" When he didn't answer she said calmly, "I'm just tying up loose ends from past lives for both of us, that's all."

He continued to stare at her and she said with obvious satisfaction, "Eat your ice cream, Jet."

After they left Morelli's, Jet drove them in the opposite direction of the interstate that would lead them home.

"Where are we going now?" Grace asked drowsily, full to the brim with ice cream.

"I thought that we'd check out the Courage Exhibit at the museum before we went back."

Grace sat up straighter, eager to see the history that had paved the way for the integration of schools. "I thought it ended in June."

"It was supposed to, but it's been so well received that the Atlanta History Center held it over."

Before long, they pulled into a parking lot teeming with cars and busloads of children on school outings. As they threaded their way through the crowd, she clung tightly to his hand. Once at the ticket window, Jet took out his wallet and purchased two tickets. Tugging Grace along with him, he handed them to the clerk, who unclipped a red velvet rope and let them in.

People walked quietly through the exhibit, showing respect for the history surrounding them. Grace and Jet stared in awe at the black and white photographs of the De Laine family. A peculiarly haunting one was that of the family gazing at their charred home in Summerton.

Grace shivered as she realized how lucky the family had been to get out alive and live to tell their story. She whispered to Jet, "I can't imagine how strong Reverend De Laine must have been to start a petition for the integrating of schools in the 1940s. I don't think that I'm made of the stuff that he was."

Jet replied, "When a person wants something badly enough, they do whatever it takes."

On the way out of the exhibit, Grace picked up pamphlets from the cases on the wall. Looking at Jet, she said, "I think that I'm going to have my class do a project about all this. They can show me how Internet savvy they've become."

"That's a good idea. A lot of times, people benefit from rights their forefathers got them without realizing what it took to get them."

As Grace slept on their trip back to Lake City, Jet mused about the day they'd had. *She's ready. I love her and I'm convinced that she loves me the way she should.*

CHAPTER 20

When Grace entered the room in her Vera Wang, Jet literally rocked back on his heels at the lovely vision she made in her peach dress. “You bought that in Lake City?” he asked as he stared at the detailed bodice and full skirt swirling around her shapely legs.

“I know,” she laughed, “who’d have thunk it?” Then she gave him a once-over and said, “You don’t look too shabby yourself.”

‘”I know,” Jet said and placed his hand on the lapel of his jacket. “My woman bought this for me and she really has taste.”

Grace led Jet to a full-length mirror and stared at their appearance. “We really do make a handsome couple, don’t we?”

Jet grinned and held his arm out to Grace. “Yes, but don’t let people hear you say that. It sounds a little prejudiced.”

When they got to Deep River Holiness Baptist Church, they saw that only a few stragglers were hastening up the steps. Jet parked the car, and they hurriedly entered the church.

When they were inside, the ushers smiled and walked them to the front. Gratefully they slid into the available space at the end of the second pew.

Grace watched the choir march in singing the processional song. Then Pastor Greene entered the church and sat among his co-pastors.

The service went smoothly from one phase to another and Grace felt a peace and happiness in the church that she'd never felt before. She leaned on Jet, who had his arm around her, and they listened intently to every word of the sermon. Once Pastor Green was finished, he called for the church secretary to come to the front of the church and read the announcements.

Jet took his arm from around Grace and reached into his pocket.

She looked at him questioning. Then her eyes widened when she saw that he held a black square velvet box in his hands. He opened it and a huge square diamond almost blinded her. The sight of it made tears course down her face. Turning to her in the pew, Jet said softly, "Grace Foxfire, I love you more than words can say. Will you marry me?"

Nodding her head she said, "Yes, I will marry you, Jet. I love you so much." Grace stuck out her hand and he slid the ring on her left finger. It was a perfect fit.

Then she stood, pulling Jet up with her, and said loudly, interrupting the church secretary, "I have an announcement. Jet just asked me to marry him and I said yes." She held her hand up for everyone to see. At first there was a shocked silence. Then a small spattering of clapping was joined by boisterous applause and choruses of "Congratulations."

Pastor Greene stood up and went to stand behind the podium. When the revelry subsided, he gave them a stern look while he pointed his finger at Jet. "It's about time. I wondered if I was going to have to call the two of you into my office and counsel you."

His statement was met with snickers and mumbled words. "You right, Pastor," someone said.

After the service, they stood outside as well-wishers came by. When Liza approached them, Grace gave her a dazzling smile. "You were right when you said that Jet and I are made for each other."

"I may not be the smartest person in town, but I knew even when y'all were little children playing that you'd end up with each other." Then she looked at them closely and said, "Your mothers would be proud."

"Thank you, Liza." Jet smiled gratefully.

"When are you getting married, and are you going to have a big church wedding?"

Grace chuckled. "Heavens, Liza. We just got engaged and we haven't worked out any of the details yet. I promise the minute we do know we'll let you know."

"That'll save us from paying to put an announcement in the paper," Jet whispered without moving his lips.

Liza leaned forward and said with her hand to her ear, "What's that you said?"

"He didn't say anything, Godmomma," Grace answered for Jet.

Satisfied, Liza hobbled off towards her car.

Jet shielded his eyes from the blinding sun and said, "I'm starving. Let's go to Pop's and get some barbeque."

"I would love that," Grace murmured, still a little bewildered by the way the day had developed.

Then out of the blue, Jet said, "I didn't see Naomi in church. When is she going to drop Ebony off?"

"Friday morning."

"How long did she say that she was going to be gone?"

"At first it was a couple of days, now it's a week."

"It'll take her longer than that to find a place in New York."

"Maybe she'll move in with her cousin."

"I doubt it," Jet said. "Apartments in New York typically aren't that big." Then he looked at Grace. "There's nothing you can do about this. Just try to enjoy the limited time that you have left with Ebony, if she does indeed have to move away."

"Okay, Jet."

Jet turned off the paved road and onto a dirt one worn by constant traffic. They soon arrived at Pop's Barbeque Shack, a small, worn structure. Jet returned a wave to a couple that he allowed to pass before he pulled into the makeshift parking lot.

"Who was that?" Grace tried to not too obviously peer into the station wagon loaded down with people.

"I don't know," Jet chuckled. "You know how seriously the people in South Carolina take their motto, 'Smiling faces, beautiful places.' "

She laughed right along with him and agreed. "They do speak to any and everyone."

In front of the building, there was a large brown barbeque pit that emitted a puff of smoke when the covering was lifted. The tangy smell of barbeque whetted Grace's already ravenous appetite.

An old, white-haired man sitting on a wooden chair smiled amiably at her and Jet as they approached him. "Son, I heard you got engaged at church today."

Jet leaned forward and shook his hand. "News sure travels fast."

"It sure does. Congratulations to you, Grace. I like it when the right people get hitched. I can tell when I see a couple whether or not they're right for each other and you two belong together." Pop grinned, showing teeth tobacco-stained from years of dipping snuff and asked, "Now, what can I get you to eat?"

"We'll have two barbeque sandwiches with hot sauce for me and mild for my fiancée." Jet turned and winked at her. A shiver of anticipation slithered down her spine. Grace loved the way Jet said the word "fiancée," and her expression glowed.

"When ya'll gettin' hitched?" Pop asked as he fixed their sandwiches and put them in a brown paper sack. "There's no need to wait, since y'all living together already."

Grace sucked her teeth in annoyance. If it hadn't been for the fact that he was an old man who had during her childhood been nice to her and many a day given her free barbeque sandwiches, she would have told him to mind his own business.

Instead, she was content with Jet's complacent answer, "We know that, Pop."

As they left the barbeque stand and drove towards the turnoff to their house, Grace slid Jet a sideways look. "Do you have any idea as to when you want to have the wedding?"

"I think that's entirely up to you," he answered. "I'll just go along with whatever you want. But I do agree that the sooner the better."

"I think so, too, but I don't need him to tell me that." She added, "I want you to be involved in the planning of the wedding."

"I'll be more than involved, but I want you to make most of the decisions since the bride really is the focus. All that's required of the groom is that he pretty much show up on time."

Grace grudgingly admitted, "You're right."

"What are you planning to do today?" Jet stood at his car door getting ready to drive into town.

She pointed at a couple of boxes in the garage that she'd brought from Atlanta. "Nothing much except I want to go through those. It's probably just junk that I need to throw away."

"I have a meeting with the city council, and I figured we could check out a movie this evening, if I'm not too late with it."

"That sounds like a good idea. We probably won't get a chance to do anything like that once Ebony gets here."

"That's what parents complain about all the time, not having enough time for each other. Once we have our own children, we'll have date night, just to keep things spicy and dicey."

"That's what men always say that they're going to do." She gave him a stern look and cautioned, "Just make sure that you follow through."

"Have I disappointed you yet?"

"I can't say that you have." She leaned over and gave him a peck on the cheek before he got into the car and backed it out the driveway.

When Jet looked up before he drove off, Grace stood in her housedress waving at him and he thought she was the most beautiful sight he'd ever seen.

Grace grabbed one of the boxes and carried it into the den. She sat on the couch and unfolded the flaps. Reaching her hand inside, she found sweaters, pants that she couldn't fit in anymore, and a couple of pairs of boots. Once the box was empty, she decided it was easier to just get rid of the lot of it and stuffed everything back into the box and put it back in the corner. *I'll have Jet drop it off at Goodwill the next time he goes in town.* Then she thought about it and chuckled. *I'll do it. Give him a break. I always have something for him to do.*

Lifting it, she took it and put it in her Jeep. Then she grabbed the next box and took it into the den. Inside there were small knickknacks that she'd had on a shelf in the bedroom in Atlanta. Then she withdrew something wrapped in bubble wrap. Gingerly, she unfolded it. The wrap held the fragments of the crystal duck that had been the breaking point between her and Delilah. Grace held the pieces in her hands and then carefully balled them up into the wrap and threw them in the garbage. *That broken ceramic duck doesn't define what Livingston and I had. No one or nothing can besmirch that.*

Going back to the box, Grace dragged out something flexible, which was completely covered in brown wrapping paper. Once she tore that off, she encountered bubble wrap. She loosened the tape binding it together and when the wrapping fell away, she choked on the bile that rose in her throat at the sight of her dirty wedding dress with a streak of her own blood on it from her fall in the emergency room. Face to face with a graphic reminder of the most horrible experience of her life, she was unable to look away. Then suddenly she lurched forward and vomited. Falling to her knees, Grace crawled with the dress in her hand to a corner and pulling it across her, she sobbed.

An hour later, Grace still sat there. Dimly in the back of her mind, she heard the telephone ring. A long time later she heard the phone ring and still she couldn't reach for it or stand up.

Eventually, she heard the garage door open and her eyes fixed on the door Jet would have to walk through.

When Jet entered the kitchen and saw Grace huddled in the corner, he was so shocked that he dropped the gallon of orange juice he was carrying. When the carton hit the floor, orange juice splattered across the front of

Grace and the dress she clutched to her bosom. "What the hell?" Then he suddenly realized that Grace held her wedding dress. Recovering quickly, he tore the dress from her hands and stormed outside to the garage, only to return a few seconds later. Lifting her, he strode to the bedroom with her. Jet went into the bathroom and returned with a damp washcloth. Lovingly, he wiped her face. Once she was cleaned up, he took her hands in his and held them tightly. "Are you okay?" he asked in a sober tone.

"No," Grace mumbled. "It was in the box." She numbly looked at him. "Who would have done something like that to me?"

Jet spoke harshly. "I don't know, but I'm going to find out."

Jet stormed out of the room and minutes later she heard him yelling at someone on the phone. Then there was silence and she heard him yelling some more. When he reentered the room he said with an incensed look on his face, "Luke said he and his brothers never saw a wedding dress and Solange said that she put it in the trash for the garbage man to take it. She wants you to call her the minute you're feeling up to it." He paused for a moment. "I assume that either Rose or Delilah took it out of the trash and later snuck it in one of the boxes when the guys were packing you up. I'm sorry, Grace."

"I'm sorry too, Jet." She shook her head miserably before she stammered, "I can't marry you," she said in a forlorn voice.

"What?" Jet exclaimed, clearly rattled. "Grace," he whispered, "it's just a dress."

She held her hands out in despair. "It's not just a dress. It's an omen. Everyone I've ever loved has died. If you marry me, harm will come to you like it did for Livingston. You'll die or something."

"Grace," he said in a voice choked with raw emotion, "you have got to be kidding!"

"I'm not going to marry you now or ever," she said with conviction. "Even if you don't have enough sense to protect yourself, I will." Then she shakily stood, ignoring the hand Jet held out to her. "I'm going to take a shower." When she tried to walk past Jet, he grabbed her arm. She jerked it away, staring at him.

"You're just using this as an excuse!" he shouted.

Grace focused on a spot on the wall behind Jet.

He shouted, "Look at me!" Jet grabbed her chin and turned her head toward him. "You need to be grateful for the love that's left behind. Grace," his tone was dismal, "I'm not a ghost. I'm right here, dammit. I'm a flesh-and-blood man. It's time for you to start living your life and stop living in the past. Livingston's not coming back."

She glared at him stubbornly. "You'll thank me in the long run. I want us to stay together, but I don't want to marry you. Things are good between us the way they are." Then her tone turned beseeching. "Let's not rock the boat."

His expression was bleak. "I didn't know that you're so weak, Grace. I thought that you didn't want to be like your mother, but you give up too easily, just like she did."

The truth stung Grace and in an effort to obliterate the pain she felt, she gave Jet a hostile stare and said,

"What about you, Jet? You don't always face things either."

"What do you mean?" He eyed her warily.

"Why weren't you driving the night of the bachelor party? Were you trying to dull the pain that your two best friends were getting married and you drank too much? Is that what happened?"

"Yes, it is," he said candidly, his eyes boring into her. "So you wish that I'd died instead of Livingston?"

"Of course not!" Grace said.

Jet continued as if she hadn't answered him and said with tears in his eyes, "You're only thinking what I'm thinking. I wish I'd never had that bachelor party. But that's not the way things turned out and I have to deal with what's left." Jet turned around and began walking out of the room.

Grace ran behind him and grabbed his arm but he shrugged her off.

"Don't go," Grace shrieked, "Don't leave me."

He stopped and turned, saying cruelly, "I have to get away from you for my sanity."

Jet continued in the direction of the garage with Grace shouting for him not to leave. He went over to his motorcycle and pulled the plastic cover off, throwing it to the floor. Grabbing his helmet, he looked at Grace and said after he revved up the bike, "I'm leaving town and I don't know when I'll be back, but when I return we'll discuss alternative living arrangements. I know that you don't really care about anyone but yourself, but try to get yourself together tomorrow before Ebony comes."

Grace shouted above the din, "The doctor hasn't cleared you for riding your motorcycle, Jethro! You can't go!"

Jet looked at her and spoke with finality, "Jethro doesn't live here anymore." Then he added brutally, "Riding you has been more dangerous than anything else I've straddled in my life, Grace."

After Jet backed his motorcycle out into the driveway and roared out of sight, Grace sank to the concrete floor, engulfed in tears.

That night after Grace took her shower she went into her bedroom and opened her dresser drawer. She took the bottle of pills from under her nightgown and, withdrawing two, she went back into the kitchen and made herself a cup of hot Sleepytime tea. Looking at the clock she realized that Jet had only been gone four hours, but it felt like four days. She placed the pills on her tongue, and then suddenly she spat them out into her hands. '*I thought that you didn't want to be like your mother.*'

Jet's words resounded in her ears and she stormed back into the room, grabbed the bottle out of the drawer and flushed all of the remaining pills down the toilet. After she watched them swirl into oblivion, with a newfound determination, staggered back into the kitchen, sat at the table and drank her tea. Once finished, she knew that she would not able to sleep in the room she'd shared with Jet, so instead she retired to her old bedroom.

Grace heard the doorbell chiming over and over again, and crossly she looked at the clock and realized that it was after one. She'd been up half the night, dozing for less than an hour at a time and finally, about seven o'clock in the morning, exhausted, she'd fallen asleep. She staggered to the front door in her boxers and T-shirt. Through the glass panels, she saw Naomi and Ebony. *Damn, I forgot. I don't want Ebony to see me looking like the cat dragged me in and the dog was too afraid to take me out.*

Unlocking the door, she opened it and as she ran back to the room to run water over her face and comb her hair, she shouted, "Come in, I'll be right out."

As she stood in front of the bathroom mirror, Grace cringed at her disgraceful appearance. Her hair was askew and her eyes red from crying. Her face was puffy, and, most of all, she looked utterly miserable. Quickly grabbing her fashion fair makeup container, she dampened the makeup sponge and ran it across her face, something she would normally have never done without washing first, but she needed some color in her face. Then brushing her hair back, she returned to the den.

Ebony was sitting on the couch next to Naomi and when she saw Grace, she scrambled down and ran to her, throwing her little arms around Grace's thighs. "Auntie Grace, can I stay with you?"

"Of course you can," Grace answered. Plastering a welcoming smile on her lips, she looked at Naomi, who was eyeing her strangely.

"Have you been sick?" she bluntly asked, staring at Grace's still disheveled appearance.

"No," Grace responded, "why do you ask?"

"For one thing," she pointed into the kitchen, "look at your kitchen floor. There's juice all over it. Also, you just don't look like a newly engaged woman."

Grace gave a start when she heard Naomi's words.

Naomi gave Grace a slightly envious look. "Yes, I heard. It's been the talk of the town all week." Naomi shrugged. "As they say, another one bites the dust."

Ignoring her comments about the condition of her house Grace said, "Is that what they say?" Grace's tone was noncommittal.

"You should be doing a happy dance. Mr. Jet's quite a catch, you know."

"I know," Grace mumbled, then changed the subject. "Did you prepare Ebony for the fact that she'll be here a whole week and not the occasional afternoon that she's used to?"

"Yes, I did." Naomi said dryly. "I should be offended that she's letting me go without so much as a whimper."

"Maybe she doesn't understand the concept of time, yet." Grace looked at Ebony doubtfully as she had already positioned herself in front of the television even though it wasn't turned on.

"She gets it, all right. I asked her, 'Do you want to go to my godmother Liza's house or Auntie Grace and Uncle Jet's?' You won hands down."

"Jet's probably the real draw. I can't see anyone really wanting to spend time with me. I'm such a mess." Grace muttered these words and then wished she could retract them because of the inquisitive look Naomi got on her face. Before she could ask her what she meant, Grace said, "What time is your plane leaving?"

"In a couple of hours." Naomi looked at her watch and said, "I'll call when my plane lands to let you know that I made it safely."

"That's a good idea," Grace agreed.

"Ebony, come give Momma a hug."

Ebony scrambled over to her mother and let herself be lifted. Naomi kissed her daughter on the mouth and then gave her a big squeeze. "Mommy loves you very much and you behave for Auntie Grace and Uncle Jet, okay?"

"Okay," Ebony answered in her high-pitched voice.

"Thank you so much for doing this for me, Grace. I owe you big time. Maybe I'll find Ebony a father and me a husband in New York," she said with a hopeful lilt to her voice.

Aggravated, Grace stared at her with hands planted on her hips. "Is that why you're going up there, to look for a man?" she scoffed. "You're better off staying right here where you know the people and their family trees."

"No, thanks. These guys are too boring for me. I want to experience life. After all, I should get some play only if it's because they'd consider me fresh meat."

"Yes, fresh meat to be devoured," Grace warned. "Don't you tell any guy you meet that you're new to New York. Try to blend in so they don't try to take advantage of you."

"I know how to take care of myself," Naomi replied self-assuredly. "Don't you worry about me. Yikes, I have to go before I miss my flight. When I get back I'll do your hair for free."

"Yeah, that really evens things up," Grace commented with mild sarcasm, which sent Naomi into convulsions of laughter as she walked out the door.

Later that night, after Ebony was sound asleep in the bed next to her, with trembling fingers, Grace dialed Jet's cell phone number. She wasn't surprised when it went straight to voice mail. She said fearfully, "Jet, I made a terrible mistake. I love you and want to marry you. Please come home."

CHAPTER 21

The next morning Grace was awakened by Ebony tapping her on the shoulder. When she opened her eyes, Ebony declared, "I'm hungry. Cereal, please."

Pulling herself out of her state of self-pity, Grace swung her legs to the floor. She looked at Ebony and asked, "Do you need to go to the bathroom?"

"Uh-huh," Ebony affirmed.

Grace pointed and said, "The bathroom's in there. Don't forget to wash your hands. As a matter of fact, I think that I'll go with you to make sure you know how to do it."

Grace stood patiently and watched Ebony use the toilet, wipe herself, flush it and then go to the sink to wash her hands.

"After we have breakfast we have to go into town because I have a doctor's appointment."

"Are you sick?" Ebony asked Grace as she trailed after her into the kitchen.

"I sure am," Grace answered sardonically.

"I hope you feel better, Auntie," Ebony said as she climbed up on a barstool at the counter.

"I hope so too, munchkin."

When they got to Martha Storey's office, Grace noted that she was a little early and decided to kill time in the

Wal-Mart across the street. For safety, she put Ebony in the cart and they went to the toy section. Ebony clapped her hands excitedly and reached for a large doll.

"You like that?" Grace asked doubtfully. "What does it do?"

"She sings," Ebony pulled the string in the back of the doll and the doll sang choruses of nursery rhymes.

"How cute," Grace said, putting the doll in the cart. Then she went to the electronics department and selected several computer disks that taught toddlers their numbers, animals, and speaking skills. Once she got to the cashier, she was stunned by how expensive these items were because she hadn't looked at the prices. She looked at Ebony as she pulled out her credit card and said, "It costs a lot to be smart these days."

"'It costs a lot to be smart these days,'" Ebony repeated what she said with a cherubic smile.

Once she was back at the doctor's office, Grace walked inside, tightly holding onto Ebony's hand. Immediately the receptionist's face brightened and she said, "I see you brought someone with you today. How cute is she?"

"She's a looker, all right. I probably should have called first, but is it okay if I leave her out here in the waiting room while I talk to the doctor?"

"Sure. May I give her a piece of candy?"

"Yes, she can have one piece," she answered indulgently, as Ebony had stuck her hand out to Janet the minute she'd heard the word "candy."

"And I'll turn on the television. I think *Dora the Explorer* is on."

"Thanks so much, Janet. Is the doctor ready for me?"

"She is as soon as you sign in."

The minute Grace sat down in the chair across from Dr. Storey, she burst into tears.

Dr. Storey calmly watched the flood of tears as they cascaded down Grace's cheeks and dribbled off her chin. When Grace began to hiccup, she handed her a box of tissues and watched Grace dry her face.

Grace kept her head bent and began to speak softly. "Jet and I got engaged to be married."

Dr. Storey said gently, "I'm sure that there's more to the story because somehow I don't think those are tears of joy."

"I messed it up. I unpacked a box of clothes and found my dirty wedding dress. It threw me for a loop and I told Jet that I didn't want to marry him, but I do. He left me and said that he doesn't want anything else to do with me."

Sympathy was etched across the doctor's face. "I can see finding something like that would make you very upset. But I don't quite get the correlation between the finding of the dress and calling off the engagement."

"I'm afraid that something will happen to Jet if we go on with the wedding as planned. Livingston got killed the night before our wedding."

"Grace, I know that was a tragedy, but that doesn't mean that you don't deserve to find happiness with another man."

Grace hiccupped and said, "Every person that I've ever loved in my life has died. My dad, Jet's dad, my mother, Jet's mother, and then Livingston. It's like I'm a carrier for death. I need to keep Jet safe."

"Do you think that Jet is a carrier for death also?"

Grace shook her head in denial. "Of course not!"

"All those people that you named were people that he loved also. He too has suffered, yet he's not afraid to continue to love."

Grace grew quiet for a minute but then she said, "I have dreams."

"Dreams?" Dr. Storey asked. "We all dream, Grace. It's a way for our subconscious to tell us things that we don't face when we're awake."

"But I have premonitions. The night before my mother, Jet's mother and Livingston died, I had the same dream. I was in a hospital, and I went to a hospital bed naked and crawled under the covers. I had the same dream before the bachelor party. I tried to warn Livingston not to go to the party, but he didn't believe that anything would happen to him. If he'd listened, he'd be alive today. I'm afraid that Jet is next."

"You've never spoken before of these dreams to me, but I'm not going to dismiss them as hysterical nonsense because of the timing. In India, there are holy men who can prophesy coming events, but that doesn't mean that they can change the future any more than you can. You can't not live your life because of what might happen. Does Jet know how you feel?"

"He knows. But just like Livingston, he doesn't believe anything will happen to him," she mumbled. "Now, I'm afraid I'll never get a chance to tell him that I do want to marry him."

"Are you going to give up your love for him that easily?"

"I can't find him. I've already called him seven times and he hasn't returned my messages. He thinks that I blame him for Livingston's death, and I don't," she said emphatically. Then she whispered, "Jet probably thinks that I have too many issues for him to want to be bothered."

"Then change his mind. If you really want to marry him and have a life with him, make him see you for the strong woman that you really are."

"That's just it, Doctor. I don't know how strong I am. Last night, I almost took two sleeping pills."

"Almost?" Dr. Storey asked, closely searching Grace's face. "But you didn't?"

"No, because I don't want to be dependent on anything. I flushed the whole bottle down the toilet. Jet told me before he stormed out that I'm like my mother," she ended dejectedly.

"But you're not like your mother because you know when to stop," Dr. Storey said compassionately. "That was an unfortunate thing for him to say because he knows the history, but you have to give him some leeway because you'd just broken his heart. The important thing is, do you think that you're like her?"

"In many ways."

"Here," Dr. Storey handed Grace a piece of paper. "I'm going to walk out of the room and when I get back I want you to have written on one side all the good things that you remember about your mother and on the other side all the bad things and we'll do a comparison."

After Dr. Storey left the room, Grace sat there, her brow creased as she tried to think. Once she started writing, she couldn't stop and was still writing when the doctor reentered the room.

Proudly Grace handed her the paper and Dr. Storey read it. "Some of the good things that you have are that your mother was a good cook, kept a clean house, defended you, went to church on the days you sang in the choir, took you to Myrtle Beach, was nice to Jet, and told you every day that she loved you. You have more than ten good things about your mother and the only negative one that you have is that she became an alcoholic. She wasn't perfect, but I see that she had a lot of good in her."

"Yes, she did," Grace mumbled in awe, "and I never saw it."

"Sometimes it's hard to see things for what they are when you're in the midst of it. That little girl out there, who is she?"

Grace was caught off guard by the question and stuttered, "She's my hairdresser's daughter. I promised that I would take care of her while she went to New York."

Dr. Storey handed Grace her list back. "You can add that your mother raised a thoughtful and caring daughter because even though she feels as if her world is crumbling around her, she kept a promise to someone not related to her and is loving to a child not her own."

That night, after making sure Ebony was in a deep sleep, Grace picked her up and carried her to the SUV. Once she'd strapped her in, Ebony stirred and Grace held her breath, willing her to remain asleep. She drove to Liza's house without music because she wanted to make as easy a getaway as possible. She cut her lights when she pulled up in the driveway at the house and saw a sleepy-looking Liza dressed in a nightgown with a scarf over her head.

Grace held her fingers to her lips and gathered the sleeping Ebony in her arms. She quickly followed Liza to a bedroom, laying Ebony on the bed. Then she went out to the truck, followed by Liza. Grace handed her a small suitcase with some of Ebony's belongings and said gratefully, "Thank you so much for keeping her for me."

"I don't have any room left," Liza complained. "That's why I had you put her down in my bed." She looked speculatively at her and asked, "What's so urgent that you have to leave in the middle of the night?"

"I have to go and get a family member, and I can't take Ebony with me. I'll be back as soon as possible to get her."

Liza's eyes almost popped out of her head. "A family member? Who are you talking about, and why is Mr. Jet not with you?"

Not answering her, Grace climbed back into her Jeep and said distractedly, "Call me on my cell if you need me," and left.

Grace sipped on a cup of coffee as she made the fifty-minute drive to Myrtle Beach, her thoughts on Jet. *He can't have fallen out of love with me yet. He wanted to marry me last week. I've got to make him see that I panicked at the sight of the dress, but I do want to marry him at all costs. I'll do whatever it takes.*

Halfway there, she hit a sudden rainstorm. When she hit her brakes to slow down, her SUV fishtailed and slid across the other lane onto the shoulder. She dropped her head on the steering wheel in an effort to steady her nerves. *Thank God there was no other car on the road or there could have been a fatal accident.*

Gingerly, Grace pulled back onto the main thoroughfare and this time slowed her speed to below the speed limit. After half an hour, the rain vanished just as quickly as it had appeared. When she saw the exit for Myrtle Beach she sent up a prayer to God. "Lord," she said aloud, "I know that I've been pretty ungrateful many times in my life, but I've had a moment of clarity. I know that you know what's best for me and though bad things have happened in my life, so have good things because you made Jet a part of my life. Please, I'm begging you to give me another chance at happiness with the man I love completely, wholeheartedly, to the very depths of my soul."

Grace pulled into the resort and instinctively drove down to the cabanas. She saw Jet's motorcycle parked outside the unit they used to stay in with their mothers when they were children. With great trepidation she parked and walked up to the door and knocked on it, tentatively at first. When there was no response, she pounded with urgency. "Jet, it's Grace. I have to talk to you." When there was still no answer she walked to the lobby and startled a sleepy-looking clerk with his feet up on the desk.

She gave him a sheepish look and said, "I'm looking for one of your guests. He's booked in #257."

The clerk said, "I don't know what to tell you, miss. The guests don't tell us when they go in and out."

"Well, I'm his sister and it's been such a long ride, I'm exhausted."

The young man searched her face with intense interest and said decisively, "You look like an honest woman so I'll believe you. If you promise that you're not up to any funny business, I'll loan you the master key so you can let yourself in. I need it back in the morning before I get off around nine o'clock."

"Thank you sooo much," Grace said and reached into her purse and gave him a $20 bill.

"Thanks," he said gratefully. Then almost as an afterthought, he said, "If his car is here and you can't find him, go down to the beach. They had a luau earlier and he may still be down there hanging out."

Grace grabbed her suitcase and cooler out of the back seat of her truck and let herself into Jet's cabana. She had a flashback to her teenage years and the good times they'd had during the summer with their mothers. Thankfully, she'd had a revelation in Dr. Storey's office and realized that Jet had probably retreated to a place that they'd shared during their happy times.

Walking quickly into the bathroom, she stripped and after donning her shower cap scrubbed every inch of skin. She hadn't given regular attention to her skin since Jet had run from her and her drama.

Then she applied lotion to her body, put on her tankini bathing suit and flip-flops, and turned around in a circle through the perfume she'd sprayed in the air so it would cling to her body. Her only effort at makeup was to outline her eyebrows and add coral lipstick to her mouth. Grabbing a towel, a cold bottle of wine and corkscrew from the cooler, she gathered up all the courage she could muster and went to find Jet.

Jet lay on his back on a beach towel. After the tenth voice mail from Grace, he'd left his cell phone in his room. He wanted to be fair about their situation, but when he got home they'd have to make a decision. Either she would stay at his house in Lake City until she found another place to live, or she could move back to Atlanta and live in the house that she'd bought with Livingston, in which she'd thought that she'd lead a perfect life. He'd heard from the bank that morning and the house was his, so that wouldn't be a problem. He didn't want Grace in his life anymore. He was tired of trying to make her see that he was the right man for her.

"Jet."

He shook his mind from his mediation. From somewhere in the darkness he thought he heard his name being called.

"Jet."

He heard Grace's lilting voice from behind him and he sat up and whirled around to find Grace standing there. An intense anger consumed him and he spoke callously. "What are you doing here? When a man leaves you, Grace, it means he doesn't want to be bothered."

She cringed from his words but would not be deterred from her mission. "I came here for you."

"I'm not interested in talking to you," he sneered. "But I must say I'm not surprised that you showed up. You've always wanted what you can't have. You're so contrary."

Grace sat down on the sand next to the blanket, afraid to move closer to Jet because he so obviously couldn't stand the sight of her.

"You don't have to talk, but if you hear me out and still don't want me around, I'll go back home."

"Home," Jet sneered. "What makes you think that place on Red Hill is a home?"

"Because you made it one," she answered contritely. "I've always been grateful for what you did for me, but when you left it and me, that's when I truly realized what the difference between a house and a home is."

Jet gave her a cold stare.

"First of all, Jet, I do not wish that you were the one killed in the car accident. When I was told at the hospital that the driver was killed and it was your car, I fainted. I couldn't believe that you were taken from me because I couldn't imagine a life without you. Mind you, I also passed out when I saw that it was Livingston dead and not you, but I know some of that was the result of shock that they'd misidentified the bodies."

Jet's eyes had narrowed and his teeth were clenched, but she could see that he was intently listening to every word she said and this buoyed her and made her press on. "Did you know the night of your bachelor party that I had the same dream I'd had the nights before our mothers passed?"

Jet gave a start of surprise, but then he quickly masked his expression.

Grace expelled a breath, then said, "I went to Livingston and waylaid him on his way to the party and asked him not to go. I begged, I pleaded, and when he wouldn't listen, I should've called you."

"Why didn't you?" Jet asked quietly.

"I don't know," she whimpered, "but because of that I've felt somewhat responsible. Maybe if I had calmly sat him down and explained my fear instead of being so hysterical, he might have taken me seriously."

Hearing these words Jet exploded, "You're not responsible. Things happen, Grace. For whatever reason, they just do!"

"I know that now, Jet." She picked up his hand and stared into his eyes. "You've loved me for such a long time, and I you. I don't know exactly when my sister love turned to something different." She paused. "Maybe it's always been there. The love I have for you is a slow, burning desire. It's the 'I want to see you every day' kind of love that utterly consumes me. It stole on me like a thief in the night. I'm asking you to give me a second chance and please marry me. When I saw the wedding dress, it petrified me. But the thing that I'm the most afraid of is not having you in my life. If I lose you, I know that I'll never love again because I won't settle. Lightning never strikes in the same place three times." She gave him a look full of love that held honesty and tenderness and asked softly, "Will you please take me back? I promise I won't let you down again."

Jet searched Grace's face and through the breeze off the shore he heard Livingston whisper, 'Don't be too proud, man. Give her one more chance. Take her back.'

Grace's head jerked and Jet knew she'd heard it, too. After a long silence he said with authority, "Yes, I'll marry you, Grace."

All of a sudden, a gust of wind came out of nowhere and they knew they were alone once and for all.

They sat on the blanket drinking the wine that Grace had brought. From out of the darkness, Grace heard the haunting melody of the song that had played the first time she and Jet had slow danced together. She looked him deeply in the eyes with a sexual yearning she couldn't and didn't want to squash. Paraphrasing the lyrics from the song she whispered, "You taught me how to love you." She took her hand and touched Jet in the chest, propelling him back on to the blanket. "Now let me spoil you." Then she began to deftly pull down his shorts.

With hooded gaze, Jet watched her and dutifully lifted his hips when she tried to bare him. "Someone might see you," he whispered.

"So what," she murmured throatily, "I'll never see these people again."

Grace began with feather-light kisses across his chest, and then gave him a long kiss on his mouth that took Jet's breath away. She lowered her head to his manhood and circled his tip before lightly massaging his testicles from underneath. She drank him in until he shuddered in her mouth, and then she swallowed.

The next morning, the insistent ringing of Grace's cell phone made her grope for it on the nightstand. "Hello," she whispered, hoping that the ringing wouldn't wake Jet, but when she felt his eyes on hers, she was exasperated that he'd been disturbed. "Yes, I hear her. What?" Grace shrieked and sat up with her hand on her heart. "We'll be there as soon as possible."

"I heard Ebony screaming," Jet said wryly.

"That's the least of it." Grace had a disoriented look that made Jet sit up and take notice. "She said that ever since Ebony woke and found out that she was at her house and not ours, she's been yelling nonstop. But before she could call me, the New York Police Department called. Naomi has been in a fatal accident. She followed another pedestrian out into the intersection and got run over by a city bus because they crossed without waiting for the light." She turned stricken eyes to Jet. "What about Ebony?"

It took a while for Jet to process everything he'd heard, but when he finally did speak he said without hesitation, "We'd better go and get her."

EPILOGUE

The cocker spaniel Shaggy started barking the minute she saw the school bus screech to a halt in front of the driveway. She stood waiting as Ebony jumped off it with ponytails flying. She rushed up to Grace, handing her a bundle of papers. "Mommy, I got an 'A' on my numbers paper."

"Good job," Grace said, bending down to greet her with a kiss. "You certainly worked at it hard enough."

"When is Daddy going to be home?" she said, putting her hand down to let Shaggy lick her hand. Then the dog took off around the side of the house to chase a bird she'd never catch.

"Soon," she said. "He called a while ago and said that his meeting at town hall was over. I have a snack waiting for you in the kitchen."

Just then Jet drove up in his Yukon. Grace held on to Ebony until it stopped. Ebony ran to him as he got out and grabbed him mid-thigh. That was as high a short six-year-old could reach. Jet bent down and scooped her up in his arms. All the while she was protesting with her infectious laugh, "Let me down. I'm a big girl now."

As Grace watched her husband, Councilman Jet Newman, stride toward her, she felt the familiar surge of pride about the man he was. When Jet reached Grace, he let Ebony slide to her feet, and leaned over and gave Grace a leisurely kiss before he placed his hand on her protruding belly. "How's my son doing today?"

"Livingston is kicking up a storm," she answered somewhat resignedly. "I think that he's already an aggressive child."

"Good, that means he's probably going to be an athlete."

Grace laughed and said, "Then we'd better make sure we keep a strict eye on him while we're raising him." She gave Jet a look. "Are you *sure* that you don't want to name the baby after you?"

Jet grimaced. "No way. I was able to overcome the name, but what if lightning doesn't strike twice? Livingston's the right name. It represents the strong spirit of a man that helped us find each other." Then, with his arm around her shoulders, he turned her towards the house and led her inside, with Ebony holding onto his hand and Shaggy leading the way.

ABOUT THE AUTHOR

Michele Cameron, a native of Bridgeport, Connecticut, is a graduate of North Carolina A&T State University in Greensboro with a bachelor's degree in professional writing and English education. Ms. Cameron currently teaches high school English in Orlando, Florida.

Cameron's first novel was *Never Say Never* was given a 4-star rating by Romanceincolor and she was named a New Face among African-American writers for the month of January 2008 by that magazine. Her second novel, *Moments of Clarity* . . . was rated with 5 stars by Affair de Couer magazine. Cameron has been featured as a guest on numerous notable BAN radio stations and has had many articles on the internet. Her fourth novel entitled, *Unclear and Present Danger,* will be released in February 2010.

Coming in September from Genesis Press:

Celya Bower's hot, new title

2 GOOD

CHAPTER 1

It was Monday morning and she was through being the fool.

Madisyn O'Riley had had it. Her now ex-boyfriend loved to push her to the limit, but this time it had backfired. Catching him in a compromising position wasn't anything new for Madisyn, but last weekend she had been strong and chucked his no-good behind to the curb permanently.

He was surprised, to say the least, but it made Madisyn feel as if she'd conquered Mt. Everest. Nothing could take away her feeling of jubilation, not even the thought of having to deal with a new boss.

She had been an administrative assistant at Brandt, Anderson and Mallory Advertising for over five years, but today felt like her first day. She loved her job and would miss her former boss, but time marched on and so did she. As she prepared for work that morning, she looked at her reflection in the mirror. Her honey-brown skin was clear. Her bright-green eyes stared back at her. People had always asked her if she wore colored contacts. She didn't. She had inherited her green eyes, honey-brown complexion and her figure from her mother. Her plump mother. Madisyn was what most people referred to as thick. But she didn't mind. She was happy with her body for the most part.

She checked out her starched white blouse, closely inspecting it for any flaws. Not seeing any, she walked back into her bedroom and picked up her jacket, then headed for her garage.

The heat greeted her as she raised her garage door by way of the remote. Why did North Texas have to be so hot during the summer? Since she lived in Dallas and it was the middle of June, she knew the day was going to be a scorcher.

Madisyn arrived at work early that morning in order to get a jump on preparing things for her new boss, who was due to arrive in a week. She needed to order his nameplate and business cards, and issue a service order for the IT department to change the computer to his specifications. She was busy working her magic when her friend and co-worker, Keisha Allen, approached her desk.

Keisha was dressed in a too-short dress that hugged her slender frame. She had a knack for wearing just about anything and making it look drop-dead sexy. She'd always told Madisyn how proud she was of her body, that she wasn't ashamed to show it. Keisha sported the latest complicated and trendy hairstyle, complete with required quota of hair weave, and her makeup was always perfect, making her pecan-brown skin almost glow.

"I like that dress, girl," Madisyn said politely. Privately, she thought Keisha looked like a call girl, albeit a high-dollar one. Madisyn had been raised to say something nice no matter the circumstance, but Keisha continually pushed that envelope.

"Thanks. But not now. Your new boss is on his way up. He is hot, girl. H-O-T!" Keisha said.

"Yeah, yeah, fine words from a woman whose thermostat is stuck on purgatory anyway. Any man not wearing a wedding band would be hot to you." And even if he was wearing one, Madisyn mused.

"Don't hate because I date. You're just jealous. I told you Darnell wasn't good enough to spit on. You're pretty, Madisyn, and it's time for the world to see the real you. Some men like a healthy woman."

Typical Keisha. Just because Madisyn didn't weigh a hundred pounds and wear a size two, Keisha thought the end of world was upon her. "You know, you might be right," Madisyn lied. "But I don't want to change for a man. I want him to change for me." Not that she thought she needed much changing. She was comfortable with her size fourteen frame.

"Hey, why don't we start that new change tonight? My cousin Aisha is giving a party."

"You mean the one that's dating the Dallas Cowboy?"

"The same," Keisha said, smiling. "You know, since she moved in with him a few months ago, I hardly ever see her anymore. Aisha said something about his friends dropping by to recruit for some of the local charities."

So that was Keisha's motivation. She would be in the midst of professional athletes. Madisyn liked her friend, but Keisha only saw dollar signs when it came to dates. That could never work for Madisyn. The next man she dated would be her soul mate.

"So, Madisyn, are you game? We can have dinner and then go to the party."

"Yes, put me down for it."

Keisha nodded and headed back down the hall. "See you at dinner," she called.

Later that day, Madisyn could finally take a breather. Her new boss, who wasn't due to report to work for another week, had showed up earlier that day, ready to work. Nothing was ready for him, of course, making her look like an idiot.

Now she had just enough time to grab some dinner with Keisha at their favorite restaurant before they headed to the party. Murphy's was a little home-style restaurant located just a few blocks from the office. The place was always packed with people from every walk of life, and tonight was no exception. Madisyn entered the restaurant and sought out her friend.

Keisha waved at her from a table in the corner. Returning the gesture, Madisyn headed to her friend. "How did you get here so fast?"

Keisha took a sip of her caramel-apple martini. "I don't have a fine new boss watching my every move. My boss is probably in his girlfriend's office right now, doing the wild thang, and with no idea what time I left."

Madisyn settled into her chair, refusing to get involved in office chatter, and changed the subject. "What are you going to eat?"

Keisha looked over the menu and smacked her lips. "Girl, I can't eat too much before we head to the party. Maybe I'll have a salad or something light. I don't want to look fat or bloated." She cleared her throat. "Not that you don't look nice, Maddie. But you should wear more makeup to dress up your green eyes. Most women would kill for eyes like yours."

Madisyn wasn't upset at Keisha's comment. She'd known Keisha since junior high and she'd always had the same outlook. Size mattered, whether it was physical or financial. To Keisha "the bigger, the better" applied only to bank accounts. Madisyn felt sorry for her friend.

Later at the party, Madisyn realized she was quite out of her safe, staid element. The gathering was being held at Aisha's home, which she shared with her boyfriend, Kerwin Gallagher, running back for the Dallas Cowboys. Madisyn had met him a few times over the last year. He didn't act the way the media portrayed professional football players. While he wasn't a saint, he was nice enough.

Every woman at the party was dressed in a short skirt or dress and stilettos that looked much too painful to walk in. Keisha was in her element with all the football players hovering around her. She was like a kid in a candy store. She hadn't said two words to Madisyn since they hit the party.

Madisyn looked down at her frame hidden in a black suit and sighed. She looked pretty boring compared to the other women. Maybe Keisha was right about the makeover, she thought.

Aisha came over to Madisyn as she held up the wall in a corner of the large house. Aisha was dressed in the requisite short mini-dress and four-inch stilettos, which made the slender woman appear to be about six feet tall.

"This is a lovely party, Aisha. I thought Keisha was kidding about the athletes being here. What on earth are these men doing here?"

"They thought it would be a great way to get volunteers for the charities they represent without it turning into a major media event. But it's not going as well as we'd hoped. Most of the women here are looking for a man, not volunteer work at a charity organization. The majority of these guys are already spoken for." Aisha snapped her perfectly manicured fingers. "Hey, you should meet Aidan Coles. He's representing Mature Alliance. It's so new they need volunteers really bad. They're still finalizing a lot of details, but I know he could use your organizational skills."

"What is the Mature Alliance?"

"It's an organization to teach adults to read and help them get their high-school diploma."

Madisyn thought it sounded perfect. She'd been wanting to volunteer, but had never known how or where to start. "And since I'm always going on about how I want to help in the community, I should volunteer for something, huh?"

Aisha shrugged her thin shoulders. "Well, yeah. Aidan could probably tell you something about it, or at least direct you to the right people in the organization. He's the founder, but I don't know how hands-on he is." She grabbed Madisyn's hand. "Come on, let's go meet him."

Madisyn didn't want to make a scene, so she allowed herself to be led across the living room to the handsome man holding court with at least ten women. He was gorgeous, of course, with caramel-brown skin, short black hair, and a thin mustache framing a large natural smile. The man was some kind of sexy. His wide shoulders were her downfall. He towered over Madisyn's five-ten frame by at least five inches.

"Okay, scat, ladies," Aisha said. "We need to talk business with Aidan."

The women grumbled but left the area. Madisyn was impressed with Aisha's skills. "Girl, you are too much. Remind me to take you shopping with me when there's a big sale at the mall."

Aisha laughed. "Just a little crowd control." She pulled Madisyn closer to the smiling man. "Madisyn O'Riley, Aidan Coles. Aidan Coles, Madisyn O'Riley.

You guys chat. I have to go police the area." She walked off.

Aidan surveyed the woman standing in front of him. She was thick, as his mother would say. She had an easy smile, shoulder-length black hair, big, expressive green eyes and honey-brown skin. "Is that your real name?" He felt as stupid as his question.

"Yes, it is. I know I should be a middle-aged Irish woman with that name," Madisyn said, glancing across the room.

He wondered what had her attention. She definitely wasn't like every other woman in the room, making him the focus of her attention. "Not necessarily. It's just very different. I think I've met Eisha, Tisha, Tameka, you know those names. Madisyn is refreshing and original."

"Well, Aidan is not your everyday name either."

"True. Blame my mother. She had a flair for the dramatic. My full name is Aidan Sidney Coles."

Madisyn laughed. "Ouch. Aisha said you're heading up the literacy program."

"Yes, I am. It hasn't really gotten off the ground yet. We're short on volunteers," he lied. He'd had a lot of volunteers, just not anyone who was actually interested in helping people. "We already have over fifty people signed up to learn to read."

"Amazing," Madisyn said, totally in awe. "I'd be willing to volunteer."

Aidan smiled. "Really? You know there's no pay."

"Duh, hence the volunteering thing," Madisyn said, laughing. "I'm doing this for me, not for money or to get close to an athlete."

"You'd be the first," Aidan said honestly.

"I've been around sports nuts all my life. Why would I want to go out with one?"

He shrugged. "Same as most of the women here. Money. Status."

"Well, Aidan, I hate to be the one to inform you, but I'm not like most of the women here. I'm my own person. I love sports, don't get me wrong. I've followed your career since you graduated from the University of Oklahoma."

"No way," Aidan said.

Madisyn had his attention now. "Yep, you attended Oklahoma University on a full scholarship, then were drafted in the first round by the New England Patriots. Then you went to San Francisco and ultimately to Dallas, about three years ago. You are one of the best wide receivers in the league and are worth the change the Cowboys had to pay for you."

Aidan stood before her, clearly in awe. "I'm impressed you've followed my career so closely."

Madisyn shrugged. "I come from a family of athletes. My dad was a high-school football coach before he retired and I have four brothers. My oldest brother, Mike, is also a high-school football coach. Liking sports is not an option in our family, you have to love sports. All sports."

He nodded, understanding. She was definitely a breath of fresh air. He was tired of those women who only wanted to be with him because he played professional football. He wanted a woman who wanted to get to know Aidan Coles, the man. Was this the woman? Only one way he would find out. "The first meeting is Friday night at seven at the center. See you there."

2009 Reprint Mass Market Titles

January

I'm Gonna Make You Love Me
Gwyneth Bolton
ISBN-13: 978-1-58571-294-6
$6.99

Shades of Desire
Monica White
ISBN-13: 978-1-58571-292-2
$6.99

February

A Love of Her Own
Cheris Hodges
ISBN-13: 978-1-58571-293-9
$6.99

Color of Trouble
Dyanne Davis
ISBN-13: 978-1-58571-294-6
$6.99

March

Twist of Fate
Beverly Clark
ISBN-13: 978-1-58571-295-3
$6.99

Chances
Pamela Leigh Starr
ISBN-13: 978-1-58571-296-0
$6.99

April

Sinful Intentions
Crystal Rhodes
ISBN-13: 978-1-585712-297-7
$6.99

Rock Star
Roslyn Hardy Holcomb
ISBN-13: 978-1-58571-298-4
$6.99

May

Paths of Fire
T.T. Henderson
ISBN-13: 978-1-58571-343-1
$6.99

Caught Up in the Rapture
Lisa Riley
ISBN-13: 978-1-58571-344-8
$6.99

June

Reckless Surrender
Rochelle Alers
ISBN-13: 978-1-58571-345-5
$6.99

No Ordinary Love
Angela Weaver
ISBN-13: 978-1-58571-346-2
$6.99

2009 Reprint Mass Market Titles (continued)

July

Intentional Mistakes
Michele Sudler
ISBN-13: 978-1-58571-347-9
$6.99

It's In His Kiss
Reon Carter
ISBN-13: 978-1-58571-348-6
$6.99

August

Unfinished Love Affair
Barbara Keaton
ISBN-13: 978-1-58571-349-3
$6.99

A Perfect Place to Pray
I.L Goodwin
ISBN-13: 978-1-58571-299-1
$6.99

September

Love in High Gear
Charlotte Roy
ISBN-13: 978-1-58571-355-4
$6.99

Ebony Eyes
Kei Swanson
ISBN-13: 978-1-58571-356-1
$6.99

October

Midnight Clear, Part I
Leslie Esdale/Carmen Green
ISBN-13: 978-1-58571-357-8
$6.99

Midnight Clear, Part II
Gwynne Forster/Monica Jackson
ISBN-13: 978-1-58571-358-5
$6.99

November

Midnight Peril
Vicki Andrews
ISBN-13: 978-1-58571-359-2
$6.99

One Day At A Time
Bella McFarland
ISBN-13: 978-1-58571-360-8
$6.99

December

Just An Affair
Eugenia O'Neal
ISBN-13: 978-1-58571-361-5
$6.99

Shades of Brown
Denise Becker
ISBN-13: 978-1-58571-362-2
$6.99

2009 New Mass Market Titles

January

Singing A Song…
Crystal Rhodes
ISBN-13: 978-1-58571-283-0
$6.99

Look Both Ways
Joan Early
ISBN-13: 978-1-58571-284-7
$6.99

February

Six O'Clock
Katrina Spencer
ISBN-13: 978-1-58571-285-4
$6.99

Red Sky
Renee Alexis
ISBN-13: 978-1-58571-286-1
$6.99

March

Anything But Love
Celya Bowers
ISBN-13: 978-1-58571-287-8
$6.99

Tempting Faith
Crystal Hubbard
ISBN-13: 978-1-58571-288-5
$6.99

April

If I Were Your Woman
La Connie Taylor-Jones
ISBN-13: 978-1-58571-289-2
$6.99

Best Of Luck Elsewhere
Trisha Haddad
ISBN-13: 978-1-58571-290-8
$6.99

May

All I'll Ever Need
Mildred Riley
ISBN-13: 978-1-58571-335-6
$6.99

A Place Like Home
Alicia Wiggins
ISBN-13: 978-1-58571-336-3
$6.99

June

Best Foot Forward
Michele Sudler
ISBN-13: 978-1-58571-337-0
$6.99

It's In the Rhythm
Sammie Ward
ISBN-13: 978-1-58571-338-7
$6.99

2009 New Mass Market Titles (continued)

July

Checks and Balances
Elaine Sims
ISBN-13: 978-1-58571-339-4
$6.99

Save Me
Africa Fine
ISBN-13: 978-1-58571-340-0
$6.99

August

When Lightening Strikes
Michele Cameron
ISBN-13: 978-1-58571-369-1
$6.99

Blindsided
Tammy Williams
ISBN-13: 978-1-58571-342-4
$6.99

September

2 Good
Celya Bowers
ISBN-13: 978-1-58571-350-9
$6.99

Waiting for Mr. Darcy
Chamein Canton
ISBN-13: 978-1-58571-351-6
$6.99

October

Fireflies
Joan Early
ISBN-13: 978-1-58571-352-3
$6.99

Frost On My Window
Angela Weaver
ISBN-13: 978-1-58571-353-0
$6.99

November

Waiting in the Shadows
Michele Sudler
ISBN-13: 978-1-58571-364-6
$6.99

Fixin' Tyrone
Keith Walker
ISBN-13: 978-1-58571-365-3
$6.99

December

Dream Keeper
Gail McFarland
ISBN-13: 978-1-58571-366-0
$6.99

Another Memory
Pamela Ridley
ISBN-13: 978-1-58571-367-7
$6.99

Other Genesis Press, Inc. Titles

A Dangerous Deception	J.M. Jeffries	$8.95
A Dangerous Love	J.M. Jeffries	$8.95
A Dangerous Obsession	J.M. Jeffries	$8.95
A Drummer's Beat to Mend	Kei Swanson	$9.95
A Happy Life	Charlotte Harris	$9.95
A Heart's Awakening	Veronica Parker	$9.95
A Lark on the Wing	Phyliss Hamilton	$9.95
A Love of Her Own	Cheris F. Hodges	$9.95
A Love to Cherish	Beverly Clark	$8.95
A Risk of Rain	Dar Tomlinson	$8.95
A Taste of Temptation	Reneé Alexis	$9.95
A Twist of Fate	Beverly Clark	$8.95
A Voice Behind Thunder	Carrie Elizabeth Greene	$6.99
A Will to Love	Angie Daniels	$9.95
Acquisitions	Kimberley White	$8.95
Across	Carol Payne	$12.95
After the Vows (Summer Anthology)	Leslie Esdaile T.T. Henderson Jacqueline Thomas	$10.95
Again My Love	Kayla Perrin	$10.95
Against the Wind	Gwynne Forster	$8.95
All I Ask	Barbara Keaton	$8.95
Always You	Crystal Hubbard	$6.99
Ambrosia	T.T. Henderson	$8.95
An Unfinished Love Affair	Barbara Keaton	$8.95
And Then Came You	Dorothy Elizabeth Love	$8.95
Angel's Paradise	Janice Angelique	$9.95
At Last	Lisa G. Riley	$8.95
Best of Friends	Natalie Dunbar	$8.95
Beyond the Rapture	Beverly Clark	$9.95
Blame It On Paradise	Crystal Hubbard	$6.99
Blaze	Barbara Keaton	$9.95
Bliss, Inc.	Chamein Canton	$6.99
Blood Lust	J. M. Jeffries	$9.95
Blood Seduction	J.M. Jeffries	$9.95

Other Genesis Press, Inc. Titles (continued)

Bodyguard	Andrea Jackson	$9.95
Boss of Me	Diana Nyad	$8.95
Bound by Love	Beverly Clark	$8.95
Breeze	Robin Hampton Allen	$10.95
Broken	Dar Tomlinson	$24.95
By Design	Barbara Keaton	$8.95
Cajun Heat	Charlene Berry	$8.95
Careless Whispers	Rochelle Alers	$8.95
Cats & Other Tales	Marilyn Wagner	$8.95
Caught in a Trap	Andre Michelle	$8.95
Caught Up In the Rapture	Lisa G. Riley	$9.95
Cautious Heart	Cheris F Hodges	$8.95
Chances	Pamela Leigh Starr	$8.95
Cherish the Flame	Beverly Clark	$8.95
Choices	Tammy Williams	$6.99
Class Reunion	Irma Jenkins/ John Brown	$12.95
Code Name: Diva	J.M. Jeffries	$9.95
Conquering Dr. Wexler's Heart	Kimberley White	$9.95
Corporate Seduction	A.C. Arthur	$9.95
Crossing Paths, Tempting Memories	Dorothy Elizabeth Love	$9.95
Crush	Crystal Hubbard	$9.95
Cypress Whisperings	Phyllis Hamilton	$8.95
Dark Embrace	Crystal Wilson Harris	$8.95
Dark Storm Rising	Chinelu Moore	$10.95
Daughter of the Wind	Joan Xian	$8.95
Dawn's Harbor	Kymberly Hunt	$6.99
Deadly Sacrifice	Jack Kean	$22.95
Designer Passion	Dar Tomlinson Diana Richeaux	$8.95
Do Over	Celya Bowers	$9.95
Dream Runner	Gail McFarland	$6.99
Dreamtective	Liz Swados	$5.95

Other Genesis Press, Inc. Titles (continued)

Ebony Angel	Deatri King-Bey	$9.95
Ebony Butterfly II	Delilah Dawson	$14.95
Echoes of Yesterday	Beverly Clark	$9.95
Eden's Garden	Elizabeth Rose	$8.95
Eve's Prescription	Edwina Martin Arnold	$8.95
Everlastin' Love	Gay G. Gunn	$8.95
Everlasting Moments	Dorothy Elizabeth Love	$8.95
Everything and More	Sinclair Lebeau	$8.95
Everything but Love	Natalie Dunbar	$8.95
Falling	Natalie Dunbar	$9.95
Fate	Pamela Leigh Starr	$8.95
Finding Isabella	A.J. Garrotto	$8.95
Forbidden Quest	Dar Tomlinson	$10.95
Forever Love	Wanda Y. Thomas	$8.95
From the Ashes	Kathleen Suzanne Jeanne Sumerix	$8.95
Gentle Yearning	Rochelle Alers	$10.95
Glory of Love	Sinclair LeBeau	$10.95
Go Gentle into that Good Night	Malcom Boyd	$12.95
Goldengroove	Mary Beth Craft	$16.95
Groove, Bang, and Jive	Steve Cannon	$8.99
Hand in Glove	Andrea Jackson	$9.95
Hard to Love	Kimberley White	$9.95
Hart & Soul	Angie Daniels	$8.95
Heart of the Phoenix	A.C. Arthur	$9.95
Heartbeat	Stephanie Bedwell-Grime	$8.95
Hearts Remember	M. Loui Quezada	$8.95
Hidden Memories	Robin Allen	$10.95
Higher Ground	Leah Latimer	$19.95
Hitler, the War, and the Pope	Ronald Rychiak	$26.95
How to Write a Romance	Kathryn Falk	$18.95
I Married a Reclining Chair	Lisa M. Fuhs	$8.95
I'll Be Your Shelter	Giselle Carmichael	$8.95
I'll Paint a Sun	A.J. Garrotto	$9.95

Other Genesis Press, Inc. Titles (continued)

Icie	Pamela Leigh Starr	$8.95
Illusions	Pamela Leigh Starr	$8.95
Indigo After Dark Vol. I	Nia Dixon/Angelique	$10.95
Indigo After Dark Vol. II	Dolores Bundy/ Cole Riley	$10.95
Indigo After Dark Vol. III	Montana Blue/ Coco Morena	$10.95
Indigo After Dark Vol. IV	Cassandra Colt/	$14.95
Indigo After Dark Vol. V	Delilah Dawson	$14.95
Indiscretions	Donna Hill	$8.95
Intentional Mistakes	Michele Sudler	$9.95
Interlude	Donna Hill	$8.95
Intimate Intentions	Angie Daniels	$8.95
It's Not Over Yet	J.J. Michael	$9.95
Jolie's Surrender	Edwina Martin-Arnold	$8.95
Kiss or Keep	Debra Phillips	$8.95
Lace	Giselle Carmichael	$9.95
Lady Preacher	K.T. Richey	$6.99
Last Train to Memphis	Elsa Cook	$12.95
Lasting Valor	Ken Olsen	$24.95
Let Us Prey	Hunter Lundy	$25.95
Lies Too Long	Pamela Ridley	$13.95
Life Is Never As It Seems	J.J. Michael	$12.95
Lighter Shade of Brown	Vicki Andrews	$8.95
Looking for Lily	Africa Fine	$6.99
Love Always	Mildred E. Riley	$10.95
Love Doesn't Come Easy	Charlyne Dickerson	$8.95
Love Unveiled	Gloria Greene	$10.95
Love's Deception	Charlene Berry	$10.95
Love's Destiny	M. Loui Quezada	$8.95
Love's Secrets	Yolanda McVey	$6.99
Mae's Promise	Melody Walcott	$8.95
Magnolia Sunset	Giselle Carmichael	$8.95
Many Shades of Gray	Dyanne Davis	$6.99
Matters of Life and Death	Lesego Malepe, Ph.D.	$15.95

Other Genesis Press, Inc. Titles (continued)

Meant to Be	Jeanne Sumerix	$8.95
Midnight Clear (Anthology)	Leslie Esdaile Gwynne Forster Carmen Green Monica Jackson	$10.95
Midnight Magic	Gwynne Forster	$8.95
Midnight Peril	Vicki Andrews	$10.95
Misconceptions	Pamela Leigh Starr	$9.95
Moments of Clarity	Michele Cameron	$6.99
Montgomery's Children	Richard Perry	$14.95
Mr Fix-It	Crystal Hubbard	$6.99
My Buffalo Soldier	Barbara B. K. Reeves	$8.95
Naked Soul	Gwynne Forster	$8.95
Never Say Never	Michele Cameron	$6.99
Next to Last Chance	Louisa Dixon	$24.95
No Apologies	Seressia Glass	$8.95
No Commitment Required	Seressia Glass	$8.95
No Regrets	Mildred E. Riley	$8.95
Not His Type	Chamein Canton	$6.99
Nowhere to Run	Gay G. Gunn	$10.95
O Bed! O Breakfast!	Rob Kuehnle	$14.95
Object of His Desire	A. C. Arthur	$8.95
Office Policy	A. C. Arthur	$9.95
Once in a Blue Moon	Dorianne Cole	$9.95
One Day at a Time	Bella McFarland	$8.95
One in A Million	Barbara Keaton	$6.99
One of These Days	Michele Sudler	$9.95
Outside Chance	Louisa Dixon	$24.95
Passion	T.T. Henderson	$10.95
Passion's Blood	Cherif Fortin	$22.95
Passion's Furies	AlTonya Washington	$6.99
Passion's Journey	Wanda Y. Thomas	$8.95
Past Promises	Jahmel West	$8.95
Path of Fire	T.T. Henderson	$8.95
Path of Thorns	Annetta P. Lee	$9.95

Other Genesis Press, Inc. Titles (continued)

Peace Be Still	Colette Haywood	$12.95
Picture Perfect	Reon Carter	$8.95
Playing for Keeps	Stephanie Salinas	$8.95
Pride & Joi	Gay G. Gunn	$8.95
Promises Made	Bernice Layton	$6.99
Promises to Keep	Alicia Wiggins	$8.95
Quiet Storm	Donna Hill	$10.95
Reckless Surrender	Rochelle Alers	$6.95
Red Polka Dot in a World of Plaid	Varian Johnson	$12.95
Reluctant Captive	Joyce Jackson	$8.95
Rendezvous with Fate	Jeanne Sumerix	$8.95
Revelations	Cheris F. Hodges	$8.95
Rivers of the Soul	Leslie Esdaile	$8.95
Rocky Mountain Romance	Kathleen Suzanne	$8.95
Rooms of the Heart	Donna Hill	$8.95
Rough on Rats and Tough on Cats	Chris Parker	$12.95
Secret Library Vol. 1	Nina Sheridan	$18.95
Secret Library Vol. 2	Cassandra Colt	$8.95
Secret Thunder	Annetta P. Lee	$9.95
Shades of Brown	Denise Becker	$8.95
Shades of Desire	Monica White	$8.95
Shadows in the Moonlight	Jeanne Sumerix	$8.95
Sin	Crystal Rhodes	$8.95
Small Whispers	Annetta P. Lee	$6.99
So Amazing	Sinclair LeBeau	$8.95
Somebody's Someone	Sinclair LeBeau	$8.95
Someone to Love	Alicia Wiggins	$8.95
Song in the Park	Martin Brant	$15.95
Soul Eyes	Wayne L. Wilson	$12.95
Soul to Soul	Donna Hill	$8.95
Southern Comfort	J.M. Jeffries	$8.95
Southern Fried Standards	S.R. Maddox	$6.99
Still the Storm	Sharon Robinson	$8.95

Other Genesis Press, Inc. Titles (continued)

Still Waters Run Deep	Leslie Esdaile	$8.95
Stolen Kisses	Dominiqua Douglas	$9.95
Stolen Memories	Michele Sudler	$6.99
Stories to Excite You	Anna Forrest/Divine	$14.95
Storm	Pamela Leigh Starr	$6.99
Subtle Secrets	Wanda Y. Thomas	$8.95
Suddenly You	Crystal Hubbard	$9.95
Sweet Repercussions	Kimberley White	$9.95
Sweet Sensations	Gwyneth Bolton	$9.95
Sweet Tomorrows	Kimberly White	$8.95
Taken by You	Dorothy Elizabeth Love	$9.95
Tattooed Tears	T. T. Henderson	$8.95
The Color Line	Lizzette Grayson Carter	$9.95
The Color of Trouble	Dyanne Davis	$8.95
The Disappearance of Allison Jones	Kayla Perrin	$5.95
The Fires Within	Beverly Clark	$9.95
The Foursome	Celya Bowers	$6.99
The Honey Dipper's Legacy	Pannell-Allen	$14.95
The Joker's Love Tune	Sidney Rickman	$15.95
The Little Pretender	Barbara Cartland	$10.95
The Love We Had	Natalie Dunbar	$8.95
The Man Who Could Fly	Bob & Milana Beamon	$18.95
The Missing Link	Charlyne Dickerson	$8.95
The Mission	Pamela Leigh Starr	$6.99
The More Things Change	Chamein Canton	$6.99
The Perfect Frame	Beverly Clark	$9.95
The Price of Love	Sinclair LeBeau	$8.95
The Smoking Life	Ilene Barth	$29.95
The Words of the Pitcher	Kei Swanson	$8.95
Things Forbidden	Maryam Diaab	$6.99
This Life Isn't Perfect Holla	Sandra Foy	$6.99
Three Doors Down	Michele Sudler	$6.99
Three Wishes	Seressia Glass	$8.95
Ties That Bind	Kathleen Suzanne	$8.95

Other Genesis Press, Inc. Titles (continued)

Tiger Woods	Libby Hughes	$5.95
Time is of the Essence	Angie Daniels	$9.95
Timeless Devotion	Bella McFarland	$9.95
Tomorrow's Promise	Leslie Esdaile	$8.95
Truly Inseparable	Wanda Y. Thomas	$8.95
Two Sides to Every Story	Dyanne Davis	$9.95
Unbreak My Heart	Dar Tomlinson	$8.95
Uncommon Prayer	Kenneth Swanson	$9.95
Unconditional Love	Alicia Wiggins	$8.95
Unconditional	A.C. Arthur	$9.95
Undying Love	Renee Alexis	$6.99
Until Death Do Us Part	Susan Paul	$8.95
Vows of Passion	Bella McFarland	$9.95
Wedding Gown	Dyanne Davis	$8.95
What's Under Benjamin's Bed	Sandra Schaffer	$8.95
When A Man Loves A Woman	La Connie Taylor-Jones	$6.99
When Dreams Float	Dorothy Elizabeth Love	$8.95
When I'm With You	LaConnie Taylor-Jones	$6.99
Where I Want To Be	Maryam Diaab	$6.99
Whispers in the Night	Dorothy Elizabeth Love	$8.95
Whispers in the Sand	LaFlorya Gauthier	$10.95
Who's That Lady?	Andrea Jackson	$9.95
Wild Ravens	Altonya Washington	$9.95
Yesterday Is Gone	Beverly Clark	$10.95
Yesterday's Dreams, Tomorrow's Promises	Reon Laudat	$8.95
Your Precious Love	Sinclair LeBeau	$8.95

Order Form

Mail to: Genesis Press, Inc.
P.O. Box 101
Columbus, MS 39703

Name ______________________________
Address ______________________________
City/State ______________________ Zip ______________
Telephone ______________________

Ship to (if different from above)
Name ______________________________
Address ______________________________
City/State ______________________ Zip ______________
Telephone ______________________

Credit Card Information
Credit Card # ______________________ ☐ Visa ☐ Mastercard
Expiration Date (mm/yy) ______________ ☐ AmEx ☐ Discover

Qty.	Author	Title	Price	Total

Use this order form, or call 1-888-INDIGO-1

Total for books ______________
Shipping and handling:
$5 first two books,
$1 each additional book ______________
Total S & H ______________
Total amount enclosed ______________
Mississippi residents add 7% sales tax

Visit www.genesis-press.com for latest releases and excerpts.